MASTERSON IN LOVE

Masterson Series Book Three

LISA LANG BLAKENEY

Writergirl Press

License Note

To All My Romance Ninjas

Books By Lisa

The Masterson Series

Devour this addictive series about the possessive bad boy, Roman Masterson, who falls hard and fast for the girl he's promised his family to protect.

Masterson

Masterson Unleashed

Masterson In Love

Masterson Made

Joseph Loves Juliette

Masterson Box Set

Masterson Next Generation Series

The crazy hot fruit doesn't fall far from the tree. Dive into this second generation of Masterson men!

Knox - Knox & Gigi

Bronx - Bronx & Karma

Seven - Coming soon!

The King Brothers Series

Dive into this series of interconnected standalones featuring 3 alpha hot brothers and the women they lay claim to without apology.

Claimed - Camden & Jade

Indebted - Cutter & Sloan

Broken - Stone & Tiny

Promised - All King Brothers

King Brothers Box Set

The Nighthawk Series

Sexy & sweet sports romances set in the professional world of football. All standalones.

Saint - Saint & Sabrina

Wolf - Cooper & Ursula

Diesel - Mason & Olivia

Jett - Jett & Adrienne

Rush - Rush & Mia

Freak - Freak & Willow

Brick - coming soon!

Introduction

They all think that I'm a phase. A fetish. A tempo-rary fixture. But I love Elizabeth, and there isn't shit anyone can do to change or destroy that … even her.

Being hopelessly in love with tatted, sexy, bad boy, Roman Masterson can be exactly what one would imagine. Intense. Passionate. Consuming. Dangerous.

After fighting so hard to be together, there still continues to be forces working against them. Yet the most difficult obstacles seem to be the ones that come from within.

Prologue

Zoe Clarkson

I can feel the tension and anxiety swirling around my shop like a witch's brew. The brooding man covered in beautiful ink, sitting rigidly across from me, is totally trying to control the room with his silence. Probably because he is used to dominating his environment by his mere physical presence, and he feels totally out of place in a room where I dictate the boundaries.

The glowing woman dressed in the pretty yellow and coral dress, sitting to his left, definitely seems to have spearheaded the decision to make this appointment, although she seems quite nervous about it. She continues to adjust herself anxiously in her seat as if she's trying to think of an exit strategy.

At first glance, I surmise that she doesn't fully comprehend or even recognize the power that she wields over the man; but I suppose that's part of the reason why she came to see me.

I specialize in just this type of work.

This is their first time here and already they have my undivided attention. The woman is classically passive aggressive. The man is oozing testosterone and probably has mother issues ... *totally* my favorite types of clients.

"So is this appointment for Miss Hill or both of you, Mr. Masterson?" I ask directly. I think he respects a person who quickly gets to the heart of the matter.

"Ask her."

"I'm asking you." I challenge.

"She booked this appointment. I don't know what the fuck is going on. She just tells me where to go and I drive."

He crosses his thick, corded forearms in front of himself. Putting up a clear wall of defense. I highly doubt that this woman *just tells* him to do anything.

"But you're planning on staying, right?"

"Of course."

"So Miss Hill–" I continue.

"You can call me Elizabeth." She smiles nervously. I think the exchange between Mr. Masterson and myself made her even more uncomfortable than she already was.

"Why don't we start with you then, Elizabeth. What made you book this appointment today? Why with me when you could have gone to a dozen other places?"

She crosses her legs at the ankles, then plays a little with her thick brunette curls, while she appears to think carefully about her response.

"Well, I have several reasons."

The man presses one of his palms firmly down on the woman's jumpy knee for a moment. The woman smiles. I can tell that she feels more at ease now.

I know that my process isn't the norm, and the man is

especially skeptical based on his prior experience with this type of thing. This is definitely going to be a challenging couple to work with, but there's something about the both of them that I like already.

I think the final results are going to be amazing.

Elizabeth

"Face against the wall ... now."

Roman Masterson is speechless, and what's truly more satisfying is that I've made him that way. I've given him four rules to follow tonight, and the promise that if he behaves, I'll reward him.

1. No talking.
2. No clothes.
3. Hands on the wall.
4. Face against the wall.

He's spectacular to gaze at when he's like this.

Naked.

Strong.

Quiet.

Vulnerable.

Beautiful.

Turned on.

I can almost see a layer of steam rising from the swirls of the massive tattoo that adorns his back. It's literally hot to the touch. Hot just for me. I gingerly use just a fingertip to trace his ink from the base of his spine, to the middle of his back, to his outstretched arms, and then to his neck.

No matter how many times I've seen Roman without a shirt on, the beauty of his ink still amazes me; and I'm drawn towards it like a moth to a flame.

I am standing completely nude, directly behind him, close enough for our bodies to touch, but not quite. Teasing him. It's a delicate balancing act as I'm standing on my tiptoes and attempting to lick, with the very tip of my tongue, the part of the tattoo that wraps around the side of his neck. I watch with satisfaction as his body shudders from my handiwork.

Then I turn him completely around. His balls hanging heavy, his cock brick hard, jutting out straight ahead towards me. Begging for me to put it out of its misery. He's been a very good boy tonight. So I think I'll comply.

"Back against the wall," I order with authority, making sure he keeps his palms flat against the wall.

"We wouldn't want you to get the idea that you can touch me without permission, now would we?" I taunt.

Roman groans lowly at the base of his throat in response, as if my words are almost too painful to bear. He's used to being in complete control of our lovemaking, but tonight he's going to learn the hard way that I run things.

I grab a down feather pillow from the bed and toss it to the ground at his feet, but I don't make a move yet. I like the tension building between us. So I slowly look at the pillow, then I stare back at him, then to his strong biceps, and then to his taut six-pack that ends in a very sexy V at his groin area.

The scar under his eye is twitching. He's staring back and forth between my mouth and the pillow. Almost as if he's trying to will me down on both knees to suck him off.

I brazenly laugh out loud.

He's not going to be able to take too much more of this. I wasn't really sure if he could. This was a test. A test of his need to dominate, and he's about to flunk it. Big time.

I decide to turn up the heat just a bit more and grab underneath my heavy breasts with both hands. Using my thumbs to rub back and forth against my nipples, and turning them hard as pennies, I make sure not to take my eyes off of his.

Roman licks his bottom lip as if it's coated with sugar. He wants to pop one of my breasts in his mouth so badly, and of course just the knowledge that he wants me like this is making me ache excruciatingly between my legs. If I could just relieve a little of the pressure between my thighs, I might be able to continue with my night of delicious torture of enforcing my four Roman rules.

Maybe if I just take one of my hands and slide a finger or two between my folds, very lightly, very slowly; I may be able to hold off long enough to make this work for the both of us. But watching me do this to myself, and not being able to participate, is probably taking things a bit too far. Roman takes an almost obsessive delight in controlling when I orgasm and how often; me masturbating in front of him is the ultimate challenge to that carnal need of his.

I know I'm right once he begins to growl at me at a decibel level that I can clearly hear. That the whole block could hear. I'm breaking him.

So this is what it feels like? I think I'm starting to see the appeal.

"Shh," I warn him. "Quiet."

"Duchess," he exhales my name like a prayer for mercy.

And then a second later he calls my name much louder.

"Duchess!"

The boom of his call frightening the bejeezus out of me. And just like that my eyes pop open and reality smacks me dead in the face. I'm still in my bedroom, but I'm not nude. I'm wearing a matching racerback tank and panty set. The one I bought from Target just the other day. I'm not standing up, but lying across my bed, and Roman is definitely here but his muscular body is hovering above me and he's grinning, as if he just won the lottery or something.

I blink my eyes several times to help get the room in focus. Not just because I don't have my contacts in, and I can't see much, but because I'm a little confused as to what's happening around me.

"I hate to wake you up, but you were dreaming about me, and it's making my dick hard as fuck."

Of course ... it was all a dream.

"I don't think—"

Roman quickly slides one of his thick fingers inside my panties and in between my folds. When he slides it back out, he pops it inside his mouth and sucks.

"Mmm, I think you were, baby. You taste like you were dreaming about me. You taste like heaven."

He's right, there's no use in pretending or being embarrassed by it. What's wrong with a little dirty dream? Plus I'm horny as hell, and he's just the man who can help me out with that. The only man.

"I was on my knees," I say with a teasing grin.

I wasn't quite on my knees yet in the dream, but he doesn't need to know that.

"Fuck, Duchess," he says gruffly. Almost in the same identical erotic way he did in my dream.

"Is that what you want right now? My dick in your mouth?"

He's so dirty. I love it, and I love him.

"Yes, Masterson," I say as I slide my body down the bed and under the sheets, "that's exactly what I want."

The first, strong pull I take of his engorged cock is smoky and spicy, and renders him utterly speechless.

Very much like he was in my dream.

2

Roman

S ex is a very powerful weapon. Historically it's been known to bring down even the most ruthless of men to their knees. Now I understand why. I'm sitting on one end of my father's dining room table while he sits at the other end, staring at each other silently because of sex. I'm not sure why he agreed to this sit down, but I admittedly did after being given a blowjob that changed my life.

Yeah, sex makes you stupid.

I feel like I'm in the middle of a Spaghetti Western stand off. The old man is blowing slowly on his spoonful of hot potato soup waiting for me to say something, and I'm doing the same as I bullshit around with my turkey on rye that Juliette fixed for me. Right before she ran out of Dodge.

Fuck it. I'm not hungry. I'll go first. But as soon as I prepare to open my mouth to say the first few words I've said to Joseph in months, the old coot beats me to it.

"So I hear that you have an issue with me."

That would probably be understating things, but okay, I'll bite.

"Which issue would that be?" I ask sarcastically.

"You think I have something to do with you not being able to secure any new clients."

He's right. I absolutely do think that. When Joseph and I parted ways last year, I wanted to make a clean break, meaning I'd start over from scratch. Yet he insisted that I take The Lotus and Mendez with me. I had to be mindful and consider my friends the Kings and not just myself when I made my decision, so I agreed. Lawyers sealed the deal. There were no hidden clauses, no backdoor deals I had to agree to, and no exchange of monies.

"It was a parting gift," he said at the time. Now I'm starting to think that there was a price for such a generous gift. He's cockblocking me big time.

Neither Cam, Cutter nor I have been able to sign a new client to save our fucking lives. No one is calling us to fix shit, and the feelers that we've been putting out there are resulting in basically nothing. Shit clients. Degenerates who want us to burn down their corner stores for the insurance money. It's fucking insulting.

"I certainly don't think it's a coincidence."

Joseph takes another slow slurp of his soup. The noise sickens me. Reminds me of days from my childhood when all I had to slurp on for days was ramen noodles, thanks to my addict mother and absentee father. After he dabs his mouth with a napkin, the old man sits back in his chair, hands folded in his lap; looking like the smug bastard he's always been. The same man I've resented but also revered for most of my life.

"If you think I had to convince people not to hire you and those *friends* of yours, you're sadly mistaken. There aren't too many people who are simply going to trust you *just* because you're my son. That is of course unless I tell them to." He smirks after making that last comment. Pissing me off even further.

"We've been working *together* as a team for years. Why would I have to convince anyone of anything, unless you're telling them shit to make them reconsider hiring me?"

"Let's get one thing straight. You and the Kings worked for me. We didn't work *together*. Having said that, let's not forget that I was grooming your ungrateful ass to takeover the business and be your own boss until you started sleeping around with family."

He's bringing up Elizabeth to get a rise out of me. That seems to be his go to strategy now to crush me in an argument. To rattle me. Throw me off my game. Wait for me to react like the hothead I can be. So he can say, "see." I'm not going to give him the satisfaction. I'm the new and improved Roman 2.0, and that's not what I came here for.

I'm here because just before I was about to blow a load in my beautiful girlfriend's mouth, she asked me to meet with Joseph, and if I said anything but, "yes baby," she made it quite clear that our very vigorous session of sucking and fucking would end prematurely.

Little brat.

Sure, I could have taken it out on her in other ways that night. It's what I do. But we've come to a few understandings over the last few months since we've been together. One of them being that I would stop being an orgasm bully (one of her ridiculous names for me) and engage in more reciprocal sexual endeavors with her. Or at least try. Although I don't see what the problem is. She's fooling herself if she doesn't see that we both get tremendous mutual satisfaction out of my control, my punishments, and of course my rewards.

"You can't seriously have a problem with me being with Elizabeth. You were never in her life growing up, and you don't really have any sort of emotional connection to her now. I mean you barely talked to her when she lived in this house. So what is your real attachment to this? To make sure that I'm a miserable fuck?"

"What you fail to realize, *son*, is that I do know Elizabeth. I've known Elizabeth since she was a kid, because her mother sent or emailed pictures of her over the years to us. She sent pictures of her first sleepover, her first spelling bee, she lost in the third round by the way; her first set of braces, the senior prom, nice looking kid took her if I recall right; and she also sent her graduation photos from both high school and college.

"I didn't need to spend a ton of time with her to know who Elizabeth was. I learned all about her through pictures, through anecdotes, and through overhearing brief but sweet phone conversations between Juliette and Elizabeth's mother."

I reach in my jeans and play around with a few M&Ms in my pocket. I pretty much always mindlessly munch on my favorite candy daily, but Joseph's words are making me feel a little guilty. Maybe if he had said all of this shit a long time ago, we wouldn't be here. Maybe if he had shared some of those slices of Elizabeth's life growing up with me as well, maybe I would have looked at her more like a family member, rather than a hot piece of ass seducing an entire club full of men the night I first saw her. Maybe I would have been the older cousin, or the big brother, who visited her on Penn's campus and scared motherfuckers like Ethan away before they could pollute her with their disease ridden penises.

Maybe. Maybe. Maybe.

But that's not what the fuck happened.

What happened was that Joseph and Juliette kept all that pertinent information to themselves. Probably because it was too painful for Juliette to talk about. The beloved niece she would hear about but could never see, because her brother wouldn't have anything to do with her.

What happened was I met this beloved cousin of mine only once when I was a kid, and she was annoying as fuck; so I buried her in the backyard to get rid of her. What happened was I didn't recognize her when I saw her again as an adult. And there was no stopping me once I saw Elizabeth in the club that night, and then again at the restaurant.

I'm not a big believer in fate. A real man makes his own destiny, but I'm no idiot either. I know that either God or some other higher power was smacking me in the back of the head back then, trying to point Elizabeth out to me. Trying to tell me that she was my girl, that I needed to claim her, and that I needed to make her see it too.

Elizabeth is supposed to be mine and she is. I love her, and nothing is ever going to change that. Why can't these motherfuckers we're related to get on board? I know I'm fucked up, but the one good thing about me, the one thing that I've gotten completely right is loving Elizabeth.

"So what, we're a little dysfunctional and don't spend the holidays together like other families. That doesn't change a single thing," Joseph continues on, "I don't care if I never met Elizabeth. By marriage or by blood, she is still my family, which means that she is your family too. She is your cousin, and while I don't necessarily care about who people choose to love, what I do care about is the fact that her parents will never accept the two of you. They will never be okay with it. Which means that they'll never be okay with Juliette. Which means that they definitely will *never* be okay with me. That's my attachment to *this* of which you speak."

I can't munch on my candy right now, since I'm positive that Joseph will get the wrong idea. He'll think that he's bothered me with that speech. Which he hasn't, but he has given me an earful to consider. So to help me process, I decide to take a bite of my turkey sandwich, instead of a handful of candy. Damn, it's pretty good too. Juliette spread some sort of secret sauce on the bread instead of mayo or mustard, which gives it just the right amount of tang.

Joseph carefully watches me as I chew and swallow my sandwich, then take a sip from my bottle of water. He still seems to be anticipating, or waiting for an outburst from me, as if his disapproval of my relationship means shit to me. It doesn't. I just want Elizabeth to be okay.

"What if I get her family on board? Bring brother and sister back together again. Will you stop sabotaging my business?"

Joseph leans forward.

"Sabotage?" he lets out a single incredulous laugh. "Do you even understand why I gave you The Lotus and Mendez in the first place?"

"So you could go travel the world with your wife?"

He and Juliette haven't spent much time in Philly over the last few months. They've been to several countries since he decided to essentially retire from the business, and from what Elizabeth tells me they're loving every minute of it. They have plans to continue traveling on and off for the rest of the year. Something about traveling to every continent before Juliette's next birthday.

"I didn't have to give you a single thing in order for me to take my wife around the world."

"So then why did you?" Since he seems to be dying to tell me.

"I gave you the easiest club to manage, the one with the highest profit margin, and I gave you the best client to manage, the celebrity with the deepest pockets and minimal drama as gifts from a father to his son. You don't have to work another day in your life if you so choose, Roman, and that's because I set it up that way. You may have earned a living over the years with some work on your part, but only because I permitted it to happen.

"I know I wasn't your ideal father, but I'm going to be perfectly honest with you since you're a grown man now. I'm sure you're very much aware that your birth wasn't planned. People that come from where we come from don't plan shit. Life just happens to us. When your mother told me she was pregnant, I didn't want you. I certainly wasn't in love with your mother, and I was too busy trying to make a name for myself and get out of the neighborhood to be concerned with raising a baby. Because of my mentality, I didn't accept you for a long time. That's my fault. It's one of my biggest regrets. I realize now that I was reacting to a situation that I didn't plan for like a fright- ened child and not a man. It just took me a minute to realize it.

"For a while, I thought just sending your mother money every month was me doing what I was supposed to do. Actually I thought I was doing what most of the neighbor- hood losers I grew up with weren't bothering to do. Taking care of mine. But once I really grew up and recognized that it takes more than a few dollars every month to be a father, to really take care of my responsibilities, I finally understood that I was doing you and myself an injustice.

"After that realization, there was no turning back for me. So when you called that day for my help, and asked me to come bring you some money, I knew that was a sign. I became determined to give you the life you deserved. A better life than I ever had growing up. The best schools. A nice house. A career. And I've done that. I'm still doing that. Now it's up to you to decide what you are going to do with all that I've given you."

"I'm not sure I understand what you're trying to say by telling me that long saga of my bastard beginnings," I say with an edge to my voice.

Joseph sighs. "Why are you looking for clients, Roman? You certainly don't need the money. I've made sure of that."

I think about that question. It's the first time I ever really gave it any serious consideration. Why am I busting my ass trying to find new clients when I don't need the money? When I could live off the interest of the money I have in the bank.

"Well for starters, there isn't just me to consider. There's Camden, Cutter and Jade. They're all counting on me."

"Jade and the boys can manage the club, or you can split Mendez with them, or maybe they should go on their own and do something else. So what's the *real* reason you're holding on? Dig deep."

I consider everything Joseph is asking. Instead of thinking of a snarky comeback, I decide to try and be honest with him. To be honest with myself.

"No one wants to just get up everyday and do absolutely nothing, Joseph. Not people like me. I need to keep busy. I need to work."

"You already work. Dig deeper," he demands.

"I want more challenging work. I want clients. More like Mendez, or better yet, even more fucked up ones. I don't want to just manage a club and babysit a baseball player. I'm better when I have a problem to solve."

"Good answer, but I think it's more than that. You just haven't accepted the truth yet."

I tell this bastard the truth, my truth, and it still isn't good enough for him. It never is.

"Are you listening to me, old man? I need clients. That's all there is. There is no other truth."

"All right then, if that's all there is, then go get yourself some clients."

"What the hell do you think we've been discussing here? I could get them if you'd stop throwing up roadblocks everywhere. No one will work with me. You've led them to believe that all I am is muscle, and that you were the brains. They don't think I can handle the jobs. That I'm not polished enough."

"And I wonder why they think that?"

"Are you blaming me for some of the carnage I've left behind for the sake of the family business? Because let's not forget that I was doing most of it under your orders. Your command. You wanted shit to get fixed, and sometimes that meant that things got messy. That's the world we live in. The life we chose. And you taught me everything I know."

"You're right, but clients don't want to know about the threats, the violence, or the fear that it takes to make their problems go away. They want to pretend that they've hired someone who can just magically make shit disappear for them, and leave no mess behind to remind them of what they've truly asked for."

"So you're saying the reason I have no clients is because I'm messy?"

"All I'm saying is that I am not purposely stopping you from getting any clients. I don't have to, nor do I have any interest in doing so. I was just hoping you wouldn't want that life any longer. I hoped that you'd take my gift of the club and Mendez and go live your life. A peaceful one. I can see I may have miscalculated your need for a crisis."

I made Elizabeth a promise and I've kept it by being here, but I've humbled myself as much as I possibly can today.

That's it.

I'm done.

I can see that this meeting has been a complete waste of my time just like I knew it would be. This is some sort of *pull yourself up by your own bootstraps, son* teaching moment for him. As if I'm some sort of spoiled trust fund baby. He fails to recognize the major part I played in the success of his, no scratch that, *our* business. Without me there'd be nothing getting the fuck fixed. There'd be no business.

He has no stomach for the dirty work anymore, and he hasn't for a long ass time. He thinks you can just throw money at any problem and get it taken care of, but you can't. Some people don't respond to money, regardless of the amount, especially when they think they can get more. Some people just need an old fashioned boot up their ass.

"All right then. Please thank Juliette again for the lunch." I take a final bite of my sandwich. "It's been illuminating speaking with you as usual, Joseph."

"I assure you that I'm doing nothing to prevent you from acquiring clients, Roman. They're just not ready to hire you. You'll have to figure that out on your own. If I do it for you, no one will respect you. Plus, it's not totally dried up for you out there. I've heard you've been getting a couple of clients."

"Not good ones."

"Do they pay?"

"That's not the only factor to consider and you know that. I have to be particular about what types of jobs I take. What work they want me to do. I've achieved a certain level of cache. I have standards."

"Oh so barn burners are too beneath you?" The old man asks.

Barn burners is what we call an arson job. Arson jobs can be a huge headache if you don't get it right, and they can get you serious time if you get caught. Those are not jobs that men at my level should even be entertaining. They're way too risky, and there's not enough profit.

"See that's the difference between you and me. I started out in this business here." Joseph holds his hand palm down at his hip.

"I took on shitty ass clients and built my business to here." He raises his palm up next to his waist.

"Important men started hearing about the work I was putting in on the streets, and I started getting hired for bigger jobs. Better clients. Ones that paid with a check, and not with cash washed through a strip club. I was quiet, I was efficient, and at the time I was cheap. And then ... I rose my business to here." He raises his palm to the side of his forehead.

"And I fought like hell to keep it at this level. But the problem with you is that you think that you're already here, when you're really here." He moves his hand back down to his hip.

"You've been living off of my reputation and my success, but you still have dues that must be paid if you want to rise to the level that I'm at. I didn't want that for you, but if that's the life you're seeking, you need to recognize where you fall in the food chain."

I've heard enough, so I stand up and put on my jacket. He's never respected me, the Kings, or what we've done to help make him the success that he thinks he is. I'm ready to get out of here. I'm going to fuck Elizabeth good and hard for making me agree to this waste of an hour.

"Wait," he says in a tone of voice that sounds almost regretful.

I finish putting on my jacket. "What?"

"The thing you said about bringing brother and sister together."

"What about it?"

"Do you think you can do it?"

"I don't know. Why don't you tell me what happened between you and her family that made them hate you so much?"

"Nothing in particular. Loving Juliette."

"Well they're seriously taking out that shit on me. Elizabeth's father made it quite clear. Their bigger issue with me isn't necessarily that I'm related to their daughter by marriage, but that I'm *your* son. They dislike me, but they despise you."

"You may be right about that."

"Plus I don't really give a rats ass if brother and sister never talk again. It doesn't affect me either way."

"See that's another area where we differ. It makes me question the depth and sincerity of your so-called feelings for your cousin. All I see are advantages to making sure brother and sister reunite. The main one being that it will make my wife happy, and I would move heaven and earth to make Juliette happy. You obviously wouldn't do the same for Elizabeth. You need to ask yourself if she's what you really want, or more importantly if you've even earned the right to have her."

I hate the old man sometimes. He's an asshole. Especially because he has the unique ability to make me second-guess myself and call me on my shit like no other. All this lunch has managed to do is piss me the fuck off. Elizabeth is definitely going to have to give me a repeat performance tonight to help me heal myself of all of the fucking passive aggressive jabs he's taken at me today.

I start walking towards the front door. I want to get the hell out of here in the worst way. He didn't really have to bother telling me *again* how my existence wasn't planned or wanted. That has always been crystal clear. Yet there's something about hearing it from his own lips, though, that makes me resent him just a tad bit more than I already did before I walked in this house.

We were never ultra close, but there were times when Joseph gave me glimpses of what a good father should look like. He took me to buy my first car. He introduced me to boating. He actually attended a couple of parent-teacher nights. He brought me into the *family* business. It's the knowledge of him doing these things, things he didn't have to do, that have always been at war with the man who left me without a second glance in the care of my crazy ass mother. The man who took years to get it *sort of* right. The man who basically just told me to my face that I don't deserve Elizabeth. That I'm not worthy.

Am I?

3

Roman

This is the second best feeling in the world.

My knuckles connecting with the jaw of a complete prick.

His face twisting and contorting from the impact.

Blood splattering across the sleeves of my hoodie and the concrete.

My heartbeat steady.

My breathing calculated.

Damn, I missed this. This kind of control. This absolute power. It's as close to an orgasmic experience as I can feel. Not to mention that I'm doing the world a public service by kicking this dirtbag's ass. Everyone out here has been talking about him under their breath but not doing one single thing about it. Somebody out here had to step up to the plate.

Today it's me.

I'm not sure how many days it's been since I've been on a run. I've lost track, which isn't a good thing, so today was hard. Real hard. My run didn't feel good like it usually does. The endorphins never kicked in. The shit felt like work.

That was until I spotted this dirty looking skateboarding kid in the middle of the park, who was tearing into his girl's ass about something. Probably something trivial. Something that didn't warrant the venom he was spewing. Annoying the fuck out of me and everyone within earshot, by getting louder and louder by the minute, and making the girl tear up in public.

The girl's a plump little thing with mousy brown hair and sad eyes. Wearing a dingy plaid shirt and ill-fitting jeans, the girl wasn't much to look at, but fuck if that mattered. She was somebody's daughter or perhaps someone's future mother. Hopefully never the mother of this devil's spawn. I literally watched this poor girl shrink by at least a foot from sheer humiliation today.

So while it is completely none of my business, I just couldn't let it stand. Like I said my run has been shitty, and so I'm already annoyed. I had to make it my business.

As their confrontation escalated, I casually finished stretching my hams and calves out, cracked my neck, and started to walk over to where the two of them were standing. Him yelling. Her shrinking. They were by the park's tallest white oak arguing, or should I say the prick was yelling while the girl cowered and took small steps back, farther and farther away from him. I can tell that he's done this before, and I'm guessing he's holding back because they're in public, because she's frightened but not surprised.

They both noticed me as I silently began to walk over towards them. The girl diverted her eyes quickly away as if she was embarrassed that I'd noticed the scene that he's making. The asshole tried to hide the fact that he's cracking the knuckles of his right fist behind his thigh. He knows everyone is watching, and he knows he's being out of line; so I guess he calls himself getting ready for a confrontation with me, but I'm ten steps ahead of his ignorant ass.

"What the hell do you—"

Before he can finish biting my head off, I make sure that my fist connects with the bottom of his chin with one quick but powerful upper cut, ensuring that he will bite down completely through his tongue when his jaw snaps shut. I hope the embarrassment and more importantly the pain will help him remember this day for a long ass time, because it hurts like a motherfucker.

I used to pull this move all the time when I played touch football as a kid with some of the older guys in the old neighborhood. It was a survival technique back then. Those assholes didn't care if I was younger or smaller. If you had the balls to play with them, then you had better had the balls to take body shots, elbows to your head, and a fist to your mouth. They didn't care.

My signature upper cut move got me respect back then. I took several of them out of a game with it, but today I'm simply doing it for shits and giggles. Well that and the fact that I want to take this bully down a peg or two. I despise guys that beat up on women physically or verbally. It's one of the telltale signs of a weak man, and I don't have patience for pussies.

"Wha da fluck did ya do that for asthole?!" he protests unintelligibly as blood oozes from his tongue.

Huh.

I crack my neck once to the side, because I'm thinking I'm losing my touch. He shouldn't have been able to say anything after that hit. I'm glad Cam and Cutter aren't here to see this shit. First my run, and now this. They'd be laughing their asses off.

As I step closer to jab him a second time, he throws his hand up in defense. "Wathe! Dunna hit me again."

"I thought you called me an asshole just now?"

"No, sssir." He shakes his head and a little more blood oozes from his mouth.

Okay, so I'm feeling a little better now. Especially because his girl hasn't screamed out of concern or kneeled down to tend to the jerk like I thought she might. She just silently watches him, then looks at me, and I swear I see a flicker of gratitude pass through her soft, quiet eyes.

"You're lucky," I say to the kid. "I have a lot on my mind today."

Which was why I was out for a run.

To quiet my head.

To figure out my fucking life.

"But then you disturbed it with all of your bullshit. I really wanted to put you in the emergency room. That's how much you irritated the fuck out of me, and everyone else in this park. So here's my gift to you, asshole.

"I'm not going put you in the hospital today for ruining my run. I'm just going to give you a piece of advice that I suggest you take. Next time you think about talking to her like a piece of shit, remember this day. Remember the hole in your tongue. Remember the coppery taste of the blood rolling down your throat. Remember exactly how I knocked your ass down, and how you begged me not to do it again like the pussy you are. And I want you to definitely remember that your girl saw it, and she'll sure as hell remember it too. She'll always know from this moment on that you're a total front. A fraud. A worthless piece of shit."

"And you—" I turn my attention to the young girl, who's still looking a bit shell shocked from what I've just done and said to her boyfriend. "Maybe you don't have a mom or any big sisters to tell you any better, so I will. You're better than this. Next time this guy calls, don't answer. Next time he comes by, tell your parents or whoever you live with to call the cops. This guy is trash, and there isn't much hope for him, unless he has some sort of come to Jesus moment in the near future. Otherwise this is your chance to get out before it gets a lot worse. You feel me?"

"Yes, sir," was her only response.

I just hope I got through to her. I wasn't lying. This thing between them would get a lot worse if she let it go on. I'd seen it a dozen times in the old neighborhood. In fact, I'd had first hand experience. My mother didn't like to be without a man and more than not, they were bums who talked to her like a piece of shit. It turned my stomach, but I was too young to really do anything about it at the time. I'd seen fourteen-year-old girls from the block who held their own better than my mother.

Nowadays I normally turn a blind eye to this type of shit. I'm not some vigilante out here fighting for the rights of young girls, before they destroy the little bit of self-esteem they may have left. But today I'm restless.

I haven't seen or really spoken to Elizabeth in forty-eight hours, because she's been in School Bucks mode. It sounds a little crazy. What's two days right? I never even used to go back to any woman for seconds, but now that I'm with her, I don't know how to act. I'm greedy. I want seconds, thirds and fourths. I want her all the fucking time.

Finally a text.

Elizabeth: Whatcha doing?
Me: Wiping blood off of my hands.
Elizabeth: Ha. Ha.

She thinks I'm kidding. This girl's too good for me.

Me: Finished working?

Elizabeth: Yep, I'm all yours.
Me: Will be there in 30.
Elizabeth: ♥♥♥
Thirty minutes. Who am I kidding?
I make it to her house in under twenty.
Brick fucking hard.

4

Roman

I smell a set up.

As soon as Elizabeth opens the door for me, the pungent and delectable aromas of Old Bay Seasoning, fresh garlic, butter, and seafood hit me in the gut. I'm hungry. Plus, I've been out to enough overpriced meals to know that I'm about to sit down to at least fifty bucks worth of ingredients. Now the interesting part of this scenario is that Elizabeth can't cook for shit.

That means something's up.

And it ain't just lunch.

"Still not using your key I see." Elizabeth says in a tone of voice I can't quite put a finger on. "Come in and sit down. Are you hungry?"

I'm here a lot. I helped Elizabeth pick out a flat screen TV for the living room. I keep a toothbrush and several changes of clothes here. I work a lot from the second office in here as well. But even considering all of that, Elizabeth knows that I never use my key to her place, because giving her room to decide on whether or not she wants to let me in her house or not is about the only space that I admittedly manage to give her in this relationship of ours. So I don't want to infringe on that. No woman is ever going to have the distinct pleasure of ever being able to call me smothering. No matter how badly I want to be up under her sweet ass everyday.

I'm pretty sure I know what's going on and I don't like it. The meeting between Joseph and I that she basically blackmailed me into attending didn't go well and now she feels badly. But it's been two damn days since I've been inside her or even laid eyes on her and she's cooking to make it up to me? She should have answered the door butt ass naked. That would have been the starting point for a proper apology.

"Is that a problem?"

"What?"

"Me not using my key."

"Just making an observation."

"Just trying to respect your space like we agreed. It's your place, not ours."

Elizabeth notices the cuts on my hand and lifts it up.

"I thought you were kidding. Were you really bleeding today?"

"He deserved it," I say matter of factly.

"He?"

Elizabeth grabs a first-aid kid from one of the kitchen drawers and begins to quietly work on my right hand. It's nothing serious, just a few cuts from the douchebag's jacked up front teeth. Obviously his mother didn't give two shits about him when he was a kid, because he's definitely never seen the inside of an orthodontist's office in his life.

I watch closely as Elizabeth pours the peroxide on my hand, then gently dabs it dry with a clean piece of gauze. Her meticulous care of my hand seems almost like a metaphor for how careful she has been with me and my heart. I'm so fucking lucky. So lucky that sometimes I don't trust it. Like I'm waiting for the other shoe to drop.

Her brunette curls are all swept up in a messy bun on the top of her head with a pencil going through it, but a few wisps have fallen out of the bun and are stuck to the side of her neck. All of this showcases that beautiful neck of hers, which is adorned with a very delicate gold necklace that she never takes off. A gift from her mother on her sixteenth birthday. A sweet story if it hadn't been given to her by a woman who probably thinks (or hopes) that I'm going to break her daughter's heart and disappear.

I shake that negative thought away and continue my perusal of Elizabeth's body. She's wearing a soft gray cotton tank top, gray leggings, and her feet are bare with red painted toenails. She looks fucking stunning and sexy as hell without even trying. So I can't help myself. I grab her like I've been wanting to do for days and wrap my arms tightly around her. At this moment I don't give a damn what she's up to or why she's cooking shit that she doesn't know how to cook. I just want my girl close.

"I'm all sweaty, Roman." She half-heartedly objects while trying to swat my arm away. "And I'm not finished with your hand."

"I don't give a shit," I growl.

And I don't. I grab her around the waist and pull her even closer into me.

"You smell so good." She giggles while burrowing her face into the side of my neck. After her text, I practically flew home in the Rover, showered, threw Tibbs in the backseat and headed to her place.

I place my hands at the base of her throat and pull her back for a long kiss. Her response is hesitant at first, but after a few seconds, I feel her body melt into mine. Like it always does. As if it's just where it belongs. Intertwined with mine. I explore her mouth with my tongue. Making sure to revisit all it's nooks and crannies. Ending it with a soft pull of her top lip.

"I missed you, Duchess."

"Me too," she replies immediately.

I pull my head back to take a long look at my girl. Elizabeth has been mine for almost a year now, and I want her more each day than I did the day before. I hate feeling like this sometimes, because I've always despised distractions. And Elizabeth has to be the biggest distraction I've ever experienced in my life. But I wouldn't do a thing to change it. In fact I pray almost everyday that I don't fuck it up. I fought really hard to get her, for her to accept her feelings for me, and to not worry about what others would think of how we met. How we're related. But sometimes I feel as if I'm fighting twice as hard to keep her.

Her parents still aren't fucking okay with me, which I know has to be tearing her up inside, even though she will never admit it. The old man even kind of mentioned that if I really loved Elizabeth, I'd be doing whatever I could to make it right. It's not like I don't think about fixing this shit with her parents, but in all honesty, I don't see why we need their approval to be together. We're grown. And frankly I can't change who my father is, which seems to be the bigger issue.

Her friends seem to be okay about us, but it's obvious that we won't be doing a lot of double dates or group outings with most of them. They're all fresh college grads that come from good homes. Normal homes. I'm from the streets. They've all got some sort of entry level job or are in graduate school, and I'm far beyond them with enough money to live on for the rest of my life if I invest wisely. And that doesn't make me feel superior to them, or inferior, it just makes us very different; in very different places in our lives.

While I know how to make money, I don't know shit about how to make money doing what Elizabeth does. I'm flying blind in that world, and sometimes it bothers the hell out of me. I wish I could help her build a million dollar tech business, but I don't seem to be much help in that department. Not in the way she needs it. She needs a few ridiculously smart computer geeks on her team, or a high-powered publicist to spread the word about the app; not someone with my particular skill set. I could probably buy her those things (in particular a high-powered publicist), but I know she wouldn't accept them. She's very independent in that way, which I totally respect. So until she needs me to punk the shit out of someone, or blackmail someone, I'm basically useless to her.

"What happened today?" she asks.

"This skater boy in the park was making a spectacle of himself by belittling his girl, and I couldn't take the shit anymore. No one else bothered to step up to say anything to him, but you could tell everyone wanted to kick his ass."

"That's interesting."

"What is?"

"Did he hit you first?"

"Hell no!" I say it like she's lost her mind. Then I pay closer attention to her facial expression and the meaning behind it. "What? You don't approve?"

"You never do stuff like this. You never seek out a confrontation. Not unless it has to do with work, and even then you try to avoid getting physical."

This woman puts me on a pedestal that I don't deserve. She doesn't have an exactly accurate idea of what I do and what I don't do.

"I was standing up for the girl. Women's rights and all

that good shit. I thought you'd be proud."

"I think being proud would definitely be overstating how I feel about this hand," she says as she finishes wrapping my knuckles in a bandage. "Clearly you sucker punched him. That's not necessarily heroic or necessary."

Her words eerily remind me of similar ones said to me by my high school counselor.

"Are you fucking serious right now?"

She shrugs her shoulders.

"What's going on with you?" I ask. I didn't expect a ticker tape parade, but I can't say that I totally expected *this* reaction.

"What?" she replies nonchalantly, using very poor acting skills.

"You're in there cooking, and let's be honest, babe, you don't do a lot of cooking. Plus, you're acting like I just committed a crime, when all I did was do the world a damn favor. So what's going on? Second time I'm asking," I warn.

"Well there are a couple of things on my mind I guess."

"Talk."

"Well the first thing isn't necessarily a bad thing. In fact, it's a great thing. You know that coder I hired a while back to work for me virtually? Well he's recently moved here to Philly. That's who I've been meeting with the last two days. We'll be able to work together in person and on a regular basis here at the house. I'll definitely get a lot more accomplished this way. You know how hard it is to work virtually with coders sometimes."

She's practically puking words. Trying way too hard to convince me. I don't like this shit one single bit.

"Uh-huh."

"Remember that this was always the plan, Roman. Hiring someone who I could work with here in the house."

"I remember," I say icily. "It was my fucking plan."

I just didn't foresee the plan playing out quite this way. I don't know jack shit about this guy who she's hired to work for her, because I promised her that I wouldn't interfere in her business. Just like she doesn't interfere in mine.

They've worked together for a while, but most of it was through chats and Skype, so I never felt the need to do a full background check on him. But him moving here. And her telling me after the fact. That's something totally different, and that's not something I can honestly say that I can just let ride. There are too many unanswered questions about the whole shit.

Did he move here specifically for her? For this job? Do they talk about more than work shit? Is he single? What does he look like? Is he attracted to her?

Wait, I've just bumped my head and lost my damn mind. Of course he's attracted to her. He's a man, and Duchess is a man's wet dream.

"I'm going to need to run a check on him obviously," I say to her. "What's his name?"

"Really, Roman?"

I ignore the attitude.

"What's his fucking name?"

"I've mentioned it to you a thousand times. Now you want his name *again*, because he's moving here?"

"Do I have to ask a third time?"

"Blake! His name is Blake Harrison," she yells.

"Now what else did you have to tell me?"

"Sloan got a promotion."

"And why the hell would I care about that?"

Elizabeth hits me on the shoulder.

"Because she's my best friend idiot, and because the two of us are going out Friday night to celebrate."

"Friday," I say stoically.

Fridays belong to us.

Elizabeth calls them our "date nights." I call them our *go out and do something, before I fuck her senseless nights*. This is something we organically established about two months ago. Something I watched the old man do with Juliette, and I figured that out of all the things he's done wrong, at least my father got his relationship with Juliette right. So I don't mind following that blueprint, even if I never will admit to the shit.

"Her idea no doubt," I grumble.

That bitch Glamazon is always plotting against me.

"I know what you're thinking, but Sloan's whole team is taking her out to celebrate, and she invited me to go too. I couldn't very well pick the day. Most office employees go out at the end of the week. It's just one Friday. We'll have plenty more."

Elizabeth talks to her whacked out Barbie doll girl-friend every damn day on the phone. Do they have to hang out on *our* night too? I'm going to have to remind the Glamazon of who the fuck I am in a little bit. I've let her get away with entirely too much meddling, and I'm sick of her shit.

"Am I invited?" I ask.

As if I was really going to fucking go, but when Elizabeth turns her lips up as if I'm being ridiculous for even asking, the shit rubs me the wrong way. At least give me the chance to say no.

"Well am I?"

She huffs. "Why would you want to go? You barely like Sloan, and you definitely don't like any of the people she works with. You wouldn't have a good time."

The brush off.

"Am I your dirty little secret, Elizabeth?" I jest. Sort of.

"Oh please. You're hardly anybody's secret. Her whole

office knows who you are. You've made sure of that on more than one occasion."

I chuckle to myself. That's true. I know all about that horny Thomas asshole Sloan works with who's been after Elizabeth since forever. I warned him once to stay the fuck away from her, but he's not a good listener. So I've had to make an appearance a few more times to remind him and anyone else who's considering making a play that Elizabeth belongs to me.

"So I'm not invited? I just want to be clear."

"Oh my God, Roman—"

"All right, all right." I cut her off, before she really gets mad and doesn't give me any pussy tonight. "You're right. I don't want to go out with those uptight pricks anyway. They act like they're curing cancer or something, when all they are, are drug pushers."

She rolls her eyes.

"Is there anything else?" I ask. "Neither of those things seem worthy of this five star meal, that I'm about to risk my life for."

"Very funny. Can't I just do something nice for my boyfriend?" she asks while twisting several strands of her hair.

A dead giveaway.

"You absolutely could, but I know better, Duchess. What's up?" I pull the hair she's twisting out of her hands and between my fingers. "If I have to keep asking, you're going to have to pay for it later, and I promise that you won't like it. You won't come at all, and I'll enjoy every minute of watching you squirm."

"All right already," she exhales a puff of air then continues, "I want you to meet with Joseph again."

I knew it was some dumb shit like this.

"Uh, hell no."

"Why?"

"Haven't you and Juliette learned your lesson yet? It didn't work last time, and it won't work again. The two of us will talk if and when we're ready to talk. We're grown fucking men. Leave well enough alone."

"If we leave it up to you, you two will never talk. You both are just alike. You both think that you don't need anything but money and sex, but that's not all you need, you two need each other too."

I almost laugh. She's watched too many family dramas where things end up neat and tidy and in a perfect bow. That's never going to happen with us. We've never been that. We never will be. And I'm very much okay with that.

"I said no."

"I'm asking you to meet with him again, because a letter came for you."

"A letter?"

"Yes, it was delivered to the house. A few days after J and J returned from their Alaskan cruise, I stopped by and Juliette told me about it."

J and J is Elizabeth's new nickname for the old man and Juliette.

"What's with all the clandestine maneuvers? Why didn't Juliette just call me to come by and pick it up?"

Elizabeth hesitates for a moment.

"Because of Joseph."

"What about him."

"He wasn't necessarily going to tell you about it."

"Is that fucking right?"

I feel a lethal mixture of tension and trepidation swirling around in my gut. There could only be one person that Joseph would give that much of a damn about me having any contact with.

"Is it from ... *her?*"

"Yes," Elizabeth answers in a careful tone.

"Did you read it?" I ask hoping that she didn't. I have no idea what the letter says, but I definitely don't want Elizabeth reading any of my mother's *crazy* until I do.

"No."

"Is there a return address on it?"

"No, but the postmark is from Vegas. If you want to read it, you should go over there and get it, Roman. It's your letter, and you're a grown man. Uncle Joseph can't just keep it from you. Just go over there and ask him for it."

So my mother's in Vegas, huh? How fucking cliché.

"So what's for dinner?" I ask abruptly changing the subject.

There's no point in talking about this further. First of all I'm not asking Joseph for shit. Secondly, I'm not opening that letter. All I ever really wanted to know was if my mother was alive and she clearly is. I did sort of want to know where she was living, and now I do. She's in Vegas. It would also be great to know why she was such a shitty mother too, why she didn't want me, but I'll never get that answer. Not an honest one anyway. So I'm thinking that I just need to let all my fucked up mother issues go at this point. She's always going to disappoint me, so what's the point of caring anymore?

Elizabeth stares at me for a moment. Waiting for some sort of reaction from me. Probably trying to figure out what kind of a mood I'm in now that I know about the letter, but I'm not going to let that shit bother me or bother us. I've got a good thing going. A great fucking thing, and I'm not going to let shadows from the past ruin that or ruin us. Never.

"Dinner?" I ask again.

"A crab bake." She smiles as if she's very pleased with herself. "I made crab legs, sausage, corn on the cob, onions and red potatoes smothered in garlic butter. Just the way you like it."

That puts a genuine grin across my face for a lot of reasons. First of all, I am actually really hungry. I haven't eaten a thing today. All I usually have before a run is a protein shake. The second reason I'm smiling is because this dinner is symbolic.

Over the summer Elizabeth and I visited the Jersey Shore several times. Like so many East Coast families, Elizabeth had been to the shore countless times with her family and friends over the years, but I wanted to show her *my* Jersey Shore, which is a little different than what she was used to.

While I grew up on cheese steaks and salt water taffy at the beach just like she did, after moving in with Joseph as a young teenager, I was introduced to a whole other side of the shore. The side where the Philadelphia elite own summer homes and private boats. The side where families vacation in beautifully restored and modernly renovated Victorian homes with rich attention to detail, on freshly paved streets, alongside clean quiet beaches and lush land-scaping. It's part of the shore I had no idea existed as a kid, because you drive past all of those areas when you're on your way to the family beaches in typical tourist towns like Wildwood or Ocean City.

So I made reservations at my favorite five-star hotel in Avalon, New Jersey with a pristine private beach where we spent plenty of days playing in the water and plenty of nights with me playing in between her legs.

One of the things we did for four nights straight was order a delicious crab bake and eat it on the deck by sunset. It's one of my new favorite memories, and I think it's so fucking cute how she's trying to recreate it. I just wish it wasn't because of that damn letter.

"I'm going to punish you tonight for this," I tease.

"For fixing you one of your favorite meals?" she asks incredulously.

"No, for thinking that you needed to do all of this in order to tell me about a stupid letter."

"I didn't think that."

"You were nervous. You thought I was going to lose my shit."

"I think I had a right to worry a little. You're already in a bad mood. You beat some poor kid's head in today for no reason. Or should I say not a good enough reason. I just didn't know how you would feel about it."

"I don't feel anything," I say as I sit down at her dining table.

"Then you're lying to yourself, because I know you, Roman Masterson. And just mentioning your mother's name makes you feel all sorts of things. Maybe one day you'll share some of those feelings with me."

I rub the back of my neck to relieve some of the tension that has built by just talking about my mother for the last five fucking minutes. Evidently Elizabeth is right. My mother is a topic I like to avoid at all costs, because the subject makes me more than just a little bit angry. It makes me feel something way more fucking scary.

Sad.

"So do you want to stop by their house to grab the letter after we eat?" she asks while placing a large, steaming bowl of seafood in front of me.

"You really don't want to come tonight do you?"

"I take it that means no. See, just the mention of your mother's name and you've already turned into the orgasm bully again. I thought we had a new agreement? Why are you killing the messenger?" Elizabeth chuckles.

"Oh, I'm not going to kill the messenger." I grin sinisterly. "I'm just going to kill what's in between the messenger's legs. I promise you that shit."

"Promises. Promises," she says in a flirty way that shoots straight from the base to the tip of my dick.

"That mouth of yours," I warn.

"Well somebody has to–"

And before she finishes saying whatever snarky comment she was about to make, I slam my crab cracker down and shoot straight out of my seat. I've had enough, and I'm about to end all this shit right now. She knows it too, because she shrieks, and makes a beeline for the loft.

"Stay away from me, you Neanderthal!"

I laugh a little out loud, because my girl's reflexes are so slow. So slow that I could have easily caught her ass right by the forearm at the table, but where's the fun in that? I allow her to reach midway up the ladder to the loft, but then literally grab her ass off of there and throw her over one of my shoulders.

"Put me down before you throw your back out!" she protests.

I give her ass a quick whack.

"What am I an old man now? It'll be a long time before lifting your tiny ass will ever throw my back out."

"I'm serious, Roman."

"I'm serious as fuck too."

With one hand holding her in place, I use the other to quickly and dramatically swipe our entire crab bake to the floor, and then I toss her ass right on top of the table that we were just eating on.

And then I eat her.

Until she finally whispers with an exhausted smile and two orgasms later ...

"You always deliver on your promises, Masterson."

Fucking right I do.

5

Elizabeth

There is sleep crusted in the corners of my heavily lidded eyes. My mouth tastes like I've swallowed a bottle of liquid chalk, and my head is pounding like a bratty little five year old has been kicking me in the temples for days.

I've come to the conclusion that being best friends with a professional partier and drunk (I mean social drinker) can be utterly exhausting for an ordinary girl like me.

Last night Sloan and I spent the majority of our evening bar hopping with a few of her co-workers to celebrate her latest promotion at work. I'm not really sure how things work exactly in the world of pharmaceuticals, but I'm pretty sure that she is now the head of her own team of sales reps, instead of being on someone else's team (or something like that).

Sloan's not really one for giving lots of details about her job, and I'm not really sure why. I guess she's just weirdly private about some things, and then on the other hand gives way too much information about things like her sex life. But whatever the specifics about her new job, she's happy about it, and therefore I'm happy for her. It means more money, which Sloan is very much used to having since she is the daughter of a professional basketball player. So it's a very good thing that she can now further keep herself living in the lifestyle that she is accustomed to.

To celebrate, last night we probably stopped by four different bars, and unfortunately I had a drink at every single one. Two drinks is truly my happy place. That's the point where I need to stop. Big girls already know their limits, but idiots like myself? Well we keep going and going. And that's how I know that at three drinks I'm twisted sideways, and at four I'm just plain old stinking drunk. Interestingly enough, I know for a fact that Sloan drank way more than I did, yet I seem to be the only one that's in a whole world of pain the morning after. So unfair. She gets legs that go on for days and the ability to drink most grown men under a table, and I get ... this.

Lying on one side of her feather soft bed (she has one of those memory foam mattress toppers), in a fetal position, wondering why I allowed myself to drink that damn much, and promising God that I'll never do it again if he'd just stop the pain. While she's over there happily humming an old David Bowie song and brushing her teeth like she hasn't a care in the world.

A sound very much like a sickly animal escapes from my mouth. I want her to stop humming. I want her to stop brushing her teeth so noisily, and I desperately want to attach several strips of tape across her mouth, so that she'll shut the frack up.

"Are you finally awake?" Sloan asks me with toothpaste suds oozing out from the corners of her mouth.

"Eww." I gag. "Would you please finish taking care of that before you start talking to me," I beg while my stomach rolls.

"It's just toothpaste you nutball."

"Just spit it out!"

Ugh, just saying those four words made my head even worse.

"We drink every time we go out, and you're in your twenties. I cannot for the life of me understand why you're acting like a fourteen year old newbie. It's alcohol, not heroin, for God's sake."

"First of all, I wasn't getting drunk when I was *fourteen*. At that age, I was still in braces and spent my free time scrapbooking with my mom."

"Cornball!" she jokingly sneezes through her fist.

"That's right, I was," I say proudly. "Which made me a newbie at drinking alcohol at the age of twenty-one, which wasn't that long ago thank you very much. You know the age when drinking is legal for law abiding citizens of this great country of ours?"

"Hardy, har, har. You told me that you used to drink your mom's wine when you were a kid, cornball."

"Not even close, person who only hears what she wants to hear. What I told you was that I would steal *sips* of my mom's wine on occasion. That's a little different than all of your high school tales of getting drunk at the local baseball field with a boy four years older than you, slut puppy."

"Okay, okay. So I'm a little more *seasoned* than you," she admits while cracking up. "But I gave you a ritual to follow. Food, then alcohol, then water. Then alcohol again, then water, then home, then Motrin, then sleep. It's foolproof. Learned it from my parents and their wino friends when they used to have house parties after the home games."

Ah, that explains a lot. Sloan's parents had a busy social life when she was a kid, and her dad was a popular basketball player for the Sixers. The complete opposite of my quiet childhood in the 'burbs.

"I never get sick at night, and I never have a hangover in the morning. You must have skipped something. Do I need to write it down for you, Babygirl?" she asks with a crooked smile.

I suck my teeth as my response, but unfortunately I think she may be right. I'm not the best listener sometimes, and it's very possible that I may have skipped a couple of steps. I definitely didn't drink all the water I was supposed to, and the Motrin bottle is still in my bag. I don't even think I ever took it out, or I probably would have left it on top of Sloan's nightstand last night.

I suck at this.

"You know what?" she asks after spitting toothpaste suds in the sink. My stomach rolls again.

"Oh my God, Sloan, what?"

Why is she still talking?

"We should do this every week!" she announces excitedly.

"And why the hell would I want to do *this* every week?"

"Well I wasn't sure how to bring it up, but I think we're a little off right now. Our friendship is a little off I mean, and I want to fix it."

What is she talking about?

"I mean I know I'm on the fast track at work, but lately I seem to be spending way too much time with the girls at work. All they do is blow smoke up my ass, because I'm the top female rep in my department. They just want my spot. They're not real. You're my only real friend, Bitsy."

"There's nothing wrong with our friendship, Sloan." I groan not really wanting to talk about this right now. Especially if the end result is me agreeing to a night of this type of ridiculousness every weekend.

"Come on. You have to admit that we've grown a bit

apart over the last few months, especially because of the bubble you seem to be living in."

"Me?"

I knew it was just a matter of time before Sloan brought up the "Roman bubble" that she believes I've been floating around in. She's mentioned that term a few times to me lately, but after fighting my feelings for so long, I'm not ashamed to admit that I definitely have fully embraced my relationship with Roman. When I'm not working on my business, I want to spend every waking moment with him.

In the car with him.

Talking to him.

Texting him.

Kissing him.

Under him.

On top of him.

I already know how that must seem to some people, especially Sloan, but I'm smart enough to also recognize that I'm in the honeymoon stage of this relationship. And that I'm still learning new things that I like, or frankly that I love about Roman every single day. And that excites me. I like the bubble.

She also needs to understand that a lot of this is probably because I'm making up for lost time sexually (which is why I'm always jumping his bones or permitting him to jump mine), and that eventually this need I have to spend every waking moment with him will eventually subside. Of course I probably need to do something proactive in order for that to ever happen. So I can't believe I'm thinking this, but maybe my crazy friend is right.

Perhaps agreeing to a weekly girls night out with my bestie would be a beneficial part of helping that process along. I need to explore other interests other than Roman if the two of us actually plan on moving forward in a healthy way. I need balance. We both do. I don't think I'd survive it if he became tired of me. Not after all it took to get here.

I'll probably have to fight Roman tooth and nail for him to agree to this though, because no matter how much I talk up her attributes, Sloan and her very large personality have not grown favorably upon my boyfriend. It's no secret that she isn't his favorite person. I think he believes she's a "bad influence" and simply tolerates her for my sake.

"Okay let's do it," I say.

I agree partly because I think it's a good idea and partly to shut her up. I just want to sleep this hangover off.

"Friday nights?"

Fridays? Oh boy, he's definitely going to hate this idea.

"What?" She notices my hesitance. "Are Fridays going to be a problem with the Dark Knight?" she asks with one hand on her hip. "Even Batman takes a night off."

"Oh would you stop it already."

I don't really want to give Sloan any more ammunition to talk negatively about Roman than she already does. Some days it's funny, but on other days it makes me uncomfortable.

"I mean Fridays are the best party nights in the city. Plus it's the easiest way I can get some of the guys from work to pay for a round of drinks, so it doesn't have to come out of our pockets all night. The whole office goes out Friday nights."

"You sure are cheap for someone who just got a raise."

"I don't care if I become a billionaire. A lady should have her drinks paid for by a gentleman. That's just how shit is supposed go down. My daddy taught me that a man who won't at least pay for a round isn't worth a second glance."

"Earth To Sloan. Your daddy is a millionaire. Of course he'd say that."

"He wasn't always a millionaire, and I know for a fact that—"

"Oh my God. I'm going to vomit in your bed if you don't shut up now. Fridays are fine, okay?"

Sloan sits on the edge of the bed while drying her mouth with a fresh towel.

"Good."

She stops what she's doing and begins to glare at the screen of her phone with a perplexed look on her face.

"What is it now?" I ask.

"I'm not trying to sound like I'm full of myself, but this is the third guy in about six weeks to basically blow me off. I mean ... I'm no hot model chick, but I've got a halfway decent ass and an amazing pair of tits, so I just can't believe that not one of these dudes is even remotely interested in seeing what I'm like in bed."

"You're right, that's not egotistical at all," I say sarcastically as I pull Sloan's feather down comforter back over my head. "Gosh, it's so bright in here. Can you please close the shades?"

"I mean look at this text." She shoves her cell phone under the covers ignoring my obvious pain.

"Sloan, please," I whine. "That screen is like a sunbeam. You could at least turn down the brightness level."

"All right, lightweight." She adjusts the settings. "Here." Then she shoves the phone back under the comforter.

215-555-7982: Hey I can't make it tonight. I'll call u when my schedule clears.

"That's all he said?" I ask.

"That's it, and I'm absolutely confused as all hell. Me and this guy had some serious chemistry percolating. Tall, built, tax attorney, and twenty-nine years old. He's perfect on paper and even hotter in person. We would make beautiful golden babies in an alternate universe where I cared about shit like that."

I hand Sloan the phone back and she tosses it in the center of the bed. "Well I guess he wasn't as perfect as you thought. Maybe your radar is off."

"Maybe you're right. Hell, maybe he's gay. I don't know what the hell is going on. Maybe I just need to chill out for a minute, and stop looking so hard for Mr. Right."

"Mr. Right?"

"You know what I mean. Mr. Right In Bed."

"Ahh, yes. Good idea," I mumble, curling back in my fetal position. Hoping she's finally done talking.

I can't deal with one of Sloan's pity parties right now, because that means she's going to talk me to death, when all I want to do is sleep off this throbbing pain in my head. Maybe I can manage to listen to her grumblings after some breakfast, a couple of those Motrin I never took, and a hot shower ... in like five hours.

I fall in and out of sleep for what seems like an eternity, but really only ends up being about ninety minutes. When I sleepily stretch and adjust my position in the bed, it clues Sloan in on the fact that I'm not in a deep sleep any longer. So she decides to pounce on the opportunity and much to my chagrin ... makes a suggestion.

"Bitsy."

"Yep," I say tersely.

"Let's go get coffee."

"Now? What time is it?"

Eww, my throat sounds raspy.

"Noon."

Ugh, I never sleep in this late. Okay that's it. I'm on an alcohol hiatus at least until Christmas.

"Did Roman call?" I ask.

"Nope."

Her gleeful response irritates me, because she's supposed to be cheering for my new relationship, not wishing for its demise, but that's an argument for another day.

"Looks like he'll be totally fine with this new Friday arrangement, huh?"

Sloan can be a real bitch sometimes.

"Oh be quiet."

I briskly grab my phone and check it for any text messages. There's nothing there, which I already knew would be the case, but I just wanted to make sure. So I decide to text him instead.

Me: Hey

Roman: Duchess

Me: Are you all right?

Roman: No

Me: What's wrong?

Roman: Why aren't you at home?

Me: Because I'm at Sloan's

Obviously, duh.

Roman: Aren't you two a little old for sleepovers?

Me: I drank too much. So I stayed here.

There's a delay in his response. That pause is his way of letting me know that he's annoyed with me for staying out and probably irritated more so with my drinking. Although I find him to be such a hypocrite.

He's fine with me drinking as long as he's around to reap the benefits of my inebriation. He can get away with murder once I've had my usual limit of two drinks. Although some of it is pure acting on my part. I'd allow Roman Masterson to do almost anything to me with or without the liquid courage.

Roman: We agreed to Fridays. Not Saturdays. I'll talk to you later.

Jerk.

Me: Fine

I refuse to engage him when he acts like this, and honestly he's been acting like this a lot lately. It's starting to make me think all sorts of crazy things. Like maybe he's growing tired of me or tired of a committed relationship. I mean this is the longest one he's ever been in, or maybe the only one he's be in. Or maybe our differences are starting to take a toll? I don't know. Some days I can see us as a gray haired couple sitting on rocking chairs, and some days I'm not even sure we'll make it past next week.

"What did the Dark Knight have to say for himself?" Sloan asks with the same disingenuous tone that Roman uses when he asks about her.

"Nothing at all."

"Mmm-hmm. So you ready for that coffee then?"

"Yep, but I'm going to need a sweatshirt and a pair of your Converse."

"No problem, girl."

As I lean against the cool ceramic tiles in Sloan's shower, I put myself through a mental checklist of all the things I have on tap for next week. I have an interview with my first national newspaper on Monday, thanks to some coverage I received a month ago from a local blogger. It will be amazing to have a spotlight interview and start getting the word out about School Bucks in a bigger way.

Sales for my app have picked up during the autumn season, because that's when parents begin to earnestly look into SAT coaching and testing, early admissions, and scholarship searches for their kids. This is a great time to actively expand the database as well as strengthen features of the app, which is why I'm so fortunate to have such a great coder like Blake (my new employee) on board.

With his help, I don't think it's too much of a stretch to have an expanded and updated version of the app ready by Christmas. A lot of students will be getting new smartphones for the holidays as gifts and will download lots of new apps when they do. I want School Bucks to be one of those apps, because who doesn't need money for college right?

On Tuesday I'll be working most of the day, and on Wednesday I've agreed to help Juliette with a little home project of hers. She wants to re-shelve and paint her pantry. Why she won't spend Joseph's oodles of dollars to just hire someone to do it is beyond me, but who am I to refuse my very kind hearted aunt. Plus it's a great way to spend time with her. We don't see each other that much anymore now that I've moved out.

I typically reserve Friday afternoons and evenings for Roman. Even though we talk to each other everyday and try to see each other several days a week (i.e. The Roman bubble), it's on Fridays that we have our own version of a date night. We try to do some sort of activity, like a normal dating couple, and then we spend the rest of the night wrapped up, around, and inside each other. I'm going to have to move that date night to Thursdays now, and I already know that Roman is going to give me hell about it. I don't look forward to that conversation.

Even though I'm doing this for us, to make sure that there is an "us" over the long haul, I don't really want to do it. Which is exactly why I should. Even if I don't really want to hang out with Sloan every Friday night. Even if I'd rather be spending my entire weekends with Roman. I cannot allow that desire to influence every single decision that I make.

Plus, I think Roman may be getting a bit used to me making decisions that revolve totally around him. I will not give him utter and total power over my life, and I refuse to let him think that he has it. No matter how much I tell myself that it wouldn't be bad at all. That it wouldn't be a problem. That I would in fact welcome it, want it, and enjoy it. Because to admit that, would be like handing over my independent woman card at the front door, and Beyonce would be standing right in the doorway, in her sparkling leotard and high heels, waiting to bitch slap some sense back into me.

So here I am.

Showering in Sloan's bathroom, about to put on some of her clothes, to go have coffee at Java, and to try and think about all the other things I've got going on in my life other than Roman.

Maybe I'd have better success at it if only I could stop thinking about that thing he does with his tongue, oh and his fingers, and then of course that massive cock of his. Yeah, not thinking about any of that would make this whole independent woman thing a lot easier.

Because right now all I feel like doing is putting on a dress, pouring Roman a drink, cooking his dinner, lighting a cigarette, and waiting for him to get home from work like one of those good little 1950s housewives.

To hell with Beyonce.

6

Elizabeth

As soon as we walk inside of Java, the smell of freshly roasted coffee hits me like a ton of bricks. My stomach begins to growl in angry protest. It wants caffeine. And what's interesting is that I'm not a huge coffee drinker, but I think alcohol does weird things to my body and makes me crave things I normally wouldn't desire.

"Seriously?" I rhetorically ask the cashier.

It's just my luck that Java is out of caramel drizzle, so both Sloan and I are going to have to order some other sort of specialty drink. I had my mouth all set for an extra hot caramel macchiato, but now I'm just annoyed. And it gets even better.

It looks like Java has recently redecorated the interior of the shop, eliminating all the comfy club chair seating they used to have. Now there are more places to sit, but it's all hard, wooden chairs with metal legs. Totally practical but terribly uncomfortable. This wasn't a good idea. I want to get back into bed.

"Let's just take our drinks and head back to your place." I suggest.

"Let's just sit here for a few minutes. You never know who we might see."

"Exactly. I look and feel like death warmed over. I don't want to see anyone I know."

Sloan ignores my complaining, as usual, and grabs us two chairs at a small circular table in the far corner of the shop.

"Just for a few minutes. To celebrate my promotion. And we'll be able to people watch at this table without people really being able to see us."

"And just how long are we going to celebrate this promotion of yours."

"Don't be a hater, Bitsy."

"Who's hating? I have no interest in selling Viagra to horny old men like you do. I just want to get back into bed."

"Remind me never to drink with you again. You are so damn cranky on the hangover day."

"Whatever. So just tell me, who exactly are we waiting for?" I ask suspiciously.

"No one in particular, inspector gadget. I just wanted to get out of the house."

"Yeah right," I mumble.

Sloan and I spend the next few minutes debriefing each other about the previous night's escapades. She tells me about a guy she met at the second bar we visited last night, and how they flirted with each other for a while then exchanged numbers. Now she's waiting to see how long it will take him to call her, and wonders if this one's going to blow her off too.

I, on the other hand evidently spent a lot of time at the

last bar we stopped at talking to a bartender named Mark. A conversation that I have very little recollection of.

"How do you know his name was Mark?" I ask Sloan in an attempt to remember what ridiculous things I may have said last night.

My memory is spotty, but when I concentrate really carefully, I think that I can remember bits and pieces of a conversation between the two of us. I'm pretty sure Mark and I attempted to have some sort of philosophical debate about the liberal agenda in Hollywood, bad reality TV, and maybe something about a kitten he adopted; but I'm not one hundred percent sure. I lost chunks of our conversation to plenty of red wine by the time I woke up this morning. Similar to waking up from a dream that you can only remember snippets of.

"How on earth can you not remember him? Every time you asked him a question you drawled out his name like you were Scarlet O'Hara holding court before the big ball."

"If you actually watched the movie, you'd know that Scarlet O'Hara didn't ever drawl her words out. She was actually a fast talker."

"Whatever." She quickly cuts me off. "You were like *Marrrrk* how long have you been a bartender? *Marrrrk,* is the house merlot good? *Marrrrrk,* can you ask the deejay to change the song?"

Oh crap. Did I say all of that?

"You're such a little flirt once you get some vino traveling through those Type A veins of yours, Babygirl. I think it helps to clear out all the Dark Knight cobwebs from your brain, and you start seeing the world for all that it truly has to offer and not just what's inside your little love bubble."

"Oh please. There's no flirting involved. I just become

a Chatty Cathy when I drink. I like to talk to people. I'm not always on the prowl like some people I know."

"Then why do you end up chatting up *only* hot looking bartenders everywhere you go? Why didn't you talk to the humongous guy who was sitting right next to you, and staring you down the whole time we were there?"

"Was he hot?"

"The big guy?"

"No, ding-dong, the bartender."

"Absofuckinglutely, but how convenient of you to not recall that part of the evening. So I guess when your boyfriend asks you what you did last night, you won't bother to make mention of *Marrrrk* will you, because you don't remember. How very convenient."

I roll my eyes upward in exasperation.

"Everyone has their weird thing, Sloan. I think flirting with bartenders may be mine."

"Either that or you've figured out the smartest way to drink for free all night."

We both start cracking up, but then I shut my mouth instantly once I hear it.

"Grab that chair over there."

My ears must be playing tricks on me.

"Why do you have that look on your face all of a sudden?" Sloan inquires.

I'm staring blankly inside my coffee cup.

I can't speak.

I can barely breathe.

I'm waiting to hear it again. To make sure.

That voice.

I don't want to do it, but I have to. I turn my head and scan the room looking for it. I need to be sure, before I lose it right in the middle of Java.

Sloan shifts nervously in her seat.

"You're freaking me out, Bitsy," she whispers quietly. "What the hell is it?"

The voice speaks again.

There's a low, callous timber to it. It's familiar and frightening. And when I hear it for the second time my blood runs ice cold.

"That one there, dumb ass."

I pray it isn't, but I think that I know that voice.

Shrek.

"Let's get out of here, Sloan," I speak quietly.

"Not until you tell me why right now," she says while looking around the room frantically for the cause of my distress.

"Don't turn your head!"

Sloan's eyes bug out.

"What. The. Hell. Is. Going. On. Dammit?!"

"He's here," I whisper with a voice dripping in fear.

"Who's here?"

"The guy who attacked me."

"Where?"

Sloan is about to pivot her head once again, until I move across the table and firmly grab her forearm to stop her.

"I said *stop* turning your head. He knows what I look like, Sloan, and I have no idea what he looks like. Only his voice. We have to get out of here ... now."

Sloan nods her head finally in realization. She knows more than anyone how my life was turned inside out after the assault, and she definitely knows just how frightened I am of my attacker. It's the sole reason why I immediately picked up and moved in with my aunt.

Like a guardian angel on my shoulder, Roman's face pops into my head. If he were here, he'd know exactly what to do and what to say to make me feel safe. Of course, if he was here, there's also the chance that he would put himself in harms way, and I definitely don't want that either.

While my man is a badass, Shrek is no joke either. He's a drug dealer, a woman beater, and bottom of the barrel scum. I've always imagined that a beast like him, with virtually no conscience, must drink snake venom for breakfast. Certainly not a hot cup of civilized coffee from Java The Hut. *What on earth is he doing in a coffee shop filled with college kids?*

Coincidence or not, contemplating why Shrek *may* be in the same coffee shop as me is not what I should be doing right now. Right now I need to concentrate on getting the hell out of here. Quietly and cautiously. So that's what I'm going to do. That's what I'm pretty sure Roman would advise me to do.

I think carefully about that. I've learned a lot these last few months talking to Roman about his many adventures when fixing issues for clients. Sticky situations he's found himself in. One of the first things he taught me was to always be diligent about assessing my surroundings as quickly and quietly as possible. Whether I felt I was in imminent danger or not.

I notice that there are two doors to Java. The glass double doors in the front and the single glass door side entrance that leads to the small parking lot. I don't know what Shrek looks like, but his voice came from the direction of the front door, and I can see with my peripheral vision that there are two large, plainly dressed men in sweats and sneakers sitting near that door. The stature of the guy in the gray sweats seems slightly familiar, and it very well could be Shrek, although I couldn't swear to it in a line-up. But just the slight peek I did get of him is setting off all sorts of inner alarms and red flags. My gut is telling me to get the hell out of here fast. Another lesson Roman has been trying to teach me.

"Listen to your gut Duchess and not your head."

I look to my left and make the decision that Sloan and I could probably exit the side door undetected if we're careful. Luckily I have on Sloan's oversized, dark blue hoodie, which acts almost as a shield of sorts. I look just like any other random, nondescript college student.

I pull the hood up, grab my latte, and try to leave as casually as I can without bringing any attention to myself. Java is bubbling with patrons, and Shrek seems to be quite engrossed with something he's either watching or reading on his cell phone.

"Now," I speak softly to Sloan. "And walk casually."

As we start moving to the door my cell phone rings.

"Hell," I fuss as I fumble to answer it.

I forgot to put it on vibrate, and I'm afraid that the volume may turn someone's head towards our direction, so I abruptly answer it without even looking to see who's calling.

"Yes," I whisper curtly.

"Elizabeth?"

Holy hell, it's my father, and he's calling from a number I don't recognize.

"Dad?" I answer the phone quietly, as Sloan and I continue to hightail it out of Java.

"Is everything all right?"

"Yes."

My father never calls. "Is everything all right with you?"

By this point, we've exited Java and have approached Sloan's new company car. Another one of the perks of her promotion. I don't dare look back inside the shop, but I just have a feeling that someone has their eyes on me through the glass pane, so I do it. My stomach still rolling with nervous energy.

What I see are a pair of eyes staring through the glass ... and straight through me.

Dead eyes.

And now I know for frackin' sure.

It's him.

I quickly divert my eyes away from his dead fish ones, while Sloan begins to pull out of the parking lot. I'm so rattled that I totally forgot I was on the phone with my father.

"You sound like you can't talk. Is that gangster with you?" my father asks abruptly snapping me back into the moment.

That *gangster* would be Roman, and of course my father's first thought is to blame any perceived distress I may be under on him. My father's opinion of Roman and Uncle Joseph hasn't waivered one single iota since the blow up at my birthday dinner. In fact, I'd venture to say that his imagination has only made his terrible opinion of both of them to become even worse. He imagines Joseph and Roman to be hard-core gangsters. Killers. Thugs. Seducing his only sister and daughter with money and sex. Needless to say, I think my father watches way too many mob movies and organized crime documentaries.

"What do you need, Dad?" I ask looking back at Java as Sloan pulls out of the lot.

"I'm calling to find out what your plans are for the holidays."

That's odd. Why didn't Mom ask me?

"*You're* asking?" I ask incredulously.

"Yes, I'm asking. Is it so strange for your father to ask if you're planning on coming home to have dinner with your family? Your uncles plan on coming this year, so your mom is going all out. Just wanted to know if you wanted to show your face for once."

Oh that explains it. He wants to put on a happy family front for my uncles.

"Are you inviting Aunt Juliette too?" I challenge.

"No, Elizabeth. You know that's not going to happen. She won't come without that husband of hers."

"Well yeah, Dad, that is pretty common with married folks. They spend the holidays together."

"Well not in my house. Not those two. I can't do it, and I won't do it. Your uncles don't want to see him either. Hell, one of them might knock Joseph out for the ridiculousness going on down there with you and that boy."

"You told them?"

"About you playing house with your cousin? I sure as hell did. And like I said, you're lucky that they didn't drive to the city the night I told them. They were ready to. Baseball bats and all."

"How very old school *gangster* of them."

I hear my father sigh heavily. "I didn't call to argue with you, Bitsy. I called to find out your plans for the holidays. That's it."

"For Thanksgiving or Christmas?"

Honestly, I didn't feel like going home for either if my father was still so dead set against my relationship. And he was right. My uncles were ten times worse than him. I'd probably get the third degree through dinner, dessert and football. Not my idea of a good time. Plus, I hadn't even talked about the holidays with Roman. I just assumed we'd spend them together, and I know he doesn't want to spend it with me in Penn-Washington. That would just be my birthday dinner all over again.

"Both."

"I don't think I can make it for Thanksgiving. Maybe

Christmas. I'll let you know." I just felt like telling him something somewhat believable, so I could get off of the phone.

"Your mother really wants you to come."

"And I'd really like to come, but I'd like to bring my boyfriend."

"That's not happening."

"Then I'm pretty sure I'm not coming."

"Think about what you're saying, Elizabeth. You've known this guy for less than a year, and I've known that family of his for most of your life. You need to consider for just a moment that I may know what I'm talking about. He's going to hurt you or worse get you hurt."

"Dad, he manages a major league baseball player and a nightclub. That's it. He's not the Godfather or a Goodfella."

"He's your cousin."

"By marriage, not by blood, and it's a marriage that you don't even acknowledge by the way. So don't force me to make a choice, Dad, because I will choose Roman. I am in love with him."

"I know you *think* you're in love with him, but time has a way of revealing the truth about people and their intentions. You don't know him yet. I'm just asking for you to give this some time. Don't make any rash decisions, like cutting your mother and me out of your life, until you've really gotten to know him. I'm still learning new things about your mother all the time, and we've been married for over twenty-seven damn years."

"I haven't cut you out of my life, Dad. I'd say that you are the one pushing that agenda. And I didn't say that Roman and I were getting married tomorrow. All I said was that we're together, and at some point you and mom are going to need to get on board with that, if we're going to be in each other's lives in any sort of healthy way."

Sloan starts to give me a narrow glare, which is a long time signal between the two of us for me to get off of the phone. I think our stealth like departure from Java has rattled her, and she needs the two of us to debrief.

"I have to go, Dad."

"Just think about Christmas if you can't do Thanksgiving. Think about us, Elizabeth. The people who raised you. Who have supported everything you've ever done. We've never spent both holidays apart."

This conversation is getting way too uncomfortable for me. My father and I never talk like this. My mother yes, but not us.

"Are you sick?" I ask in my attempt to understand where this is coming from.

"Sick?"

"Do you have cancer or something?"

"Oh good lord, Elizabeth, no."

"Okay then good. I'll call you guys later, Dad. I promise."

"Bye, sweetie."

It hits me hard after the call disconnects. I think I'm starting to realize just how big the chasm between my parents and I is growing. Even though my mother and I communicate semi-regularly through texts, she must have put my dad up to that call, because she is still worried about me.

Great.

And now I feel guilty.

My father sounded really disappointed towards the end of our conversation. I know that he's right to some extent. Eventually I'm going to have to do something about it. I can't just let my relationship with my parents disintegrate. I mean they're my parents for God's sake. But what about Roman?

"Earth to Bitsy." Sloan snaps her fingers near my ear. "Hello? Earth to damn Bitsy!"

"Oh, my bad."

"Yeah, your bad. I get you have daddy issues, but what just happened back there at Java is way the hell more important for us to discuss right now. We need to tell somebody what just went down."

"Tell somebody? Tell who?"

"Are you on crack?! The police for starters, and then maybe the Dark Knight. Hell, let's tell everybody."

"Uh, that would be a no and a hell no."

I haven't involved the police (stupidly) in this thing from the beginning. I guess it was my way of protecting my ex-boyfriend Ethan at the time. I knew on some level in my gut that he had something to do with the attack based on his reaction or rather his lack of one. So bringing the police in at this point would probably raise more questions than it would solve.

Why didn't I call 911? Why didn't I report the assault? Why didn't I go to a hospital? Why did I keep so much cash in the house? All very valid questions with no logical answers, other than I was a blooming idiot.

And telling Roman? I'm petrified of pulling him into this. It's been a while now since he and the Kings have had a new client to *fix* something for, and it's so obvious that he's itching for a new challenge. Especially a confrontational one. If I told him about this, he'd definitely go looking for Shrek. He'd probably kill him or come very close to it.

It took me forever to talk him off the ledge when I first told him about everything that happened inside my apartment that night. I practically begged him not to interfere, and that was before we fell in love. Now that we're together, I don't think he'd listen to me *at* all. He'd just react.

Telling him about what just happened would only thwart all of my efforts to keep him out of it. Not to mention that he'd probably put me on some sort of lock down for "my own safety" which would drive me completely nuts. I won't be able to take a poop without him knowing. I can't live like that.

No ... telling him would definitely be the wrong move.

"Why not?" Sloan asks as if I've lost the last little bit of sense I had left. "What is the likelihood that some street thug, some around the way drug dealer, who knocked you out cold in your own fucking apartment, just happened to be grabbing a coffee at Java? That's pretty much our hang out. A Penn hangout. Smart college kids. Why would he be there if it didn't have anything to do with you or *he who will not be named?*"

Sloan refuses to mention my ex Ethan by name, since he dropped off the face of the planet yet again. She feels like he used her to find out information about me, and then dropped her like a hot potato once he was finished. He's on her ever-growing shit list of people whom she has "no words for." Especially because she had given him the benefit of the doubt.

"There's no way Shrek could have known that I was going to be there, Sloan. We just decided to go an hour ago. Not to mention that *he who will not be named* told me that he used to sell pills for the guy. Which means that he has to be familiar with the campus and campus hangouts. How else do you sell drugs to college students if you aren't familiar with the area that you're selling them in?"

I just answered my own question as to why someone like him would be at Java. If I think rationally about things, he's probably been there many times. Roman's told me a thousand times to *"follow your gut then follow the trail,"* because it usually leads to the truth.

"Okay, okay. Excellent point." She seems to finally exhale a bit. "So it could have been a total coincidence, *but* the fact remains that he knows exactly who you are. And while you definitely were covered up in the hoodie, there's no guarantee that he didn't notice you. I mean we look at people all the time when they come in and out of Java. It's just human nature to look at people when they come in and out of a small shop like that. I'm not trying to scare the shit out of you, Bitsy, but I'm just thinking that you should at least mention this to somebody. Somebody that could keep an eye out for the douchebag or at least on you."

"I hear you," I say.

And Sloan's right. Telling someone would be the smart thing to do. The obvious thing to do. But I know that person shouldn't be the police, and it definitely shouldn't be Roman, so that leaves me only one other choice right now.

Not to say a word.

7

Roman

The most beautiful woman in the fucking world is sitting butt naked, cross-legged, on the floor of my living room in front of my massive glass window that highlights the beauty of the Philadelphia city skyline. In her right hand, adorned with a single gold bracelet (which I gave her tonight) and petal pink nails, she's holding a glass of cabernet in a long-stemmed glass.

I watch with rapt anticipation as she motions to take a sip.

And then another.

She's so fucking sexy.

Her body is covered in a thin layer of sweat that gives her skin an intoxicating satiny finish and makes her glow like a Christmas bulb. That and the last orgasm I just gave her, have a lot to do with my girl's glow. She's breathtaking, and it makes my dick rise in appreciation, actually for the third time tonight.

If I didn't know better, I'd swear that every physical movement, every twist and turn her body makes in my presence seems very much like a deliberate and expert seduction of me.

The total consumption of me.

But I do know better. I know that my dear sweet *cousin*, my Elizabeth, doesn't have a deliberate bone in her body when it comes to her sexuality or the art of seduction. In her case it's effortless.

It just is.

Body and soul. She's mesmerizing inside and out, and I'm definitely one lucky son of a bitch. It's also one of the reasons why I can feel my insides winding and twisting like an angry, knotted ball of yarn right now. I don't want her to leave this apartment. This room. I don't ever want her to go. I hate the shit.

But every Friday night since the Glamazon got a promotion pushing even more drugs to overpaid doctors, I've let Elizabeth's pretty ass talk me into the rawest deal imaginable. She's been hanging out with the biggest pain in my ass for no good reason other than the fact that the two of them claim they need some "bonding" time.

What the fuck? I don't get it.

I'm either working to make some money, or I'm in between my girl's legs. End of story. I don't need to hang out with my boys just because. I'm not fourteen years old. That shit is dumb. Why would I pick getting drunk with a bunch of assholes over pussy? My pussy. A warm and wet one that strangles my cock, because it loves for me to be inside of it.

Or why would I watch a ball game and eat Buffalo wings with the King brothers, when we could be handling something for a client and billing them? Making some fucking money.

The shit just doesn't compute to me. It's either one or

the other. Money or pussy. Not some fuzzy gray area where you don't get either. That just seems un-American.

But I'm not a woman, and I've come to the conclusion, since starting a relationship with Elizabeth, that not every decision she makes is for me to understand. She may actually want to spend time with the man hungry princess, because she truly enjoys spending time with her (although I realize I will never totally understand that relationship). Sometimes I think this is just another way that the Glamazon has chosen to fuck with me. I wouldn't put it past her shady ass.

But while it's imprinted on my fucked up DNA to suspect, to not trust, to always be on guard; I also need to try and trust that feeling deep in my gut that tells me that Elizabeth doesn't have any ulterior motives. That she's not like the usual club skanks I've spent many of my nights with. Temporary bed warmers. Scheming gold diggers.

Or like my mother.

She's nothing like that woman either.

Elizabeth isn't using me for sex, for money, or to fix her daddy issues. She isn't emotionally draining me like some needy leech. She doesn't need me to make her feel prettier or more important. She feels all of that on her own. She draws from her own well.

I've dealt with some crazy, fucked up women in my life, but that's not Elizabeth. It's not even remotely who she is. So that's why when she sat me down, after trying her damnedest to cook me the worst crab bake I've ever had, I couldn't resist complying. I couldn't say no to her or her inedible bribe. Or at least part of it.

I trust her.

As much as I can trust anyone.

Sure, I gave her a little shit for this Thursday "on," Friday "off" idea of hers. And I may have spanked her ass a little extra hard that night, but all in all, I gave her what she asked for. I always do. It's just that when I gave it to her, I didn't realize how much it was going to fuck with me in the coming weeks and months.

No wonder men run from commitment. From love. Especially men like me. This shit is hard. It definitely ain't easy. It's hard to control, and I'm used to making the rules. I want Elizabeth by my side every second of the day, and not because I don't trust her or because I don't trust all the assholes out there (which I sure as fuck don't), but because I like how I feel when I'm with her. I smile when she's with me. I relax. And I spend a great deal of time actually contemplating things that I can do to make sure that I hear that infectious laugh of hers again and again. All of that is scary territory for someone like me. I've never had a healthy relationship with a woman in my life. Well maybe Juliette and Jade, but they're different.

Other people in my life can see Elizabeth's effect on me too. In fact I might have to dock Jade's pay if she mentions one more time just how much of a pussy I become when Elizabeth is in the vicinity.

"Maybe we should talk about this when Elizabeth comes home. Since she'll hopefully be arriving with both of your balls in her handbag."

That's what the little devil said to me two days ago when I was giving her the third degree about a vendor issue at the club. I swear I'd fire Jade's ass some days if I didn't think the Kings would shoot me in the nuts for it, especially Cam.

Speaking of Cam, the dance between he and Jade is actually starting to get pretty sickening. I wish he'd just man the fuck up and finally claim the shrimp. I'm not entirely sure why he hasn't yet, nor will I ever probably know. It's not like the two of us talk about our innermost feelings over pints of ice cream, while brushing each other's hair. That's for pussies. Although that's what I'm pretty close to becoming any damn way.

"What are you looking at, Duchess?" I slide behind Elizabeth on the floor and sit directly behind her with my legs in a V formation. She slides back farther and leans into my embrace.

"The sunset. The lights. Everything is so beautiful from up here, Roman. I'll never get sick of it."

"Sounds like you may be ready to see this view every night," I suggest closely by her ear. "I know I am," I say referring to her beautiful ass and not the skyline. "You're dying to move in here with me aren't you?"

Very smooth, asshat.

Yeah, I'm definitely a butter soft punk. Actually asking a woman to move in with me? No really, that was more like begging. I think I'm even actually trying to pull some sort of badly executed Jedi mind trick on her, so that she'll think she came up with the idea on her own. I'm so ridiculous right now. I don't even recognize myself sometimes. This thing with Elizabeth is mind-bending. It's making me think things, say things, and do things that I normally would have never considered. Especially now that I've allowed Joseph to get in my head.

Lately we've been debating over that uber confident, smart-ass, dick she hired. Just his name alone, Blake, is enough to make me want to slap him. I think he was the name of a character on some nighttime soap my mother use to watch in the 80s. That's not a real man's name.

Being able to read people swiftly and accurately is a skill, and I've been paid a lot of money to be able to size people up quickly. I've been doing it for as long as I can remember. That's why I knew almost immediately upon meeting him that Blake wasn't a hustler or someone trying to take advantage of Elizabeth. That would have been too easy. That's someone I know how to handle. Unfortunately this guy is ten times worse.

First of all he's totally legit. Not a hustler or a scammer. Second, he's a pretty boy. A lot like that swimmer friend of Elizabeth's, Jagger, that used to have a hard on for her. No battle scars. No tats. No edges to him. Third, he's also smart. He uses words that I've never heard of half of the time, and he definitely knows his coder shit. Yet something about that squeaky clean motherfucker rubs me the wrong way.

On paper he's everything a woman like Elizabeth should be with. She bragged the other day to her girlfriend Tiny over the phone that he graduated from some university with honors and had worked for some major tech company in New York. Maybe she said all of that for Tiny's benefit, but she sounded majorly impressed.

He's also helping her create ideas for her business that are making her practically cream her panties. Ideas that I can't help her with. I know how to shake somebody down or pistol-whip their asses, but not how to code. I don't know shit about computers except for how to buy them. Cam kind of speaks his language, but according to him the work that they both do is very different. Blake helps Elizabeth "build code." Cam's specialty is "hacking code."

This Blake prick also knows a lot of shit. Useless but fascinating shit. He could probably go on that game show Jeopardy and win. He's traveled outside the United States several times, and not to the tourist traps where I've vacationed, but places that are less traveled. More "authentic" according to Elizabeth.

I'm going to be honest and admit that roughing it in a third world South American country or back packing across a snow capped European mountainside is not my idea of relaxation. I like the beach, I like to sail, I like to gamble, and I like to fucking party. I'll make no excuses for that. That's what normal motherfuckers like to do on vacation. But Elizabeth seems to be quite fascinated with all of this prick's stories about how he barely made it out of a Peruvian bar with his life or how extraordinarily kind the people of Hallstatt, Austria are.

Fuck me.

When does this asshole have time to work? Just hearing the level of excitement in her voice when she listens to his stories makes me want to kick Mr. Perfect straight in his nuts.

Don't get me wrong. I'm so fucking happy that Elizabeth has found someone that will help her take her School Bucks dream to the next level. It's what she wants. It's what she deserves. She's worked so hard for this, and if this pain in the ass can help her get there, then I'm all for it, but I'm not stupid either. I know that I need to keep a very close eye on him, because as non-threatening as he may appear to be, something tells me that he knows just how perfect he is for Elizabeth too.

One look at me, scarred, covered in ink, rough around the edges, not knowing shit about making apps or code or whatever the fuck he does. One long sideways glance from him, and I can tell that he thinks he knows me. That I'm some sort of uneducated, unrefined, low life with new money.

Not good enough for her.

Not smart enough for her.

One look at me, and he thinks I'm a temporary fixture.

A fetish.

A phase.

I know that's *exactly* what he's thinking. I've met hundreds of guys like him. That's why after shaking his hand for the first and only time, I felt it. I felt in my gut that he is just biding his time. Plotting and planning on how to steal Elizabeth away from the likes of someone like me. To save her from herself. From me.

Funny thing is I don't blame him.

Sneaky little motherfucker.

8

Roman

Elizabeth giggles reservedly as if she's walking on eggshells with me. Bringing up the topic of living with me, is probably the likely cause, but it's almost as if I can't stop the bullshit pouring out of my mouth. My need to claim her permanently is driving me to say and do really stupid things. Things she may not be ready for.

I'm not sure if Elizabeth's noticed, but her ass and hips are spreading. She looks even more delicious and more fuckable than the night we met, and I'm taking full credit for that. Definitely due to a mixture of high calorie restaurant eating and the pounding I'm putting on her pussy on a regular basis.

Last night I dreamed about tatting her ass with two words: "Masterson Made," because while it was a beautiful piece of art when we met, it's only gotten better since I've gotten my hands on it. The dream was crystal clear. One word per ass cheek in one of those elegant script fonts. I woke up grinning and stiff as a board.

I'm definitely fucking losing it.

"We have the perfect arrangement already." She

annunciates each word carefully. Like she's speaking to the village idiot and needs to slow it down so that I'll understand. I'll tell you what I don't understand. What I refuse to understand. And that's her use of the word *arrangement*.

What the fuck?

I hate that word. It sounds temporary. As if at any moment during our *arrangement* that she can just get up and walk away. Like I would ever let that shit happen. She's my ultimate addiction. My absolute fix. And just like a meth head, I'll do whatever I need to do to make sure that I can always get my drug of choice. I'll kill a motherfucker for it.

"This is an arrangement is it?" I growl as I skillfully tweak both of her nipples. I know I'll have her full attention once I start this, and maybe she'll start to see the error of her ways.

She takes another quick sip of her wine and places the glass carefully down on the floor beside us, pushing it slowly away from our bodies. Then she raises her arms up and behind her and locks her hands behind my head, chest poking out, giving me full access to her tits.

"An arrangement of the best kind."

She purrs like a kitten, and I growl in response like her lion king. My need to claim her now and forever grows and twines within me inch by inch like a wild weed threatening to choke me from the inside out.

"You still plan on leaving tonight?" I ask with more bite to my voice than I intended, as my hand gently wraps around her throat.

Ownership.

Mine.

"Mmm-huh."

Part of our new bullshit agreement is that Elizabeth gives me all of her on Thursdays, and I do mean every inch, but then she gets to leave and wake up in her own house *alone* on Fridays.

One of the reasons for this absurd arrangement is because according to her she likes to wake up at home, so that she can start working early with Blake a.k.a the Sneaky Motherfucker, and then later goes out for *ladies night* a.k.a. clubbing, bar hopping, or both with the Glamazon.

Needless to say I'm starting to hate fucking Fridays.

Just the thought of all the eyes that are probably on Elizabeth drinking, twirling, and laughing every Friday night is making me seriously consider shutting this whole dumb plan down. Dictator style. But the kinder, gentler Roman a.k.a. The Pussy is going to try influencing her decisions by way of a tried and true method.

Fucking her to the point of exhaustion.

I pinch and roll her left nipple, the sensitive one, with a little extra pressure. Teasing her this way is one of the only things keeping me from doing what I really want to do, which is tying her ass to my bed and keeping her here for the entire weekend.

"You sure you want to leave?" I ask in a teasing voice. I'm starting to despise some of the drivel that comes out of my mouth. It's pretty pathetic. I've resorted to begging.

"We had a deal, Roman Masterson," he says as she arches her back into me farther. "Why are you acting like I enjoy leaving you?"

"If you don't like it, then don't do it." I say as I continue to knead her breasts.

Elizabeth grabs my hands to stop them from their devilish mission, turns around to face me, and looks me straight in the eyes.

"Because I could stay in this beautiful apartment, under you, every single day of the year. I could get lost in you Roman, and we both know that is not good for either of us. We both have businesses to run. We both have other relationships to nurture. We have lives outside of each other."

"I don't know what the fuck you're talking about. I have one client and no relationships I give a fuck about but this one."

You are my life.

Elizabeth smiles brightly. "You have one very high maintenance client, a very popular club to manage, and several friends who you definitely care about and who are used to seeing you everyday. You have a lot of stuff to nurture."

"I know what I have. Don't really need an inventory check from you." I pout like the little bitch I'm becoming.

"Don't be like that."

She moves in closer to me, naked, glowing, and wrapping her arms around my neck. She thinks cuddling like this is going to make me agree to anything she says, when all it's doing is making me angrier than I already was, because she's still leaving. Well making me angry *and* making my cock jump to full attention.

"Be like what?" I ask.

"A grump."

"If I'm a grump, it's your fault."

"My fault? It's been months that we've been together now, and I feel like for most of it, we haven't come up for air. I'm just trying to make sure we don't get sick of each other."

"Do you actually believe that shit, or is that the Glamazon talking?"

Elizabeth turns up her lips. She doesn't like me insinuating that she doesn't have a mind of her own. Either that or she hates when I speak negatively about her friend. Probably a bit of both.

"Sloan doesn't tell me how to feel, Roman. Contrary to what you may think, I do have a mind of my own and not just for computers and books. I've got plenty of common sense too. While I haven't been in many relationships, I do know that couples who see each other as much as we do run the risk of getting sick and tired of each other."

There's a rise to her voice as she fusses at me. She's trying emphatically to make her point. It's cute. Makes me want to kiss her mouth really hard, but that wouldn't solve shit right now.

"Are you sick of me?" I ask.

"Obviously not."

"Exactly, and I will never get sick of your beautiful ass either." I grab her chin. "Not possible, baby."

"I'm still leaving." Her eyes look down and away from mine. This is stupid. Her body is telling me that she doesn't want to go, but she's fighting this for some reason.

"The Glamazon is always looking for dick," I blurt out.

Her head pops up. "What's that got to do with me?"

"Men are going to think that you are too. Why else would you be hanging out at bars every Friday night? You know the saying. Birds of a feather. That's what they're going to think."

"I have no control over what your species thinks."

"You're drinking, partying, shaking your ass in something tight, and you think that's not sending a certain signal to a man? It's not like you two are staying home and watching a chick flick marathon."

"So what? I'm not supposed to ever go out again as long as you and I are together?"

As long? There she goes again with all of that temporary fucking language.

"You can go out with me. We'll dance. We'll drink. I'll

even let the Glamazon tag along if you want. If you remember, I do own the hottest club in the city."

When the Kings and I left Joseph, he gave me The Lotus as a parting gift. It was the club with the most potential at the time, and now it is one of the highest grossing clubs in the metropolitan area. And we're not just killing it on money nights, but on off nights like Tuesdays and Wednesdays too.

Cutter just about peed in his pants when hip-hop artist Drake stopped by the night after the city's annual Mayor's music festival. He easily blew five grand on bottle service and tipped the waitresses really well. But the real bonus was the after effects of him visiting the club. People heard he had been there, which of course makes them hope and pray that he may come again, which in turn makes The Lotus seem all the more exclusive. The result? A line down the street.

"Is everything all right with you?" she asks reservedly.

Damn, she really thinks I'm crazy now. It's official. I've crossed into a place I'd only thought I'd heard about.

Pussy. Whipped. Ville.

"Yeah, Duchess. Everything is fine. Come here."

I pull her in for a kiss. It starts off slow and Rated PG. Soft pecks on the corners of her mouth. A lick across her lips that encourages her to part them for me. Then I plunge my tongue deep inside of her mouth and languidly caress the inside of her mouth. It's a leisurely, sexy dance of our lips, tongues and hands. It makes me want to do more and get Rated R with her real fast, but I've decided to change my course of action. I need to salvage what little dignity I have left.

I pull away from our kiss and order her to, "stand up." She already knows from my tone of voice that this will play out nicely for her if she just takes my instruction without resistance.

"Now go walk over there and stand in front of the mirror, and don't say a word. I know you're itching to say something smart."

I have a massive but sleek, silver metallic framed, floor mirror that leans against a wall in my living room. It was one of my first purchases when I moved into this place a few years ago.

I give Elizabeth a minute to walk over to the mirror and stand quietly staring at herself. She's fidgeting and totally uncomfortable. It's not that she doesn't have self-confidence, she does, but I find that most women have a problem staring at themselves nude in a mirror for an extended amount of time. Eventually they start spotting shit that they don't like or want to look at. All you have to do is closely follow the direction of their eyes and watch where they linger. It's a very quick and easy way to learn about a woman's insecurities.

I rise up and walk behind her. I tower over her so much I could easily rest my chin on the top of her head. I begin to run my hands down the side of her head, stroking her hair. I lift a few locks of her hair with my palm and gently sniff them. Like jasmine and sunshine.

"Cup your breasts," I order.

She complies albeit with some hesitation.

"Look at yourself in the mirror while you do it. Look straight ahead. If it's difficult for you then look at me in the mirror."

She looks up at me.

"Do I make you happy, Elizabeth?"

My hands begin to run down the slope of her shoulders and then continue to travel down to the dip of her waist.

"Yes," she answers with hooded eyes.

"Eyes open. Put them on me or yourself, but they need to stay open."

Her eyes pop back open, but her pupils are dilated. She wants me just as much as I want her.

"Squeeze both of your nipples with your thumbs and pointer fingers."

She complies and moans a little in the process.

"That's it, baby."

I watch as her breathing becomes a bit shallow. Her eyes fighting to stay open as she gives herself over to me. I bend down on my knees behind her, as my hands continue to travel down her hips until they've landed on her thighs. Deliberately skimming her ass and just lightly brushing by her pussy.

"Legs apart."

She spreads her legs farther apart, but I can tell that it's killing her. She wants to squeeze them together to help dull the ache between them.

"Now let me tell you what's going to happen, Duchess."

Just the words make her shut her eyes again.

"Open. Those. Eyes."

She slowly opens them again.

"So this is what's going to happen. You're going to spread your legs apart a little bit farther apart for me."

I move my hand back and forth in between her thighs to give her some guidance as to how far apart I want them.

"Good girl. Now this is what's going to happen next. You're going to gently rub back and forth over your clit with your fingers. Can you do that for me?"

"Yes," she whimpers. It's the sexiest sound I've heard in a long time.

I allow her to do that for about a minute until I notice

her hips are thrusting slightly to meet her strokes. She's going to come soon if I let this continue.

"Stop."

She does.

"Don't turn your head. Keep your eyes straight ahead on me in the mirror. I want you to look at yourself right now, Duchess. So fucking beautiful. Pussy so wet and so very damn greedy for me."

My words are sending her just a little closer to the edge.

"Do you know how beautiful you are, baby?"

She's silent. Her eyes pleading for me to shut up and just give her a much needed release. Just how I want her. Needy and only for me.

"That wasn't a rhetorical question, Elizabeth. I asked you if you know how beautiful you are?"

"I think so."

"You think so? Look again."

I catch her eyes as she stares at herself further in the mirror. She's focusing on her stomach and her hip area.

"This little pouch right here," I spread one of my palms completely across her stomach. "This pouch is going to grow all of my babies inside of it one day."

She tries to hide a small grin as she shakes her head silently no. A private joke between us. We've laughed several times over how she's scared shitless of kids, but how I plan for the two of us to have a whole damn football team or cheerleading squad.

"And these hips," I bend down again and run both of my hands along her pear shaped, hourglass figure. "Sweet Jesus. These hips. I kiss one side of her hips and then the other. There's not a man in this city that doesn't watch these hips sway from left to right when you walk by. Perfection."

She tries to hide another smile from me as I work my way up the side of her body. Kissing the curve of her waist. Raising her arm and kissing the side of her breast. Then continuing my way along the length of her arm and ending with a kiss on the inside of her wrist. Her eyes closed in rapture.

"What do you want right now?" I ask her softly.

"You inside of me."

"Well I want a whole lot of shit too, but I don't always get what I want and neither will you."

Her eyes pop open and immediately find mine in the mirror. Her irises are swarming with a mixture of question and need.

So insatiable.

"This is what's going to happen next, greedy girl. You're going to rub out your clit again, then I'm going to jam two of my fingers inside of you exactly at the moment that you need me to, and then you're going to scream my fucking name as loudly as you can. You got me?"

"Yes," she whimpers as if she's already exhausted by our exchange. I might just come in my own hand if I don't watch it.

"Yes, what?"

"Yes, Masterson."

"Do it."

It doesn't take long. Her clit is so sensitive that as soon as she starts touching herself again, her eyes roll in the back of her head. She's going to literally blow in like T minus ten seconds.

That's when I firmly slide two of my fingers inside of her pussy, bend them inside to reach her special spot, and use the other hand to smack her ass simultaneously.

"Fuck!" The moment she screams the curse word I

almost come all over myself. She never uses that word. That's how good it is between us. It gets better every time.

"Who do you belong to?" I demand to know.

"Masterson." My name drifts from her lips with echoes of desperation and gratitude. "You."

She falls forward and braces her release by placing her palms flat on the mirror. This gives me easier access to her slit from the back, and I clean between her legs from front to back with several laps of my tongue. The taste is the sweet and salty flavor I've grown to crave, and it's all for me. It's all mine.

My thorough clean up job with my tongue brings my girl to an orgasm again, and now I'm so fucking horny that I sit back on my knees and heels and guide her down swiftly on my cock. I can get deep inside of her from this position, and I have to squeeze my eyes shut in blissful agony as she goes right to work and begins to slide up and down on my rigid length.

Riding me like a pro.

"Open your eyes," she orders as she watches our movements in the mirror.

Fuck if that doesn't turn me on even more. Her throwing back my command on me. Me quickly losing control and me stiffly thrusting up inside of her with a frenzied purpose.

"Aren't *we* beautiful?" she pants and then throws her head back to lean on me as she continues to slide home to her third orgasm of the night.

"Yes, Duchess."

So fucking pretty.

And then I come harder than I ever have in my entire life.

Elizabeth

Ethan Anderson
To: Elizabeth Hill
Re: Hey

Call me: 215-555-8532
We need to meet about something.

-Ethan

Elizabeth

I love the Philadelphia skyline at sunset. It's an awesome sight to behold if you're perched in the right location. I love to observe the tranquil swirls of pink, purple and blue all intertwining with each other as the end of another day approaches. Especially against the backdrop of oak and maple trees that are over one hundred years old as well as buildings, which are even older than that.

Unfortunately Roman likes to watch this beautiful sight when he goes for a run, and he's brought me along today. He keeps assuring me that he loves my voluptuous hips, thighs and butt, but I feel like he's purposely making me run off every calorie I consume any chance he gets. Whether we're running, walking Mr. Tibbs, or having amazing sex, I feel like I'm always breaking a sweat whenever he's involved.

The exercise has been good for me though. It's been helping me think; because the email I received from Ethan the other day has been weighing heavily on my mind. I'm not sure what to do about it, so I've erred on the side of caution and have done absolutely nothing. Not until I'm sure what the best course of action is.

Roman, Mr. Tibbs, and I have finished our run and have collectively made it back to the Rover where I have a picnic dinner packed for us in the trunk. His idea, because he's the best boyfriend, not to mention that I'm always talking about picnics. I brought along a cold pesto pasta salad and wine for us, and a pack of half-frozen, raw chicken gizzards for Mr. Tibbs.

Roman drives us a little farther down the path of the drive where there's a nice area for us to spread a blanket. We have our pick of locations, because there's no one here due to the fact that it's the middle of October. Even though it's a record breaking warm day, no one has a picnic in October in Philly ... except for us.

I feel a little rushed to eat, because the sun sets pretty fast at this time of year, and I don't want to have to munch on my penne in the dark. We were actually supposed to be back here before the sun set so that we could set up the picnic, but I had to stop too many times to catch my breath during the run. Running is definitely not my exercise of choice, but Roman swears by it, so I promised him I'd try. I can't even lie, once it's over, it feels really good, and I'm glad that I did it. It's just the entire time *during* the run that sucks.

"You did good today, baby. Your time was better than the last."

I don't believe a word he's saying.

"If you say so."

"I swear that if you give it thirty days that you'll love it. It will help you write better code. The whole mind, body connection thing is real, Duchess."

"Thank you, Dr. Masterson," I say facetiously.

He playfully swats me on my butt, and after we finish

our last few bites of pasta, Roman lies down on his back and I lie next to him with my head on his bare chest. I find it utterly amazing and rude as hell how women walking by us on the trail are gawking specifically at Roman, as if I'm not laying all over him. Like I'm invisible.

I try not to think about it much, but I've never been with a guy that garners this much attention from women. I mean Ethan could pull in the sorority girls for sure, but Roman is on a whole other level. Women of all ages, all ethnicities, all sizes take notice of him.

There are a million reasons why. He towers over most women. He has beautiful ink across his back. He looks formidable, and delicious, and sexy, and when he walks into a room he owns it. It's a good thing I'm confident about our relationship, or else I'd be one of those crazy stalker girlfriends who checks everything from email to Instagram everyday. Although now that I'm thinking about all the women who drool all over him, I can't help but start a conversation most women eventually have with their men. Today it's our turn to have it.

"When did you first have sex?"

"Oh so we're having that conversation," he says as the low vibration of his words tickles my eardrums.

"Yep."

He chuckles.

"I was thirteen."

"Wow." I lift my head to look at him in slight shock.

"Put your head back down and keep me warm. I don't have on a shirt, remember."

"Put one on then."

"I don't need a shirt when I have you. Now lay back down while I tell you my story."

I lay my head back down on his powerful chest and wrap one of my arms around his middle. I could stay like this all day. Listening to the steady beat of his heart makes me feel so connected and so safe.

"Mmm, that's better," he says while playing in my hair. "Okay, so you have to understand, I was a *mature* thirteen-year-old. I'd been practically taking care of myself for years."

"Were you scared to have sex for the first time?"

"Shit yeah, but only because I was afraid of getting caught by her daddy."

"What do you mean?"

"I was on a business run with Joseph. Puberty had given me a shot in my ass overnight, and I had grown practically three feet over a weekend. He decided it was time I start learning the family business, mostly because I looked the part. Not necessarily because I was ready.

"Sometimes he'd go by someone's house for a game of cards and drinks to loosen some tongues, get some information, and it was my job to entertain whoever else was in the house and keep them out of the way. At my age, that meant help in the kitchen or play with the other kids that were already there. But at this one house in particular, where Joseph played poker every blue moon, the owner of the house had a seventeen-year-old daughter who was hot in the pants. She'd been fucking for years, according to her anyway, and she felt the need to pass her vast wealth of knowledge onto me. Needless to say, my thirteen year old horny ass was deeply grateful." He grins.

I smack his chest.

"She was gross," I say. "It was practically statutory rape her sleeping with you."

"She was just a kid too."

"Give me a break. She knew better."

I know I shouldn't ask the question, but I do.

"How many women do you think you've had sex with?"

"Too many to count, Duchess. I lived a wild life for a long time, but just know that I never understood what sex could be like with someone you love until I met you. I've had good sex, and I've had great sex, but sex with you is fucking amazing. Every single time, all the time, and that's because you are made for me. We fit perfectly."

I hate how he's been with so many other women, although I know that I'm not being fair, because on the other hand I love that he knows exactly how to give me what I need. And that only comes with experience right?

"Why are you so quiet?" he asks.

I hesitate to give a response.

"You can tell me anything, Elizabeth, you know that right? There's nothing you can say that will seem stupid to me."

"Well ... sometimes I wish you hadn't been with so many women. I can't help but compare myself to them."

"There is no comparison."

I'm still quiet.

"I wish you never laid down with your ex," he says matter of factly. Filling the silence. "I should have been the first, because I'm sure as shit going to be the last."

"That barely counts. I just laid there and then minutes later I was knocked out cold by a drug dealer. Trust me. I don't consider that my first sexual experience at all."

His body tenses a bit from me mentioning that day. He hates talking about it, because he wasn't there to stop it. To save me. Of course we didn't know each other then, but that's just Roman. Always wanting to protect me in the past as well as in the present.

My guardian.

My champion.

Talking about all of this, and listening to him say how we fit each other so perfectly, is starting to wear on my conscious. I'm keeping something from him, and I'm finding ways to justify why I'm doing it to myself. I don't want him to overreact. I don't want him to put me on lock down. I don't want him to get hurt. The email probably means nothing. He who will not be named is no longer a factor in my life. So why bring it up.

I grab Roman's jaw roughly with my hand and pull him in for a kiss. I'm not usually this aggressive, and I can see a fire quickly build in his eyes by this uncharacteristic action on my part.

"I love you, Masterson," I say, but the words are dripping in guilt.

"You better," he growls.

His hand reaches around me and he pulls half of the blanket over us so that no one can see as his hand snakes under my sweatshirt and wraps around one of my breasts. My eyes immediately close from the exquisite pressure of his fingers rolling my nipple through the cup of my bra.

"Look at me," he orders. "You're under the blanket, baby. No one can see you. So I want you to slide your hand inside your panties, and let's do a quick check."

I know what that means. I've done Roman's *checks* plenty of times before. I do as I'm told as he continues to roll and pinch my nipples with varied pressure. I pull out my fingers and slide them into his mouth.

"Mmm," he says. "Tastes just like heaven. You've passed your inspection, Miss Hill. I think you're ready for a test drive. Let's get you home and fuck you properly."

I'm aching for him now.

My core dripping.

My breathing heavy.

Roman's a big tease, but then again he always delivers on everything he says. I just have to wait a little longer for it than I would like.

"Yes, sir," I respond. "Let's go home, so you can fuck me properly."

He raises his eyebrow at my use of the F word in mock appreciation.

"Good girl." He grins from ear to ear. "You're definitely learning. Come on, Mr. Tibbs. Let's take our girl home. There's something I need to shove inside of her dirty mouth as soon as we get there."

11

Elizabeth

I've taken refuge behind a tall, cinder block pillar at the Penn-Washington train station in an effort to avoid the high winds picking up outside. The meteorologist predicted an incoming storm when I checked the weather during the morning news, but I ignored her warnings. It was more important for me to wear this outfit. Blush tank top, black jeggings, over the knee black suede boots, and my favorite cinched waist, blush colored, jacket.

This certainly is not the most sensible fall outfit for a cold, blustery day like today, and I definitely don't have on the warmest coat I own, but I'd definitely rank the entire outfit high on the *that outfit looks damn good on you* scale. And right now, that's all that's important as I eagerly wait for the four thirty train to take me from my hometown, back to my place in downtown Philly.

I'm cold, but I look damn cute. So cute that I'm not even bothered that my train is running twenty minutes late. So cute that I don't even care that there is a homeless man, periodically talking to himself, to me, and also to a third person who definitely isn't visible to the human eye.

After two weeks of torture (I mean visiting) my parents, I'm finally going back home to my amazing apartment, my life in the city, and most of all to my boyfriend Roman. I missed him terribly.

My visit home was only supposed to last one week, but due to circumstances beyond my control, it turned out to be a little over two weeks, and let's just say that Roman was not very happy about it. Luckily for the both of us, I have a thick skin, and I let a lot of his acidic comments slide right off of my back. Let's face it, if I were the super sensitive type, we'd have broken up a long time ago.

I decided after the uncomfortable phone call between my father and I the last time I was at Java, that I would make my parents happy by paying them a visit. Especially since I decided that I wasn't going to be able to make it back during the holidays. If Roman wasn't invited for Thanksgiving or Christmas dinner, then neither was I.

While Roman wasn't exactly jumping for joy about my last minute visit home, he wasn't mad either. He knows that I am my parents' only child, and that I want to make things right between us, even if they're acting like stubborn jackasses right now. So even though we both knew that we were going to miss each other like crazy (this is the first time we've been apart since becoming a couple), he made sure that it wasn't half as bad as it could have been by making sure that we shared a few racy, video phone chats.

Roman: I'm about to Facetime you. Pick up.

I locked my door and turned the TV on in my room for background noise, just in case my father decided to walk by my room.

Me: Hello?

Roman: Hey, Duchess.

Me: Hi

Roman: I feel like I haven't seen you for weeks.

Me: I know. I miss you so much. It's so weird being away from you.

Roman: Yeah, it is. Let me see your room real quickly.

I walked around my old bedroom holding up my phone and showed Roman my canopy bed, the old pictures and mementos I've collected over the years on cork boards, my favorite stuffed panda bear, my weathered IKEA desk, and the view outside of my window.

Roman: Very sweet. Now put the camera back on you. What do you have on?

Me: This? An old T-shirt. I'm getting ready for bed.

Roman: I need to tuck you in first.

Me: Okay.

Roman: Lose the shirt.

I took off my shirt and slipped under my covers with just my panties on.

Roman: The panties too. I want to tuck you in properly. Don't put the phone down this time. I want to watch.

I pulled down and wiggled out of my panties with my right hand while holding onto the phone with my left. I noticed that Roman was intensely watching me while licking his bottom lip, and I could feel myself becoming wet in between my legs. We were both growing hungrier for each other.

Roman: Good girl, but wait, don't get under those covers; because I need you to go get my vibrator for me.

Me: What vibra—

Roman: Don't lie, Elizabeth. I know you took it out of my duffle and packed it in your suitcase.

I was caught. I left for Penn-Washington from Roman's house and decided at the last minute to pack a vibrator. My personal one was home, so I made the decision to take the one he bought to play with on me. How I was supposed to know he checked his inventory regularly?

Roman: That's right you're caught. Now go get it. I thought the two of us had an understanding, Elizabeth. I am in charge of and in command of every orgasm you have. No vibrators, no fingers, unless they're mine.

I pulled it out the side pocket of my bag.

Me: I've got it.

Roman: Now get on the bed. No sheets, or I can't see shit. Hold the phone high up with one hand and turn the vibrator on with the other. Get comfortable though. It's going to take me a while to tuck you in properly.

The verbal exchange between us, the tone of Roman's voice, and the sound of the vibrator already had me terribly needy. I was afraid that I'd come the second I touched myself with the silver bullet.

Roman: Spread your legs wider.

I did as I was told.

Roman: Your slick little pussy couldn't wait to come home to get what it needed. You needed to take care of things yourself while you were away, huh?

Me: Roman—

Roman: Quiet. Don't touch yourself with the vibrator yet. Just keep it on and ready for when I say you can.

Sometimes Roman liked to play with sound. Sometimes with silence. All I could hear was the motor of the vibrator and the sound of my heart thumping loudly. And that's all he wanted me to hear for a moment.

Roman: Now I obviously would rather have your hair threaded between my fingers, my balls deep inside of your cunt, while you ride me

reverse cowgirl style. You like that position right?

Me: Yes.

Roman: I know you do. I'd pull you hair a little harder as you diligently worked me, the perfectionist that you are. The muscles of your pussy squeezing me so tightly, that I'd run the risk of coming way too soon. Or maybe I'd spread your legs wide, tie your ankles to the corners of my bed, and tongue fuck you until you started speaking gibberish.

A moan escaped from in between my lips.

Roman: Is your pussy throbbing yet?

Me: Yes

Roman: You want some relief.

Me: Yes.

Roman: I bet you do.

Me: Please

I begged.

Roman: Spread wider.

He waited a few more moments.

Roman: Vibrator. Now.

I placed the bullet on the side of my slippery clit and immediately began clenching my teeth in pleasure. My hips bucking. My sex dripping. I was sweating so much that my sheets were going to be soaked.

Roman: Come for me, Duchess.

I wanted to scream like I normally do when an orgasm rocks me to the core, but I couldn't because my parents were literally a few feet away down the hall. So I arched my back, bit my lip, and damn near crushed my phone to smithereens from holding it too tightly.

Roman: That's it, baby, it feels fucking fantastic to me too. I'm about to come in my hand. I wish it was all over your face.

He grunted loudly to his own release, and after a minute or so of heavy breathing, he said the four words that informed me of just what my punishment would be for swiping his toy.

Roman: Now let's start again.

It was obvious that the slight tension caused by our separation had probably been exacerbated by two things: my anxiety over Ethan's email and the presence of my new employee, Blake.

I've been on edge since I received that damn email and decided not to tell Roman about it. When I hold things in, such as anger or anxiety, I don't do well. I crave alcohol, carbs, tend to overwork myself, and sometimes I run for the hills.

Of course I have my reasons for not talking. I haven't told Roman about the email for the same reason why I didn't tell him about seeing Shrek. There's no point in upsetting him about things that don't warrant a code red. The whole Java incident is over. Nothing happened. He didn't approach me. I'm not even sure those dead eyes of his recognized me. The email from Ethan only matters if I respond, and I haven't, so why can't I just pretend that I never received it? Why tell Roman and risk poking the sleeping bear? To make myself feel better? That wouldn't be right.

The other issue I've been dealing with is the arrival of Blake. My new coder who was referred to me months ago by Jessica Miller. She's an old classmate from high school with curly red hair and a kind smile, but someone I only really said "hi" and "bye" to, because we traveled in two very different social circles in school.

She was the overachiever and outgoing popular type, and I was the under the radar, nerdy type. That's why I was a little surprised when she messaged me through Facebook, but evidently it was because she saw a post I made on the school's alumni page looking for a coder. I wanted someone local, and thought there may be a small chance that an old classmate of mine may have a referral. Lucky for me I was right.

Blake is a close friend of Jessica's family. He's twenty-nine and has got at least seven years of real world, solid experience as a coder; way more than any U.S. based free-lancer I've ever hired before. He's recently moved into the city and is willing to work for my rate. I'm not sure why. He's way overqualified, but I think he's in between *real* jobs.

In the fall, my old high school throws a big homecoming celebration and football game that most alumni try to make every year. I'm talking even senior citizens who live a hundred miles away will still come home to support it. It's really one of the biggest events of the year in my township, so there are also people from nearby towns who also participate. And it's complete with all the festivities and food that you'd pretty much see at any town fall festival or winter carnival. It never even dawned on me when I first interviewed Blake over the phone a few months back that he'd be attending homecoming just like me, but it makes total sense. He's from the neighboring town of Washington Falls. Our high schools have a long-standing rivalry, and we actually play his alma mater in the homecoming game every year.

So when I told Roman that I had to stay an extra week, because my mother's bad back started acting up again, but that at least I'd get the opportunity to be productive because Blake was also in town, he flipped.

He's never given me specifics, but there's something about Blake that rubs Roman the wrong way. It can't be anything serious, because knowing him, he's already run a thorough background check on Blake. It's probably what Sloan told me the other day.

"It's because Blake is smart and looks Viking yummy!" Were her exact words. I just laughed at her at the time, but now I'm starting to wonder. Could my uber confident boyfriend possibly feel threatened by of all people Blake?

Now flipping out for Roman is not yelling at the top of his lungs or punching holes in walls, like many people assume he does based on his bad boy appearance and temperament. At least that's not what he does with me. Flipping out for Roman means dead silence. A scary, uncomfortable silence. Then when he does finally say something it's laced with expletives, spoken in an eerily deep voice, and it feels like shards of glass slicing someone's gut open, especially when those words are directed at me.

"The fuck."

"What do you want me to do, Roman? My mom can't move. She's stuck in bed. I have to help out for a few more days while my father is at work. He's can't take off until next week."

"What the fuck would they do if you weren't there?"

"You just want me to leave my bedridden mother! And what they would do if I wasn't here is not the point."

"All right then let's talk about what the real point is. Why the fuck are you taking work meetings with Blake, when you're supposedly staying there to help your mother out? Why is he even FUCKING there?"

"Supposedly?"

"Is that the only word you heard from all the fuck I just said?"

"You're being stupid."

The moment the word flew out of my mouth, I wished that I could have grabbed it in midair and gobbled it quickly down my throat.

The word stupid.

He doesn't like when anyone uses it in reference to him, if anyone is crazy enough to say it out loud like me. Especially when he's angry. He takes it way too personally. I have no idea why. People call each other stupid all the time. But maybe the word hits a nerve because someone called him that when he was a kid, or maybe a lot of people did? So for me to call him that ... well I suppose it's tantamount to him calling me a bitch. I know better, but it just slipped out.

"Go work then. My stupid ass has shit to do," was all he said after my faux pas and then ... nothing.

He was gone.

Total radio silence.

No more phone calls, no more texts, and definitely no more R-rated Facetime chats. He cut me off cold turkey. I tried apologizing via voice mail, text and frackin' email for twenty-four hours, but after receiving no response at all, I was done. If he was going to be a stubborn ass about a simple mistake, so could I. In fact we didn't communicate with each other for three entire days and two nights. It wasn't until the third day of our cold war, that I finally received a text from him.

Roman: You coming home yet?
Me: Friday.
Roman: Time.
Me: Not sure yet.

That was a lie. I knew what train I was taking, but I didn't want to tell him. Partly because I was still annoyed with him for acting like a total asshole about this for three days, and partly because I wanted to surprise him and see the sexy grin spread across his face when I did.

Roman: Text me when you know.

I didn't respond to that last *order* of his, because I didn't want to have to lie to him again. Or rather omit part of the truth. Blake was traveling back to Philly with me, and I really didn't need Roman seeing him if he picked me up.

Talk about a train wreck. (Pun totally intended.)

"You want my coat?" Blake asks since I'm obviously shivering.

"Thanks, but I'm okay."

He gives me a perplexed look, because it's crystal clear that I'm freezing, but thankfully he decides to let the subject rest.

"Homecoming was kind of all right this year."

"Yeah, you would say that." I grin. "Your team won."

Blake laughs, "That's true, but we win every year don't we? What I meant was that the turn out was better than usual."

"You're right, it was a really good turn out. Must have been one of the biggest crowds yet. I didn't even see you once."

"You should have texted me. I would have met you somewhere," he said. "I haven't been in two years, so I hung out with some old friends from school back at their places mostly. I wasn't on campus that much. We only went to the game, not to any of the other stuff. Speaking of the game, did you try that carrot cake from the food truck over by the North field? You like sweets, right?"

I'm learning more interesting facts about Blake as we work together. He often brings up restaurants he's visited or new recipes he's tried. He's a foodie.

"Oh yeah, I've had it before. It's delicious. That's Ruby's truck."

"Ruby?"

"She was a lunch lady at Penn-Washington High for years. She always said she was going to start a business of her own, and she did about two years ago. The food truck was her dream."

"You keep in touch with her?" he asks as if he's kind of impressed that I still keep up with the lunch lady. I almost hate to disappoint him.

"No, nothing as nice as that. It's just that my mother knows everything about everyone in Penn-Washington. She's in every organization, club, and Facebook group that the town has. So she keeps me abreast of all goings on." I laugh.

"Ah, I see," he chuckles. "Sounds like my mom and your mom probably have a lot in common. That's how we know Jessica's family. Her mom and my mom are in MADD together."

"Mad?"

"Mothers Against Drunk Driving. My older brother was killed by a drunk driver when we were in high school."

"Oh, I'm sorry. I didn't hear about that."

"Well I'm a few years older than you and my brother was three years older than me. So chances are you were watching *The Disney Channel* when it happened."

"Of course." I smile warmly. "You're right. I probably wouldn't have heard."

Our train finally pulls in and without asking Blake grabs the handle of my carry on and motions for me to step ahead of him on the train. It's kind of nice. He's almost like the big brother I never had, except for the fact that I pay him. I need to remember that. Maybe he's nice, because he likes his job and wants to keep it.

"Are these two okay?" he asks about a set of seats towards the back of the train.

"Sure, those are fine."

It's a section of four seats facing each other. So he gestures for me to take a window seat, then he takes the other facing me, and places my carry on and his backpack on the seats next to us on the aisle.

My phone buzzes to life.

Sloan: I miss u

Me: Not for much longer

Sloan: You're on your way home?

Me: Yep

Sloan: Yippee! Fun fact ... I got blown off by a man yet again.

Me: Just quit already

Sloan: I can't now. It's the principle of the thing. So what time does your train get in?

Me: I'll be home in about an hour. I'll call you later.

Sloan: Cool

Blake watches silently as I shift around in my seat, taking off my jacket, and sending a last emoji text to Sloan. I feel a little self-conscious, like he's studying me closely, but not in a creepy kind of way. Just a curious one.

"How's your mom feeling?" he asks as he pulls his shoulder length blond mane back behind his ears.

"She's much better, thanks for asking. She has to rest her back a bit more, but my dad took off of work next week. So he'll be there to wait on her hand and foot. Thank God."

"Ready to get back home were you?" he says in a funny *Star Wars* Yoda-like voice.

"Definitely." I giggle at his geekiness. "Oh and I meant to say that I'm sorry we weren't able to get as much work done as I thought we would. I didn't realize how much my mom still does at home. Even with just the two of them now, they really needed my help. She still does all the cooking, the cleaning and is part of like a thousand organizations. I was emailing on her behalf for hours."

"It's cool. We're only a week or two behind your release schedule. We can make it up by putting in a couple of extra hours this week and next week. It'll be fine. Actually in a perfect world, I should be able to do everything, and you just check that it all works in the end."

"Is that your roundabout way of saying that I should stop looking over your shoulder?"

"No," he chuckles. "I'm just saying that you should be able to take care of your mom without worrying that the app is going to get behind. You hired me for a reason. You should trust that I can get it done."

"I do trust you. It's just that I'm watching everything you do, because I want to learn. I don't just want to delegate."

"You already know the basics of most of what I'm doing. You just haven't put a lot of the theory you learned to actual use yet."

"I suppose you're right."

"That Penn degree is a good résumé builder, but in this business, experience is everything."

"That's exactly what I'm saying. At first it was entirely me working on School Bucks, but my lack of real world experience was holding the project back. I think it may have played a part in why I didn't get money from an investment group that I pitched earlier this year. I guess there's something to be said for knowing what you don't know."

"Very true, but why don't we agree that you pull back for the next two weeks, and let me finish the updates. Then after the release we can spend the next two weeks getting you ready to help me code the next update by yourself. I'll just supervise. Deal?"

I really like that idea.

"Okay, deal."

Blake reaches inside of his backpack and pulls out two bottles of spring water.

"Want one?" he asks.

I nod and accept the bottle. We've got about a forty minute ride, because the train is a local one and will make plenty of stops.

"Cheers." We both toast to our new business arrangement.

"Can I ask you something, Blake?" I ask as I take a long swig of the water.

"Sure."

"I didn't really hound you for a real answer when I first hired you, but why exactly do you work for me? It's plain as day that you're completely overqualified for the position. You should be running a tech department for an established company. Not working for a web start-up like mine."

He takes a long sip of his water as if he's contemplating exactly whether or not tell me the truth or a lie. At least that's how I'm interpreting his facial expressions.

"The truth?"

"Absolutely," I reply.

"As you know, my last job was in New York, but what you don't know is that I left kind of a mess behind. I had a thing with my boss Erin, and it ended badly." He grins sheepishly. "She basically blackballed me afterwards. At least at the companies that she'd knew I'd try to interview with. Management is pretty much out of the question for me right now."

It's not funny, but I can't help but laugh a little to myself about the thought of Blake ruining a job because of an affair. I definitely didn't peg him as the type to be having a lurid affair at work. My first and second impression of him was that he's a free spirit, with little time for serious relationships, but that shows how much I know. We all can make fools of ourselves when it comes to love.

"Did you cheat on her or something?" I ask.

"No, that's not my style. In the end we were just too different. I know they say that opposites attract, but ultimately I don't think opposites can sustain a long-term relationship. Too many compromises."

"So she's a real bitch, huh?"

"Definitely." He cracks a wide smile. "Problem is I think I still love her."

I take another swig of water after that comment. Poor guy.

"That's unfortunate," I say.

"Eh, I'll probably always love her. I just don't like her very much. So anyway, I couldn't find work without a decent referral from her, and my ego refused to allow me to wait tables, so I broke my lease in New York and came home to mom and dad instead. None of us were happy that I was back in the house. I wasn't regimented enough for them, and they were driving me nuts with their expectations. So we cut a deal.

"They will support my moving out by paying half of my rent for a while, and everything else is on me. Luckily I have a bit of savings, so I found a decent apartment here in the city through a friend. My folks pay half of the rent, and now you're helping me pay the other half, *boss lady*."

His gray eyes dance a bit when he calls me boss lady, and even though I know he's not trying to be, there's something about his playful personality that gives off major flirty vibes.

Between his natural charm and the fact that Roman already feels some kind of way about the guy after meeting him only one time, I make the decision that I need to keep the two of them as far away from each other as possible.

Blake is great, but I already know that Roman won't like him no matter what I say. And frankly I don't want anything to ruin this new alliance that Blake and I have formed. I could learn so much from him, and he's got great ideas for School Bucks. There's no way I'm messing that up.

"So how do you like working for a start up like me?"

"I like that my work really matters, and that the company is doing more for people than just making a profit. Plus it doesn't hurt that that the person in charge is easy on the eyes." He smiles.

Very flirty.

"Is that what you said to Erin?" I ask in jest.

"Probably." His grin grows even wider. "My mouth gets me in trouble a lot of the time."

Yeah ... it would probably be best if Roman and Blake stayed very far apart from each other.

12

Elizabeth

Since I haven't called or sent a text to Roman about my arrival time, I figure it's fine for Blake and I to share a cab ride from the train station. He only lives about ten minutes from me. Plus, I'm probably overthinking this. He works for me. This is business, not pleasure. So we arrange for the cab to drop me off first and then continue on to his house.

I try to pay the driver the fare for both of us, but Blake adamantly refuses. So I pay the driver my half, and then wave good-bye as they pull away. I've concluded, based on our time together on the train that my coder is a really good guy, and that old boss of his is probably an idiot for letting him go. I wonder when I can arrange for him to *accidentally* meet Tiny. They'd make a cute couple.

I drop my bags at the front door, as I angrily begin searching the bottom of my purse for my house keys. So frustrating. I meant to switch handbags before I left for my trip to Penn-Washington, but I kept forgetting to do it. I can never find my keys in this one. The base of this black leather bag is too wide and deep.

Finally I feel the cool metal ring of my keychain, and a wave of relief floods me. The fact that this little thing irritated me tells me that I'm way more on edge than I thought. I'm happy to be back home, but my body is practically thrumming in anticipation of seeing Roman. So as soon as I walk through the threshold, I'm going to put my things down, quickly water my three sort-of-dead plants, freshen up a little (mouthwash and a little spritz of body spray), and then run by The Lotus to see if he's there. The club tends to be where he spends the majority of his time when he isn't handling something for Mendez. He doesn't like to stay holed up in his apartment by himself.

Speaking of Mendez, sometimes I think that he's just an overpaid major league pitcher who wants Roman around as some sort of glorified security guard. The big *saving his ass from major league baseball* job Roman did for Mendez has been completed. The baseball commissioner isn't going after him for illegal steroid use anymore. Now baseball has moved on to some other totally guilty player. So it really makes no sense why Roman has to spend so much time with the guy other than to justify the amount of money Mendez pays him. That and the fact that Roman seems to be bored out of his mind.

Before I can get my key inside the door, I suddenly feel something large and furry with strong, hot breath nudging the backs of my knees forward, almost making them buckle. I'd know that rough play anywhere, and that means his even rougher master can't be very far behind.

Butterflies fill my belly.

And my skin grows warm.

I turn my head and immediately lock eyes with Roman who is leaning against the passenger side of his Range Rover directly in front of me. I guess I was so preoccupied with finding my keys, that I didn't notice that he pulled up in a totally illegal parking spot; there's a fire hydrant there right in front of my house.

My heart races.

He looks better than I remember if that's even possible.

He's wearing my favorite dark jeans, a black leather jacket, a thermal underneath that, and hard bottomed boots. Everything about him looks worn, hard, and weathered. And after being home for two weeks and only seeing guys I grew up with, with soft bodies and bloodshot eyes; it's like a true reward to lay eyes on a *real* man who doesn't depend on his parents to take care of him, who is as hard as a rock, and who looks at me like I'm the hottest woman breathing on the planet.

Well normally he does.

Right now he's looking at me more like a dead man walking.

Even wearing his leather coat, I can still see the outline of his thick, roped arms that are crossed tightly in front of him in defiance. His scarred face shows little emotion, and his bottomless black pupils are battling back and forth between my eyes and my body. He's pissed, and knowing him it could be about a myriad of things, but my educated guess is that right now it's because I didn't tell him I was back in town.

All right, so this is not exactly how I thought our reunion was going to go down but, whatever. Here we are. And I honestly don't care how it goes down. I'm just so frackin' happy to see his mean butt.

"Masterson." I smile and nod my head hello in an effort to diffuse the tension.

His lips twitch.

He's happy to see me too, but he's really trying to be a hard ass. So I drop my bag and my keys and run towards him. Jumping high and wrapping my legs around his waist. I start peppering the sides of his face with kisses.

"I missed you." I practically squeal. Totally happy to see him, while also hoping that my over the top greeting will thaw his icy greeting.

He grabs me immediately by my hips and butt to hold me up, but he still doesn't say a word, as he moves us both forward towards the door. Still holding me, he silently bends down into a squat, picks up my keys and opens the door.

Damn, he's strong.

Once we're inside, he sets me down carefully on the large table I have near the door and orders me with a raw voice "not to fucking move." Just those four words alone are enough to make my insides clench in anticipation.

I watch as he pulls my handbag and carry on inside the apartment and slings them forcefully across the floor after shutting the door. Even Mr. Tibbs flinches in surprise for a moment, but then moves leisurely and silently to his favorite corner of my living room and lies down. Dogs aren't dumb. He can feel the tension rolling off of Roman too, and he's trying to stay out of the line of fire.

"Masterson—" I try to say sexily.

He moves swiftly back to me, wraps his entire palm around my throat, cradling it as his thumb starts stroking my bottom lip. It's a dominant, but very controlled move. Almost as if he's trying to stop himself from doing what he really wants to do. I take a quick inhalation of breath.

"Don't say another fucking word," he commands.

I clamp my mouth shut.

He lets my throat go and casually begins to take off his jacket. His favorite one. A worn but very expensive, black leather, motorcycle-styled jacket with silver hardware. Then he carefully hangs it up on one of the silver coat hooks I recently had him install by the door. All his movements seem very slow and deliberate.

Making my angst swell.

Underneath the jacket, he's wearing his gun holster, which is somewhat unusual for this time of day. If he carries, it's usually at night when all the crazies are out. Especially for the club.

He pulls a gun that I've never seen before out of the holster, puts on the safety, unloads the clip, and takes a bullet out of the chamber. He places all the various parts down very carefully and methodically next to me on the table. I want to ask him if it's new, but I'm not a complete idiot. This isn't the time or place to talk about new purchases. This is a time to be quiet. I think he's trying to calm down.

I can't keep my eyes off of the way his shoulders, his arms and the muscles in his back ripple, as he takes off the holster and lays it across the back of the sofa. Next he lifts up his left pant leg and pulls a small hunting knife out of his left boot and places that on the table as well.

The clank of the knife landing on the table and Roman's continued silence is making me somewhat anxious, yet I'm also sopping wet between my legs. Probably because now my eyes have locked in on the very large bulge in his jeans, angrily trying push it's way through the zipper.

I'm not sure that it's in my best interest to start making inquiries, but I can't help myself. I want to know what in the ham sandwich is up with him. Is he trying to seduce me or scare me? Frighten me or fuck me?

"What is going—"

"Didn't I say not to talk?" he asks with a frosty edge to his voice.

"I know what you said but—"

"You never listen," he says roughly as he stares at me intensely, licking the corner of his mouth.

The tension is so thick between us that I can hear every random noise inside of my house. The kitchen faucet has a slow drip, which I've been meaning to get fixed. The heat just kicked on as I hear it roar to life through the vents. Mr. Tibbs just scratched his chin with his foot, thumping the floor in the process. Hell, I don't know what he's talking about. I think my hearing is just fine. I've got frackin' bionic ears. I can hear every damn thing.

"It's been fifteen days since I've been inside of you, Elizabeth, so I'm going to make this brief. Your mother is sick and needs you. I get it. You trying to make a work retreat out of it, I sort of get, but I don't like it. That's not what you were there for."

"Roman–"

"You not following a simple request to text me what time you were bringing your little ass home, I don't get. And you and that sneaky ass motherfucker sharing train rides and cab rides home together like you just got back from dinner and a show. That shit isn't going to happen again. That's non-negotiable."

Just how long has he been here?

"I think–"

"I think if I started sharing rides home with the girls from the club, you'd have a big problem with it, and you fucking should. Plenty of them have been and probably will always jump at the chance to get their lips wrapped around my dick. I'm a paycheck to them already, but they think I'm an even bigger one if they start sucking me and fucking me. And they're right. I would be."

My mouth hangs open in shock, but then I close it. The image of what he's just said is enough to make me ill. I've never given much thought to it, because I totally trust him, but I don't think I'd survive it if Roman ever cheated on me with some skank.

But almost as soon as he finishes saying his last word "be," he forcefully spreads my legs apart and pulls me forward along the table, until we're flush against each other. I can feel his rigid length between my legs, and part of me wishes that he would just get inside of me, but I know it's not going to be that easy.

Nothing with Roman ever is.

13

Elizabeth

On top of the fact that I didn't tell Roman when I was coming home like he requested, now that I think about it, I was probably smiling from ear to ear inside the cab with Blake when I got out.

Laughing even.

Blake says a lot of funny things, and Roman probably saw all of that. I can only imagine the thoughts running through his head right now. I'm sure it looked a lot worse than it was. Especially because we had just been arguing about him a few days ago. Which I need to constantly remind myself is no fault of my own. Blake works for me. He's harmless. His only crime is probably that he looks too good.

"Can I speak now?" I ask carefully but with a smile.

"I don't think I want to hear shit from that mouth of yours except you screaming my fucking name for the next three days."

"Three days? That's wishful thinking," I jest.

Another lip twitch.

"You want to test me on that? I will literally tie your ass

to my bed for three days, and I assure you that you will make plenty of those loud and hard screams you make when you're coming for me. You know the ones." He smirks cockily.

"Why can't we get through fifteen days apart without your attitude? You can't seriously be jealous. What's going to happen when I have to travel without you again?"

"You won't be traveling with him, so it'll be fine."

"And what if I had to? It's possible you know. Investors want to meet the brains behind the technology."

"You're the brain."

"You know what I mean."

"You sound way too dependent on that prick."

"I'm just being smart. He needs a job right now, and I need him."

"You only *need* me."

"You know what I mean."

"I want you to fire that asshole tonight."

"Absolutely not."

"Then you must want me to kick his ass, because those are your two choices."

"Absolutely not," I say while I begin rubbing his head with the palms of my hands. He begins moving his head underneath my hands like a cat. Rubbing his ears between my fingers. Low growls emanating from the base of his throat. I sigh to myself in relief. He isn't even really that mad about Blake. He just missed me. We're fine.

"Roman."

"What, Elizabeth?"

"Surprise!" I say cheekily.

"Surprise, huh?"

"I didn't tell you when I was coming, because I wanted to surprise you. Now you've ruined it with your bad behavior."

"I ruined it?"

"Yes, you ruined it."

"Let me fix it then. Arms up."

I raise my arms high, so that Roman can pull my top over my head. I'm wearing a black lace, demi cup bra. It was a gift from him, and it's one of his favorites. I would have worn the matching panties, but my leggings looked better without them. No panty lines. So, I'm commando.

He pulls the cups of my bra down, and he bends his head down to latch his lips onto one of my nipples. I quickly gasp when he does this, and mew even more as his thumb gently glides back and forth across the other. Making both of them firm as pebbles.

As his pull on my breasts becomes stronger, my breathing becomes more labored, and I start to squirm. I want him badly. For some reason my body is even more responsive than usual to his manipulation of my breasts; and now the crotch of my leggings are flooded with desire.

Maybe I should have worn panties.

As if he can read my mind, he takes one of his hands and uses it to slide three of his magical fingers inside the front of my pants. He immediately stops for a moment when he notices how drenched I am. He does this all the time, as if he's discovered something new. As if he's actually surprised or amazed by it. Like it doesn't happen every single time I'm with him.

"You're sopping wet," he says in a voice thick with need and wonder. "And you don't have on any fucking panties."

Oh yeah. He might be surprised by that. I rarely go commando.

"You were in the car with that prick with no panties on," he growls.

"I missed you," I whisper back. "I knew panties would just get in the way when I saw you today."

"Shit," he exhales.

He plunges his tongue inside of my mouth at the same exact time that he plunges two of his fingers inside of me, and I almost scream loud enough to wake the dead. I can't even believe my own reaction. I guess two weeks was a really long time to go without sex, now that I'm used to getting some on a regular basis. To my delight, he continues to work his fingers inside of me for a few moments before giving me a Masterson-styled interrogation.

"Didn't I tell you to text me the time of the train?"

He immediately pulls his fingers completely out of me.

I exhale harshly, "Yes."

"So why didn't you?"

He completely unhooks my bra and tosses it across the room. Which I laugh shortly to myself about. Why his belongings get neatly folded and placed down, and mine get thrown across the room is a conversation for later.

He begins kneading my breasts with both of his strong hands, making sure that his thumbs caress my nipples the way I like assuming this will get him the answers he's looking for.

"I–"

"You what?" he interrupts.

"I was trying to surprise you."

"Bullshit."

His massage grows stronger and deeper. Then he pinches one of my nipples tightly between the pads of his thumb and pointer finger. The mixture of pressure and pain feels exquisite.

"I–"

"The truth between us always. Isn't that what we've always said?"

His hands drop from my breasts completely, and he

walks a few steps away from in between my legs. I immediately miss his warmth.

He's watching me intensely, sort of how he used to when we first met. Looking into my eyes for some sort of explanation or answer I haven't given him yet. I panic for a moment that he can see that I'm keeping things from him. That I am not being totally truthful, but then I quickly talk myself down. There's no way. I'm just being paranoid. I've got to get a grip. There's no way he could know about the email or Shrek. Even if he did find out, what's the big deal? I try to rationalize. It's my business to tell, not his to know.

"I was pissed, all right?"

His lips turn up a bit. "Ah, there it is. Honesty. So you were pissed at me?"

"Yes."

"And are you still a little pissed with me?"

"Yes," I respond firmly.

"Why?"

"You cut me off."

"I didn't think you wanted to have any more conversations with someone as *stupid* as me."

I roll my eyes.

"I'm sorry okay? I just blurted it out, and later I tried apologizing repeatedly for it. Which is a bit ridiculous by the way, because you never seem to apologize for anything dumb that you say or do."

"What have I done that I need to apologize for?" he asks as he moves forward again and lifts me off of the table and onto my feet as if I weigh nothing.

He immediately bends down on his knees before me, and begins to gently pull down my leggings. Then he taps my ankle when he's ready for me to lift each foot to step out of them. I can't even think straight when Roman is down on his knees like this, because I know what's going to come next, and I'm going to like it a whole lot.

"I asked you a question, Duchess."

I try my best to keep my mind on the conversation at hand, and not on the fact that his breath is dancing across my breasts when he speaks. Not to mention that once again he's flung a piece of my clothing across the room.

Complete honesty? Well I've already broken that agreement, but I guess I can give him a little of the truth.

"You act like a bratty two-year-old when I tell you something you don't want to hear, and you never apologize for it."

"Explain," he orders as he plants tender kisses on my hipbone.

"I don't want to talk about it now, Roman."

I'd rather he concentrate on what he's doing so well right now.

"Who did you say?"

"Masterson," I moan as my heart begins thundering inside of my chest in anticipation. "I meant Masterson."

"So when do you want to talk about it?"

"After."

"After what?"

"After you give me what I need."

That statement gets me a genuine smile from him.

"And what do you need, Duchess?"

Roman gives a stellar massage, and his powerful hands begin working my butt cheeks. I probably would come right now if I didn't have superior mind control. That and the fact that he'd probably make me pay for it for the rest of the night. He still loves to control every last one of my orgasms. Both of us know that I will lose that game each and every single time. Which is precisely the point.

"Your mouth all over me."

I barely get the words out before Roman flattens his tongue and licks my slit until he reaches the hot core with three very long, broad strokes. Just enough to make me quiver, but not quite enough to send me over the top. He knows my body so well and strums it just like a fine instrument.

"And does your greedy little pussy care about what I need?" he asks with gravel and grit to his voice.

"Yes," I pant.

"Yes, what?"

"Yes, Masterson."

"Well right now I need to see it. Inspect it. Examine it. Make sure nobody else has been touching what's mine."

I'm aching now.

His possessive words making me crazy with need.

"What would you like me to do, Masterson?"

"Very nice." He pats my right butt cheek in approval. "Spread your legs shoulder width apart."

Roman begins to run his hands up and down my legs as if he's conducting a real inspection. He spreads my labia apart, kisses my clit, then maneuvers his head around me and kisses the side of my hip. Then he moves farther away from me and gives me another order.

"Pull your hair down out of that bun, turn around, and place your palms flat on the table."

I immediately do as he says.

"Very nice, but spread your legs a little farther apart."

After I adjust myself, I rest my head and arms on top of the table, keeping my butt high and my legs spread apart.

"Did I say you could get comfy? Head up. Ass up. Legs apart. Let me see your greedy cunt."

"Roman—" I try to protest.

Whack!

He slaps me across the butt with an open palm. I wasn't expecting it so it startles me, but the vibration of it ripples through my body and sends every hair on my body on high alert.

"I think you're confused, Elizabeth," he grinds the words out through his teeth. "I haven't seen you in two damn weeks. You don't tell me when you're coming home, when I asked you very nicely by the way to text me your arrival time. You come home in a cab, laughing and shit like you're at the end of a damn date, and now you're trying be a lazy fuck? I don't think so."

He whacks me again.

This one's even harder and goes straight to my clit.

And before I can get three words out of my mouth in protest, his mouth descends upon my pussy. Licking, sucking and biting me rapidly to the first orgasm I've had from his touch in two weeks.

Needless to say, this is one major damn orgasm. The contraction of my uterus is so powerful, that it renders me speechless for a moment. Breathless. And I begin to see small flickering lights behind my eyelids, much like the quick bursts of light of a camera flash. And that's when the dizziness starts. Almost like I have vertigo. The objects in the room start to liquefy. I quickly grab the sides of the table to steady myself.

"Duchess?" I hear concern in his voice.

I blink my eyes several times and take a moment to catch my breath.

"I'm okay," I assure him.

His hand slides up my back and to the back of my neck then back down to my waist. He uses both hands to gently turn me around, and lift me back up on the table. Instinctually I spread my legs.

"Good girl. Now put your legs around my waist." His

voice is heavy and raspy as I clasp my legs around his waist and my arms around his neck.

"Who do you belong to, Elizabeth?" He looks deep in my eyes. Willing the answer from my lips.

"You. Only you."

Then he slides home exactly where he belongs.

Inside of me.

My mouth gapes open. He almost seems thicker than I remember.

"You're so fucking tight." He groans in appreciation.

"Oh my God," I say harshly.

It doesn't take much longer for Roman to rock and stroke me into another earth shattering orgasm and almost into tears. It's going to be a long night. I can tell that he's not even close to being finished with me.

"Welcome home, Duchess," he says. "Now turn over."

14

Elizabeth

I hear a raised male voice, rumbling sentences heavily laced with expletives regarding something about compromised contract negotiations, lawyers and disrespect. While the words are being delivered in a purposefully harsh manner, the texture of the voice is sand and stone; it makes my body ache in a delicious way. A pleasantly familiar way.

The voice belongs to the man who is a very important part of my daily life, or perhaps rather an essential part. Like breathing. A man who's in *his* office (the spare room of my home), talking on his cell phone at a decibel level much louder than necessary. Practically barking.

For a split second I worry that Roman's bad mood could be a result of him knowing that I've been keeping secrets, but then I quickly come to my senses and realize that there's no way he would know about either of those incidences and not have said something to me by now. It's just my guilt messing with me.

I have to remember that while Roman usually speaks volumes with few words, that he definitely has his moments when he clearly *just* wants to be heard. He gets loud from time to time when he's frustrated or trying to make a point with people. Certain people. But what can be intimidating or brash to some is in fact quite comforting to me. His brand of bravado lets me know without a doubt that he's here and that he is as they say "in the building". His personality fills the room of my home from corner to corner, ceiling to floor. I think it's one of the many things that women find attractive about Roman. It's definitely one of the things that attracted me to him.

Not much has changed since I've returned from Penn-Washington. I haven't called Ethan per his terse request, and I also haven't seen Shrek again. I have done a little digging online, but I don't see anything remotely current in Ethan's Facebook stream, so I think I was overreacting. I must let this whole subject rest. I'm creating more stress in my life where there doesn't need to be any.

My relationship with my parents is still strained, and I don't really see that improving in the near future. Even after my recent visit home, they still aren't open to having Roman visit over the upcoming holidays, which is a deal breaker for me.

Roman hasn't mentioned the letter from his mother again, and he certainly hasn't made a move to go over to the house and ask Joseph to read it. So I'm probably going to have to talk to Juliette about that. Sometimes he just needs a little push.

Unfortunately Roman still doesn't like Blake, and every time I ask him to give me a good reason why, it only makes him hate him more. In fact, I'm pretty sure that Roman's crappy mood right this second is because I'm working in the living room with Blake; and knowing him, we may have laughed a little too loudly or a little too long for his liking.

It doesn't take much for my guy to become all blustery when it comes to my spending time with Blake, but I'm getting used to his comments now. I attribute his behavior to Roman just being Roman. A little crazy in the head. Definitely possessive. Somewhat unpolished. And a beautifully, flawed man whom I simply adore. Faults and all.

Things would be easier though, if I could get Roman to change his mind about my one and only employee. Blake has been nothing but a Godsend to me over the last few months. Not only has he cleaned up some of the messy code of my previous freelancers, and has come to the table with some great ideas of his own for further development of the brand and promotion of the app; but he's also picked up and moved here so that we can continue to work as a real team.

I'm going to give things with him a few more months, and if we're still working this well together, I may even consider making him my partner. He could definitely help me take School Bucks to the next level. He sees the big picture in the same sort of way that I do, and I don't mind sharing the profits with someone who also shares my vision. Especially because I know he could handle the demands of the job. In another world, a guy like Blake would be my boss, not the other way around. I know Roman will probably hate the idea, but one thing I'm perfecting as the weeks and months go by is the delicate art of loving Roman Masterson. And trust me, there's an art to it.

"Seems like your guy is having some sort of heated negotiation in there," Blake says with a tinge of curiosity in his voice. Not fear though. Interestingly enough, Blake may be one of the only men I've run across who doesn't seem the least bit intimidated by Roman.

I like that. It means his feathers won't be so ruffled

when Roman eventually says something wildly inappropriate to him. Which hasn't happened yet, but I know it's coming.

"Yeah," I laugh off his observation casually. "Excuse me for a moment, Blake. Let me go speak with him for a moment."

"No problem." He smiles brightly. "I'll work on this segment of the database until you get back."

I smile in return. "Cool, I shouldn't be long."

All right, so I'm not even going to lie. There is something about my new, calmly cool, employee, which is definitely attractive or should I say appealing. He's tall with long lean muscles, and a head full of lush, dirty blond hair which he usually wears loose or in a messy ponytail. Definitely reminiscent of a Viking as Sloan pointed out.

He also has this pair of distinctive, beautiful gray eyes that always look like they're processing information. I think his eyes mirror a mixture of his very funny personality and his exceptional brain, and if I had an older sister, I'd definitely hook her up with him. He's boyfriend material for sure. Not high-powered or polished enough for Sloan though, which is why I haven't even bothered trying to hook them up. And for some reason, Tiny hasn't returned any of my texts for the last week. Sometimes she just goes radio silent, so I haven't been able to make the introduction I wanted to make between the two of them.

I rap on the door to Roman's office as a polite gesture, but then I walk in without waiting for a response. Ultimately it's my house, and he's being disrespectful. My defenses are up, because I know he's itching for a fight, one that will end up with me spread eagle and begging for release. And they always begin with that turned up mouth of his. A cocky grin that I'm sure has worked it's voodoo magic on many an unsuspecting woman. Now it's especially reserved for me.

"Elizabeth," he greets me then turns his head and gives whoever he's on the phone with a curt good-bye. "We'll finish this later."

"Why are you so loud?" I start in on him as soon as he ends the call. Picking the fight first is my strategic offensive play.

"I needed to be loud in order to drown out all the fucking giggles coming from the living room."

"You're ridiculous." I huff.

"You're a flirt."

"Well you're an ass."

"So you're admitting that you're a flirt then?"

"No, jerk off. I'm not."

"You're pushing it with the name calling."

I say with defiance, "Not as hard as you're pushing things."

"Strip." He playfully grins. I'm pretty sure he's laughing at the fact I used the words hard and pushing in the same sentence. He has such a dirty mind.

"No."

"What did you just say?"

"I said absolutely not, Roman." I get serious for a moment. "I'm not stripping. In case you didn't realize, I'm working, and the person I'm working with is literally ten feet away from this frackin' door. If you think I'm going to—"

"That's why you're going to be as quiet as a mouse, while I take care of your little giggle problem. In fact let's make this interesting. If you come on my face, real quiet like, I'll buy you a matching Rover, so you can stop taking those damn Uber cars. They don't even screen those drivers properly. They're probably all serial rapists."

"You need a therapist," I say only semi-seriously.

"For what?" he rhetorically asks me as he slowly backs me into a corner of the room.

I throw up my hand in defense of his approach.

"I can help you find one at a reasonable rate if money is the issue," I jest.

"Is there something wrong with me asking my girl to strip?" he asks while gesturing to me with a head nod to raise my arms, but I hold steady and refuse.

Roman often uses sex as a power play, and sometimes I give in because I get just as much pleasure out of it as he does, but then there are times that I just have to stand my ground if I'm ever going to get anything done.

Like work.

I usually try to make sure that Blake isn't in my house when I know Roman is going to come by, but today it didn't work out that way. So I give him a silent but firm head shake no.

"No?" he growls dipping his head into the side of my neck.

"Uh-uh." I try my best to answer with conviction as I close my eyes in rapture. "I only came in here to tell you to keep it down. We both need to respect each other's space if we're ever going to work in here at the same time."

Of course while I'm putting up all this verbal protest, I clasp my hands around the back of Roman's neck as he burrows his head farther into the side of my neck. I can't help it; because I love the way my body vibrates when he speaks against my skin.

"You look fucking spectacular today, Duchess. This tight skirt." He slides his palm up the side of my thigh. "This fuzzy cream sweater." Brushing the backs of his fingers across my waist underneath my sweater. "No wonder captain nerd can't stop laughing at every fucking thing you say out there. He's probably mesmerized by your pretty ass."

"Why does everyone I know have to be a nerd in your eyes except for you?" I ask amused.

"Is that actually a serious question?"

"Oh, shut up."

"I know men, Duchess."

"And? I'm not sure what that has to do with my question, but now that we're on the subject, let's discuss it real quickly. I'm going to ask again. What's your problem with Blake? You're the one who wanted me to hire an employee. Hell, you bought me this apartment, so I could have space to make it happen. So now that I have, you haven't given him a single chance. You met him once and now you won't even talk to him for five minutes. I already know nothing came up in your investigation."

"I knew all that I needed to know the minute he decided to relocate here."

"I want you to talk to him."

"I do talk to him. I say hi and bye. I just won't give him the opportunity to bite me in the back."

"What the heck does that mean? Bite you in the back?" I ask in frustration. "You know what? Forget it. You're being ridiculous. Adorable but ridiculous."

"Mmm, you're adorable," he whispers in my ear. "I'm ready to spread your limbs from east to west right on this desk and fuck you sideways. Would you like that, baby?"

I squeeze my eyelids tightly closed and lie through my teeth, "No."

"You don't mean that. You know how I know? Because ever since you walked in here, you've been staring at me like a piece of chicken," he chuckles as he throws one of my old sayings back at me. "Arms up, Duchess."

I shake my head vigorously no again.

"Uh-uh." I lean away from him and say with a smile. "I'm going to walk back out of this office with all of my clothes on, and you're going to behave for the next hour or so, so that Blake and I can finish."

"Blake," he parrots back gruffly. "Who the hell names their son *Blakkke*." He exaggerates the pronunciation of the K sound.

"Umm, a lot of people do and would you please quiet down."

I move from underneath and away from Roman, knowing that if I don't put some physical distance between the two of us, that he will take great pleasure in totally embarrassing the hell out of me in front of someone I pay a salary. Someone whose opinion of me matters. I've already been in here way too long. It's embarrassing.

"Where are you going?"

"Over here," I say with determination.

He stalks over towards me.

"You know I don't beg for pussy, Elizabeth," he says into my ear with a grin spread across his face.

"So you keep saying, but I don't think you even really want it right now anyway. You're just trying to prove some sort of point."

"Don't be mistaken, pretty girl. I always want *it* when it comes to you."

Roman leans his forehead into mine, and I can't help but wrap my arms around his waist as he moves in for a kiss. He's holding back, thank God, but he still makes sure to take a moment to savor my mouth in a way that makes me imagine that I taste extremely delicious.

"You taste like bubblegum," he says in the low, gravelly voice that hardens my nipples every single time.

As his tongue plunges deeper into my mouth, I instinctively rise up on my toes and rest my hands along the back of his buzzed-cut head. Rubbing back and forth as the kiss grows more passionate. He loves it when I rub his head this way, and I can tell by the deep groan coming from deep inside his chest that I need to stop this right now before it gets totally out of hand. I'm sending seriously mixed signals.

I break the kiss and step away from him, although it takes every ounce of will power I can muster. It's so easy to get lost inside of the deep physical attraction we have for each other. It's basically all we've been doing for the last few months. Indulging in our baser instincts, our deep sexual connection, as well as our burgeoning emotional relationship.

"I'm not kissing you anymore until you promise to make a dentist appointment," I say suddenly.

"Well that shit came out of no where," he laughs. "Does my breath stink?"

"I can't kiss a man who doesn't take care of his teeth."

"Jade texted you, huh? She's been on my ass about that appointment for two weeks. Listen, Duchess, my teeth are fine. I haven't had a cavity since I was seven. Stop trying to change the subject, and bring your spectacular ass back over here where you belong."

"How do we know your teeth are fine? Jade said you haven't been in two years. That's a long time not to have a checkup."

Roman crosses his massive arms in front of himself. Every delicious inch of his firm biceps hugged and accentuated by the tight white thermal shirt he's wearing. I can already tell that he's about to say something that I'm not going to like. It's written all over his mischievous face.

"Well I did date a dental student a few years back. I think she just settled into a practice over in Chestnut Hill. Maybe I should give her a call. She gave amazing—"

"Hey!" I yell as I slap him on the arm.

Roman chuckles again.

"So fucking pretty."

"Oh just be quiet," I snap. "And behave for another hour or so. Blake has to leave early, and then we can play for the rest of the day like we planned."

"So now you've stooped to bargaining with me? Go to the dentist and I'll get some pussy. Wait another hour and then I'll get some. What happened to you telling me that *this* was mine?"

Roman swiftly walks back towards me and immediately slides his hand underneath my pencil skirt and in between my legs. The flimsy triangle of fabric I'm wearing underneath is unable to hide the pure heat emanating from my crotch. It's just the nature of the beast. I'm always hot for him. That and the fact that the kiss we just shared turned things up a notch.

"And that I could have *this* any time I wanted." He slides his hand back out, then back in again. Each time, hiking up my skirt a little farther up. Playing carefully in between my legs like my slit is a delicate string instrument.

"I'm not your possession, Roman." I try to say this with conviction while his hand still plays wickedly in between my legs.

We both know that was unconvincing.

He possesses me body and soul.

"Listen to me closely, Duchess," he says as his brow creases. "Everything about you from the top of your head to the tips of your toes belongs to me." He kisses me softly. "And I belong to you. All that's left for us to do is make it official."

The intended meaning of his words and the tone that he uses to deliver them are the most beautiful things anyone has ever said to me. That's why my resistance grows weaker, and so I say the most ridiculous thing a woman could say right in the middle of her workday. Especially with her employee sitting in the next room.

"I'll give you ten minutes."

"Stop playing around," he chuckles. Pleased with himself that he's won our game of wills between us. "You know you'll want me inside of you for at least an hour. You always beg for more."

I roll my eyes. "Okay fifteen."

"This negotiation is going downhill real fast, because in three fucking seconds I'm going to take you right here on this desk, right the hell now, for as long as I want, and I don't give a shit who's listening in the other room."

"This obviously isn't a negotiation," I whisper angrily while jabbing my finger in his chest. "This is you bullying me!"

"I'm not sure why I have to bully or beg for time with my girl on a Thursday any fucking way. Thursday is my night per our new arrangement is it not?"

"I'd hardly describe these last few minutes as you begging, and yes Thursday is your night, *not* the entire day."

He ignores me as usual when I tell him something he doesn't want to hear.

"What were you two laughing your asses off about out there anyway? Is coding that fucking funny? What's the damn joke?"

"So we're back to Blake now? I think I have whiplash. You can't seem to focus on one topic. Do you want a quickie or do you want to talk about my employee?"

"I'd like to focus solely on getting inside that ass of yours if you'd stop talking about that prick for just ten seconds."

"Honestly, Roman," I cock my head to the side, "jealousy doesn't look good on you."

"This is not me being jealous, Elizabeth. This is me paying very close attention to what's mine. I didn't become who I am by not paying attention. You should know the difference."

"Blake is not a prick, and you know it. He's a good guy, a great coder, and I like him. Not to mention that you're the only one who's been talking about him incessantly for the last few minutes, not me. Listen, I don't have time to argue with you. He's waiting out there for me, and I'm trying to build a business in case you forgot," I whisper angrily.

"Build it tomorrow," he growls. "And let his ass wait."

A knock on the door surprises us both.

"Hey, Beth, I need to check some of Ravi's notes. Do you mind if I check the emails between the two of you?" Blake asks through the closed door.

Immediately my eyes fly up to meet Roman's. I already know what he's thinking before he even opens his mouth. The fact that Blake is in my house, interrupting our conversation through a closed door, regardless of the topic or the reason, is probably rubbing him the wrong way. Really wrong. He confirms my assumption when his body grows tense, and his eyes lock on mine.

"Yes, Blake." I call out with my eyes still completely on Roman. "Check the School Bucks Gmail account. It's already open in my browser. Just search for Ravi's name."

"Cool."

Now Roman's mouth is taut just like his tightly strung body. My guess is that he's about to cuss poor Blake out something awful, so I quickly press the tips of two of my fingers against his lips to quiet him. And then Blake speaks again.

"Umm, are you all right?" he asks.

"Totally," I say through the door in the brightest voice I can muster at this point, "I'll be out in a sec."

I can see Roman's jugular vein pulsating. Blake may never have the ability to have children if I don't calm crazy boy's nerves. He's told me plenty of times that he doesn't fight fair.

"Shh, he doesn't understand Masterson protocol quite yet."

"The fuck he mean are you all right?" he says through my fingers which are still covering his lips.

"This isn't just some shit I make up in my head, Elizabeth. Any man would know that he's overstepping right now. Purposely overstepping. We're in here talking. Whatever he's doing out there can wait a goddamn minute. And what's with him calling you *Beth*? He's known you for all of two damn minutes. That's not even your fucking name."

"Would you quiet down. You're acting a bit–"

"A bit what?"

"A bit ridiculous, Roman. Crazy. Nuts. I'm not going to battle with you like this every time Blake is over. You bought me this place, so that I could work from home didn't you?"

He sucks his teeth.

"I know *why* I bought you this apartment, Elizabeth. I don't need you to remind me of my generosity."

Now I'm getting mad for real.

"Oh please! You're acting like I asked you to buy me this place."

"You didn't say no."

"So that means you're going to throw it up in my face every damn chance you can? Or that I have to do whatever you say, because you gave it to me as a gift?"

"I didn't say that."

"You didn't have to. I don't even want to live here after that frackin' comment."

I place my hand on the doorknob of the door to leave.

"Don't turn that fucking handle. We're not done."

I stop my movements, but I keep my head facing forward.

"Stop telling me what to do, Roman. I mean it. I'm not playing with you right now. You bossing me around in bed is one thing, but you trying to control my life outside of the bedroom is another. You're embarrassing the hell out of me."

"So I embarrass you now?" he asks harshly as he walks up directly behind me. "I'm stupid and I *fucking* embarrass you?"

I've never heard Roman speak to me using this tone of voice before. It's hurtful. I don't even know how we got to this place. Hell, I'm the one who has the right to be angry. He's being irrational and overly territorial. As if I've done something to warrant this behavior. As if I'm someone who can't be trusted.

My hand shakes as I continue to grip the doorknob tightly with my right hand. I'm not sure why. I'm not frightened of Roman. He would never hurt me. I'm just really frightened of the direction that this conversation may go in if I say anything else.

He is physically close enough that I could easily end the tension between us by leaning my head back against his chest. It's what my first instinct is telling me to do. It's what I've done many times before, to stop things from escalating between us. It's my surrender. My bow to his domination.

But I don't want to acquiesce today. I don't think I should have to. My employee is out there waiting for me. I've wanted School Bucks to work for so long, and I finally have someone on board that can really help me get it to where it needs to be. Besides Roman, it's all I want. Yet it seems for some reason, he doesn't want it for me. He can't possibly. Not if he's acting like this.

I don't take the easy way out this time. Instead of leaning my head back to diffuse the tension between us, I stand erect, turn the knob to the right, open the door and exit.

"I think we need a time out," I say, not really sure what I mean or for how long I mean; but what I do know is that I don't want to talk to him for at least the rest of the day. That's how disappointed I am in him right now.

He doesn't say a word in response, but he doesn't have to. Something is very wrong with him, or with us, and Blake is a symptom not the sickness. Maybe a little space between us will be just the medicine we need to help whatever it is heal on its own.

15

Roman

"Well this is down right interesting."

"What?" I ask Jade as I instruct her to take a seat with my pointer finger. "Sit."

"This place."

She plunks her tiny ass down on the bench next to me and places a dark brown messenger bag that's bigger than her entire body next to her. I laugh to myself as she sits, because she knows me so well.

"What's so interesting about this place, Jade?" I ask already knowing her answer.

"Well for one, it's pretty as fuck out here. Hallmark movie pretty. Also we are actually sitting *outside*, far away from civilization, where there's not even bottle service or a slutty girl shamelessly gawking at you. Totally the opposite of your usual day in every way unless you're running," she snickers. "Shall I continue?"

I'm sitting in an area that is about thirty minutes out of the city, called Longwood Park, people watching of all things. In my work, I have on many occasions watched, followed, and stalked people for days on end. Paying attention to where they go, who they talk to, what they buy, and what they throw away. It's necessary for me to try and learn everything about the person I'm working for as well as any people who are in the way, before I *fix* a situation.

But I've never done this type of people watching before. Which is basically watching people for no reason at all. Well let me take that back. I guess it's all how you look at it. I do have a reason for being here at Longwood, but it's not due to the usual work related reasons.

I overheard Elizabeth mention how much she loved this park a while back, when I was eavesdropping on a phone conversation that she was having with the prick also known as Blake. The pleasant lilt in her voice when she described one of her visits here peaked my curiosity. That and the fact that she was having this conversation with *him* and not me. I know about her favorite playground near Penn, we've visited it several times, but she's never told me anything about *this* place. And this place is the total opposite of that playground. That fact alone tells me a number of things.

One, that Elizabeth has something else in common with this brand new pain in my ass. Something common between the two of them that we don't share. Two, that for whatever reason, she doesn't think I have any interest in sitting in parks and watching pretty shit. Which I don't, but that's not the fucking point. I am highly interested in all things and everything that have to do with Elizabeth Hill. So I've made it my business to inform myself about this Longwood Park place all on my own.

I've been sitting on this wooden park bench, which evidently was bought and dedicated to some dude named Cecil back in 1985, for about twenty minutes tonight, and I think I'm starting to see what my girl loves about the place.

Every branch on every tree in the park has been meticulously decorated with tiny, white Christmas lights, lighting up the entire area and making it look almost like a mystical getaway. As if we're not literally minutes away from the grit of the city. That's probably part of it. Maybe Longwood reminds her a bit of home. All the nuclear families walking around out here. Holding hands. Taking pics of each other under the lights. I hadn't put much thought to it before, but a girl like Elizabeth probably wants all of that. A perfect family. White picket fence. Family time in the park. Unfortunately I don't know shit about that. All I've got is some money and Mr. Tibbs.

Now while I admit it's almost picture perfect out here, I find it especially interesting how each and every kid under the age of twelve seems to stare up at the lights in utter amazement. As if the park is magical. As if they could blink their eyes and all of a sudden see Santa.

I never had a moment as a kid where I looked at anything with amazement, or wonder, or awe. Most of what I saw everyday was old, drunken, worn men on the block who life had beaten the hell out of. Craving a drink every moment of the day.

And then there were the older guys that kids my age were suppose to look up to. They'd already graduated or dropped out of high school, and were living their lives with no real purpose. Getting high on meth, selling meth, getting girls pregnant, and talking shit all day about how badass they were.

This is the type of daily, depressing shit I had to regularly see on my way to the store to pick my mother up a pack of menthol cigarettes, or to buy myself my meal for the day, which was usually a pint of milk and a small box of Froot Loops.

Needless to say, my outlook on life was seriously jaded

very early on. None of the kids in my neighborhood saw anything with stars in their eyes. There was no pretty shit on my block. And while I'm doing my best to reprogram all of that, I wonder if Elizabeth will understand if I can't be *that* guy even though I want to be. Or at least a better version of myself. Better for Elizabeth. Better for myself.

"So why are we here?" Jade asks in an annoyed and rushed tone. As if it's not her damn job to be at my beck and call.

"I'm sorry you bitter little Brussels sprout. Am I keeping you from something?"

She sucks her teeth in annoyance.

"I'm just trying to figure out why we're meeting in West Bubblefuck. Whatever this is about could have been handled from the comfort of your Penthouse Suite or at least that makeshift office you have in your girlfriend's house."

"I'm putting the band back together again," I say satirically.

This is actually a meeting that was long overdue. Since the break with the old man, the Kings and I only have one client and one club. While we are talking about a very profitable client and club, the three of us didn't go into this whole arrangement together wanting to create some sort of "boutique" agency serving one elite client.

We want to wreck shit.

We want to dominate.

We want a real business with multiple clients and acquisitions.

We just didn't want Joseph's business or rather I didn't. I knew that if we were ever going to make a name for ourselves, independently of Joseph's reputation, then this was necessary. A clean break.

None of us anticipated at the time (well maybe Cam

did) that Joseph would make it very difficult for us to get new clients. Every time I let my guard down and forget for a moment what a dick the old man can be, he always takes great pleasure in reminding me. So this meeting is about us needing to regroup, get focused, and figuring out exactly how we're going to turn this whole thing around.

The old man challenged me the day we met to convince people to hire us as if there was not a chance in hell it could happen. So that's exactly why my mission is: to get a shitload of clients without one bit of assistance from him.

"So is the dynamic duo coming here too?" Jade asks.

"They should be here in a few."

"I'm surprised your friend agreed to a meet anywhere outside of Philly."

She had a point. Camden rarely ever leaves the city. He barely steps outside of the ten-block radius around his house or The Lotus. He likes to keep put, and his brother Cutter likes to roam free. That's why they work so well together.

"You mean *your* man." I joke with her (but not really).

Jade glares at me.

"Just because your friend likes to watch my ass from time to time doesn't make him *my* man."

"He definitely does watch your ass," I laugh.

"Of course he does. I have a fantastic ass. An hour a day on the elliptical makes it that way, and most men like to watch it."

I laugh exaggeratedly.

"What? Are you trying to say it isn't fantastic?" she asks incredulously.

"What ass?" I ask rhetorically while laughing heartily.

Jade smacks my shoulder.

"Oh right, you like them juicy."

"Hell, yeah," I agree. Elizabeth has the perfect pear shaped ass that jiggles when I'm banging her from behind. No other ass compares.

I can see the Kings pulling into the parking lot adjacent to the park entrance. After a quick scan of the area, they spot us, and start to walk over. Camden looks cautiously around the area. He hates unfamiliar surroundings.

I notice that Jade immediately bows her head and whips out her cell phone to start texting furiously. Her thumbs moving so fast, it's obvious that she isn't texting anyone at all. She's bullshitting. Pretending to be busy for appearance sake. And there could only be one person that she's doing all of this pretending for, because it certainly isn't me.

"The King is here!" Cutter gives his usual ridiculously vain announcement of himself whenever he greets me.

It sort of sounds like when Will Smith chants, "The champ is here," in that movie *Ali*. I laughed at it once when he first started doing it, and now he won't stop. Everyone has to be sick of it at this point, but because his antics attract the attention of many a club rat, I don't think he'll ever stop now.

"There are two Kings," I remind him. "When are you ever going to acknowledge that fact in that grand entrance of yours?"

"Only one of us is worth announcing," Cutter chuckles looking at his brother.

Another thing I notice is that Camden doesn't quietly stare Jade down, like he usually does when she's around. Instead he averts his eyes away from her, gives me a head nod hello, and then sits on the bench. Jade doesn't say a word to him either. Their silence speaks volumes. Something definitely went down between the two of them, and while I have no interest in the details, it just better not get in the way of work. Or our friendship.

"So you asked us to meet you out here in fucking Whoville. What's up?" Camden asks.

"Oh that's funny," I say. "Jade called it West Bubble-fuck. Aren't you two both creative with words."

Jade is staring daggers at me. This is going to be fun fucking with the two of them.

"I'll get straight to the point. It would be stupid for us to depend only on the income of Mendez and the club. While we are in a contract with Mendez, he only needs us if he's playing. If he's valuable. If he's still being talked about on Sports Center. Because if he gets hurt or suffers some sort of career altering injury, then he won't need us anymore. We need to be prepared for that day. It's inevitable. He's a pitcher. That arm won't last forever."

"I thought we have his endorsement income? What does it matter if he gets hurt or retires?" Cutter asks.

"We do have it, but only for eighteen months. The money is good now, but what happens when that contract is over?"

"Eighteen months?" Camden questions.

"It was Joseph's deal."

"Of course," he says annoyed. "He never mentioned that it was only for eighteen months."

"It's still a lot of money," Cutter adds.

"And we did a lot of work to keep his steroid using ass squeaky clean."

"He only used them to heal up. Not bulk up." I think Mendez is one of Cutter's favorite players. He makes excuses for him all the time.

"Joseph brought Mendez to the table," I remind every-one. "You know how shit works, Cam. What is your fucking problem other than the obvious?"

"The obvious?"

I look over at Jade, who is again on her phone pretending that this conversation is none of her business, then back at him and grin.

"Fuck you." He throws his middle finger up.

I grin but continue on with our conversation. "I'm just saying we can't depend on that income forever."

"We've got the club," Cutter adds. "And it's doing damn good. The bar made a killing last night."

"That's cool, but you know how it is in this town. Clubs in Philly aren't as long-lived as ones in New York or Los Angeles. People here party at one place then move on to the next hot place and when that happens, The Lotus will be dead and stinking in the water."

"So why don't we make sure that doesn't happen?" Cutter asks.

"I don't think that there's anything that we can do to make sure that never happens, brother. It's inevitable. But let me say that there is something else we can do, and that's to make sure we have other streams of income flowing in."

"So we're going back to our original plan," Camden says.

"Yep. I think we need to focus more on developing the client side of the business like we always intended. It's way easier for us to find a couple of more Mendezes than to invest part of our savings into several more clubs or restaurants. All the headaches with leases, licenses, hiring, and stealing. Crossing our fingers and hoping that they make money. Fixing client problems always makes us money, and we're good at it. Let's stick to what we know. Let's do what we do best."

"Well, duh. That sounds good in theory, but isn't the whole reason we're sitting here is because you all are twiddling your thumbs at the club every night. Obviously you can't get clients," Jade finally speaks up. I guess she was listening the whole time.

"Twiddling our thumbs," Cutter repeats back appalled by Jade's characterization of what we do all day.

"Excuse me," she mocks. "I meant playing with your dicks."

"You can play with this big dick right the fuck—"

"Never mind with that," Camden cuts his brother off, "what do you have in mind, Rome?"

"I'm not totally sure yet, but I have a couple of irons in the fire. Thinking outside the box. I just want to make sure that we all are on the same page. Are you two coming to Juliette's event?"

"I might have a run to make, and Cutter's got to hold down the club that night," Camden says.

I notice how Jade gives Camden the curious side eye the minute he says something about making a run. I must admit that I'm curious too. Camden rarely withholds information from us, but whatever he has going on is none of my business.

"All right, let's meet again after the gala. I should have something in the works by then."

"Cool."

"Do we have to meet all the way here like we're planning a heist?" Cutter jokes. "At least in *Oceans 11* they met in Vegas. This is the middle of no-fucking-whereville."

"That's what I'm saying," Jade chimes in, in agreement.

"Depends," I say annoyed with all three of them at this point. "If I feel like fucking meeting here, then that's where we'll meet."

"Touchy bastard," Camden mutters. "Let's go Cut."

As soon as the Kings are out of earshot, I start grilling Jade.

"What the fuck was that all about?"

"What?"

"I don't have the patience for your shit today, Jade. I'm already going through it with Elizabeth, and I'm not going to deal with your crap too. Something is very wrong between you and Cam, and I want to know what it is."

"And why would it be any of your business if there was something going on? What are we *girlfriends*?"

"Listen you little lima bean, I want to know because I don't want your shit interfering with my business."

"Your business is in the shithole already, Einstein."

"That's funny. I don't remember you complaining about not getting paid last month."

"Ooh, you're funny too. You always have to take it there don't you. Always throwing the fact that *you* pay me over my head."

"I'm not throwing anything anywhere. Just stating facts. But stop changing the subject. What happened?"

"Nothing important. Nothing worth mentioning."

Of course that meant that it was important as hell. I'm not an idiot. I speak *woman*.

"Well at least tell me if you're all right."

I'll kick Cam's ass if he's fucking with my little shrimp's head.

"I'm all right. The question is are *you* all right?"

"Why wouldn't I be?"

"You're the one who said that there's trouble in paradise with your sun, moon and stars."

"Nothing I can't handle."

"Did you two break up?"

"Hell no. We just had a disagreement, and we need a little time to cool off."

"Her idea or yours to cool off?"

"It was mutual."

"Uh-huh."

I sense disapproval from that uh-huh.

"I thought you liked Elizabeth?"

"She's cool."

"You're way too overprotective of me, Jade."

"Says pot to kettle."

She's probably right about that.

"I need you to do a couple of things for me before Juliette's party," I say as I walk away from her and towards the Rover. "I'll text you."

"I'll be waiting with bated breath."

Jade is definitely one of my closest friends, and I love her teeny, tiny butt, but there's no doubt in my mind that whatever went down with her and Cam was one hundred percent her fault.

That mouth of hers is something special, and *not* in a good way.

16

Jade

"Thanks for stopping by."

I'm reluctantly standing at Elizabeth's front door. I don't want to be here for a variety of reasons, but I can't wait to see what little miss perfect is going to say.

"No problem. What's up?"

I'm being unusually short with Roman's beloved because number one, we're not besties by any stretch of the imagination, and two, as if I don't have enough shit to deal with than become her beck and call girl. I don't work for her. I work for Roman. And I don't think she totally understands the concept that they're not a package deal.

And then there's the other thing ...

"You want lunch? I make a mean Cesar salad. Or maybe a glass of vino?" she chirps.

I casually glance at my new Apple watch in an effort to drive home the point that I'm not here to *hang*.

"I don't drink before five, and I don't eat before one."

"Not in the mood for small talk then?"

"Well I really hope you didn't ask me here for small talk," I say as I look around her living room, noticing the various changes she's made to her place since I was here last.

It's been a while. I've seen Elizabeth here and there at the club, or we've talked briefly over the phone, but I haven't been back at her house at all. Roman hasn't had us over here for a meeting in a long time.

"Why do I get the feeling that I've done something to make you angry," she astutely comments.

"What makes you think that? You're cool, and Rome seems to like you a whole hell of a lot, so that makes us good." I lie through my teeth.

"I guess I thought since you were his best friend, and he and I are seeing each other, that maybe the two of us would hang out a little or something. When I first moved in here you came over a couple of times, and then all of sudden you backed off."

"We talked the other day," I say bored with this conversation already.

"That was like three weeks ago, Jade, and that was about Roman's teeth."

"I'm not the kind of girl that chitchats on the phone about her problems or celebrity gossip with other women."

"I'm not that kind of girl either," she replies defensively.

"This is no disrespect to you, Elizabeth, but I've got a shitload of things to do today. So if you could just get to the point of why you asked me to swing by that would be awesome."

"All right," she snaps. "You say you have a lot of things to do today. Are any of them work related?"

Where is she going with this?

"Yes, why?"

"Well I think Roman is losing his ever loving mind, and I think it's because he's bored to death. I'm not sure what you're doing, but he's not working or working enough. It's off-season in baseball, and Mendez has been keeping his nose clean. So that's over. And I don't know what the three of them could possibly be doing at The Lotus every week. They have a manager that takes care of all the day-to-day stuff. So it's obvious to me that he needs a new client. Maybe a few new clients. They probably all are going a little crazy."

My phone dings notifying me of a new message.

King Kong: We need to talk.

The last thing I need is to have *that* conversation with Camden King. I'd be fine if we never spoke on it again.

"Why are you telling me all of this?" I ask Elizabeth. "You should talk to your boyfriend if he's getting on your nerves. And if you have a question about his business, then ask him about it or meet with the King brothers. I have nothing to do with whether or not they take on new clients."

"I know who I can ask, Jade, but I'm asking you. Do you agree with me or not on this?"

I ignore the fact that she's irritated, and walk over to her small fiddle leaf fig plant and rub on one of the smooth leaves. I'm familiar with this type of houseplant, because my nana owned three of them. It was one of her favorites.

"Sure I agree, but there isn't much I can do about it. The old man was the pro at finding new clients. The boys were better at fixing their problems."

I don't bother telling her that the three of them have already met about this very topic. If she doesn't know, then things are still strained between her and Roman. It's his business to tell. Not mine. So I'll just play dumb.

"So they need someone to scout out new clients. That's what you're saying?"

"Yeah, I guess that's what I'm saying." I walk over to

another one of her houseplants. "Your plants are really healthy."

"Thanks, it's the fertilizer."

I cruise around her living room. Never sitting down. Never really looking Elizabeth in the eyes since I've set foot in her house. I'm too angry with what she's done. I didn't want to have this conversation with her yet. I wanted to wait. I needed more information. More time. I'm doing a horrible job of holding my cards close to my vest.

"Jade," she says my name to get my attention.

"Yeah," I turn my head in her direction.

"What is your problem with me? Did Roman say something to you about the two of us?"

I raise an eyebrow at her last comment and then take a seat on her couch. Of course I know something is up with her and Roman. He tells me most things. They had some sort of falling out, although he seems pretty confident that it's nothing. I'm just not sure that he's seeing things clearly when it comes to this cousin of his. It's like she has a golden chalice in between her legs.

"Has Roman ever told you how we met?" I ask her.

"He's mentioned some of the story."

"Well to make a long story short, my ex was beating my ass and spending my hard earned money on drugs for a long time. I was young, dumb, and a walking after-school special until Roman got me out of there."

She nods as if she has any idea what it means to be abused. To be scared. To desperately need someone to give a fuck about you when you don't care about yourself. Of course she doesn't get it. She comes from the cushiest, white-washed life ever, and she's still getting shit handed to her on a silver platter thanks to Roman. This apartment she doesn't pay for is case in point.

"It wasn't easy to admit to him what was going on. He was the only true friend I had, and I never wanted him to think less of me, but eventually I knew I had to trust someone. I made the best decision of my life when I finally admitted to him what was going on. I trusted the right person with my secrets."

Her eyes just dropped to the floor. She knows exactly what I'm getting at, but I'm sure she's going to continue playing the dumb, doe-eyed, suburban thing of hers to the hilt. She does it so well.

"So what does that have to do with you and I, Jade?"

Yep, she's going to play it this way.

"You need to learn who to trust."

"I trust Roman. I trust the Kings. I trust all of you—"

"No you don't." I immediately cut her off. "So if you want me to keep it really one hundred percent real with you, I'm keeping my distance from you until you get it right or until you're gone."

Her eyes widen.

"I wish you would just spit out whatever you're skirting around right now, because you're kind of pissing me off, Jade. Do you like Roman or something? Did you two used to date?"

I laugh to myself.

"Did you ask Roman that?"

"No, should I?"

"Have you been thinking that about us this whole time?"

"Not until just now."

"Do you know what I do for Roman?"

"I guess you do whatever he asks you to do, Jade. You're his assistant. I know what assistants do. What are you trying to insinuate?"

"That's right. I do whatever he asks me to do, and most

of what he asks me to do lately is to keep a watchful eye on his cousin."

As if he really pays me enough for this shit.

"I'm sorry about that, but you need to take that up with Roman if you have a problem with it. I have no control over what he asks you to do. I have no control over him at all."

"The fact that he asks me to do it is not the problem, Elizabeth. You're missing the point."

"So what's the point?" she asks raising her voice slightly.

"Part of watching you has always involved me keeping an eye on that drug addict ex of yours. I'm familiar with drug addict boyfriends, so Roman knew I'd do a good job. Who knew you and I had the same taste in men."

I notice immediately when her stomach drops, and I grin at her inability to lie well. She'd never make it in our world if her life depended on it. It only confirms my feelings that Roman is making a huge mistake by being with her.

At first I thought it was a bad idea because she is his cousin, and then I thought it was an even worse idea, because he was much too serious about her. Far from the carefree womanizer that I was used to seeing. But now I know for sure that she's a bad idea, because she can't be trusted. In our world, that's the kiss of death.

"I know that Ethan recently contacted you, because I'm paid to monitor his emails, Elizabeth. Imagine my surprise when I saw that he emailed you about a meet and you *never* said anything to your boyfriend about it. My boss. Imagine the position that puts me in now that you and I are supposedly *cool*."

She continues to stare at me. I'm not sure if she's attempting to come up with a really good lie to cover her ass, or if she's simply speechless that I called her on her shit. It's hard to tell. I just don't know her well enough yet to say.

"Are you going to say something to him?" she asks nervously.

"Are you?"

"I wasn't planning on it. Especially now. I didn't respond to the email, so I don't see what the point would be in upsetting Roman with it."

"If you don't think it's a good idea to tell the man you sleep with on a regular basis that the dickwad ultimately responsible for an assault and robbery on you in your home has recently contacted you, then you are even stupider than I ever imagined."

"Let's not get into name calling, okay? I know he's your friend, and you care about him, and you're obviously loyal to him, but I love him too. We both just have different ways of protecting him. I'm asking you to try and understand that."

"I don't understand that sort of logic. I'll never understand that. The only explanations that make sense to me are that you either have unresolved feelings for your ex or that you don't trust your man. Either scenario is not good for Roman."

"Wait I–"

"And what if Ethan still does drugs? Chances are that he does. What if he actually does something to hurt you or get you hurt, and I could have done something to prevent it? Roman will have my ass. And I'm talking about both my job and my friendship with him are on the line. Two things worth more to me than I'm willing to risk."

"So what are you saying?"

I see the panic setting in her eyes.

"I was waiting to see if you were going to email the

asshole back. If you were stupid enough to do it, I was going to tell Roman immediately. But since you haven't, and he sent that email a while ago, I'm going to give you the chance to tell him yourself. And when he asks me about it, like I know he will, I'll lie and tell him that I must have missed it. I'll cover for you, just as long as you cover for me."

"I didn't want him doing anything crazy, Jade. I didn't want him to get hurt or arrested." She tries to plead her case. "I don't want to tell him. Not right now."

Probably not ever if she had her way.

"Then we have a problem."

"But I haven't contacted Ethan, and I wasn't planning to," she argues.

"Maybe so, but now that we've had this conversation, it can't be unsaid."

"Oh my God, Jade, you're putting me in an impossible position."

"Seriously? I'm giving you the chance to save yourself and you still don't get it. If there's one thing I know about Roman, it's that a person does not gain his trust easily. And once it's broken, it's damn near impossible to get it back."

Even though I know he loves her, I'm pretty sure that the same rules will apply to her too. I know it's just an email, but to Roman it will mean much more than that. Roman expects total loyalty if he lets you in. He demands it, because he gives it.

"I need more time," she says.

"How much more? You want to stretch this out so long that neither one of us will ever tell him? Is that your plan?"

"You never wanted us together in the first place did you?"

"No I didn't, and I never made that a secret to Roman. It's nothing personal, but Rome is a very complicated man.

Distractions throw him off his game, and you have become his ultimate distraction. You think it's because he doesn't have any new clients that he's acting crazier than usual, but that's not it. It's you."

"He's changing, and you don't like it. It scares you."

What. The. Fuck.

"I'm sorry, but last time I checked you weren't a fucking psychologist. He's not changing, and I'm not scared. You should be though."

"I thought you and I were good."

"We were cool ... until this."

A text comes in from none other than the topic of our discussion.

Roman: Where's my old address book?

"Excuse me one second," I say. "Speak of the devil."

The look on Elizabeth's face is priceless. She's scared shitless.

Me: The dinosaur?

Roman: Yes, I need a number out of there. I didn't transfer all the contacts to my phone.

Me: Why?!

Roman: JADE!

ME: All right. It's at the club in the back of the second drawer of the file cabinet.

Roman: Where r u?

Me: A meeting

Roman: I'm not paying for you to spend the day getting your nails done. Get back to the club.

Me: You need to get laid.

Roman: You're fired.

Me: That's too bad because I have the key to the file cabinet.

Roman. Get your ass in here NOW!

• • •

I chuckle out loud and then turn my attention back to Elizabeth. By the look on her face, she seems to be upset by our text exchange. She's probably paranoid that I've already said something to him.

"I didn't say anything if that's what you're worried about."

"Did you tell him you were here?"

"No."

"What can I do to convince you to help me?"

"Nothing."

"Jade, please. I need more time to tell him."

"You've got forty-eight hours. You want Rome busy with work? You want things better between the two of you? Then tell him about this shit, and you'll see just how fucking busy he'll become. The old Roman would have taken care of that loser the minute you told him what happened, but you must have a magic box in between those legs of yours, because I've never seen him leave loose ends like this."

"I can see that you are very loyal to Roman, and while that is to be commended, the fact remains that I can handle my life in whatever frackin' way I choose to. If I choose not to tell him about a harmless email that would only upset him, then that's my business. Not yours."

"He didn't email you for nothing. You can't be that stupid. If he's reaching out, there must be a reason. That's the issue. It's not going to stop with this one email."

"I don't know if it will stop or not, but I'd like to be allowed the opportunity to see if it does before I'm forced to involve other people. So in other words, I want you to mind your own damn business."

Finally! The girl is starting to grow a pair. Her eyes tell me that adrenaline is coursing through her body, and she's had it with this visit. She's livid. She walks to her front door and opens it for me. My cue to leave. I look at her for a moment, stand up, and walk towards the door.

"Nice to see you have a little bit of a backbone, Elizabeth, I wasn't sure if your sweet, suburban ass had it in you. But two days is still all you've got. If he doesn't threaten to fire me about this in the next two days, I'll know that you haven't said anything."

I think I got my point across. If she had slammed the door any harder behind me, she would have taken off one of my fingers.

Some nerve.

17

Roman

"**D**id you get it?" I ask Jade.

"You know theft was never part of my job description when you hired me," she says as she sips on a bottle of some weird diet green tea.

"Your job description is to do whatever the fuck I tell you to do. I'm sure that's written down somewhere on your paycheck."

"And I'm SO sure that I could sue your ass for the way that you talk to me."

"You sure keep finding creative ways to get out of keeping your job. I think you're itching for me to fire you."

"It'll never happen. I know where the bodies are buried."

"You keep thinking that. So did you get it or not?"

"I got it, I got it. Here."

Jade hands me a stamped letter-sized envelope with my name on it. It's the letter from my mother. I had a hunch I knew where Joseph was keeping it, and I asked her to go over there under the guise of picking up some old vendor paperwork for The Lotus. Many of the old files are still in

Joseph's home office, and I knew that he wouldn't be there on Tuesday. He always heads over to the boathouses on Tuesdays.

"Did you have any problems?"

"Of course not. Juliette let me in and gave me free reign. I made sure to take some Lotus files too, so it would look legit."

Jade hands me several old Lotus files. I toss them on the floor and continue looking at the letter. It's been opened and then resealed with scotch tape. Clearly Joseph read it, didn't like what it said, and kept it from me. I'm not totally sure why he didn't rip it up though, but I'll be the first to admit that the old man is like an enigma to me. I'll never figure him out.

"What's up with Elizabeth?" Jade asks totally out of the blue.

I raise my eyes to meet hers. Why is she suddenly so interested in my relationship with Elizabeth?

"What do you mean what's up with her?"

"Just haven't seen her in a while, so I was asking. Is that a federal crime?"

I cock my head to the side and squint my eyes. I've already told her that we were taking a little time off.

"She's fine," I say suspiciously.

"All right already. I'm leaving. You can never say that I don't ask you shit about your life, because I just did, and you acted like I was about to rob you."

She's up to something.

"Thanks for the letter, lazy lima bean."

She grunts some sort of good-bye as she heads out.

After she leaves, I pour myself a shot of Patron and then chase it with a lowball of Jack. I need to take the edge off if I'm going to read this letter. I have no idea what it's going to say, but my mother never had a great way with words. I'm sure it's not going to be filled with heart-felt sentiments. She's incapable of that. Whatever it says though, I'll deal with it. I'm a big boy.

♥ ♥ ♥

Dear Roman,

If you're reading this letter it means that, that son of a bitch Joe is getting soft, or I'm dead. I'm writing this letter as a part of my amends to you. My sponsor suggested that I write it. She's a bitch on wheels, but she's successfully sponsored like fifteen people who are still clean, so I'm sticking with her.

I'm sure you're wondering why I didn't call or visit with an apology for fucking up your life, but the truth is that I'm not ready to face you. Not when I'm still working stuff out. Not when I know that Joe gave you everything that I couldn't. It would just make me feel entirely too shitty if I faced you now. And when I feel shitty, I get high. It's one of my patterns.

So I'm just going to tell you all the things that I'm sorry for here in this letter. In fact, there's something that I've wanted to tell you for a long time now. Actually there are a few things. The first thing is that while it isn't an excuse, there is an explanation for my behavior. I have a dual diagnosis of bipolar disorder and narcotic addiction. That's what my doctor said.

In other words, I am a very sick woman, and I always have been. No one was able to help me up until now. For a long time no one knew that I had this thing wrong with me. This defect. I'm sure you already know all of this by now, but I just wanted to make sure you understood it. I didn't choose to be such a mess. I was genetically cursed with it. You may want look it up one day in case you have kids or something.

Second thing is if you are angry with me. Stop it. Being angry with me will only make your life a living hell. I know because I was angry with my own mother for so long. I still am. But I'm working everyday to try and stop being so mad, so that I can be better and maybe one day be better to you.

The last thing is the hardest thing I've ever had to say. To admit. I haven't been truthful with you and this might make the second thing I told you to do (stop being angry) a lot harder, but here it goes. Joe is not your biological father. Before you ask, I do know who it is, but he's dead, so it doesn't make much sense to look for him or his family. I wouldn't even begin to know where to tell you to start anyway. He wasn't really important to me. He was just a guy.

Joe was everything to me back then. I felt like I was drowning. I was up, then I was down. Because of my mood swings, I couldn't keep a job and I didn't understand why. I couldn't keep a man interested in me for long unless I gave them sex. The only guy in the neighborhood who treated me like a person with feelings was Joe. He was nice. He was my friend.

When I found out I was pregnant, I panicked. I didn't know how the hell I was going to support a child. I didn't even have the money to get an abortion. Your real father acted like he didn't have it or couldn't get it. So I admit that I thought Joe was my ticket.

I made sure to sleep with him once, and then I made him think that he was the father. I had fooled myself into believing that once I did, he would all of a sudden want to be with me. Want to marry me. And raise you together. But that wasn't reality. And when reality bit me in the ass, I wasn't prepared, and I tumbled really low for a really long time. You saw a lot of my low and I'm sorry for that too.

I never said anything to him, because he took care of you. He sent money and he'd send you a birthday gift every year. That's more than my father ever did for me. More than your real father was ever going to do.

So there you go. All my sins. All my regrets. I hope you can find some peace in what I've written. It felt kind of good to write it. Now I just have to get the guts to send it. Which if you're reading this right now, means I must have grown a pair and did the right thing.

I live in Nevada now with a real nice man who treats me well. He's a postal worker and is set to retire in a few years. If I can stay clean, we're going to get married and I'll invite you to the wedding. I may have never said it much, but I do love you, Roman. You're my son and nothing will ever change that.

Be Happy,
Your Mother

♥ ♥ ♥

I'm not a feely, touchy type of man. I don't think it's part of my genetic make up; I'd be lying if I didn't admit that my mother's letter has rocked me to the core.

Even if she's off the pills and the booze, it is painfully obvious that she is still obsessed with only how she feels every fucking minute of the day. As if her feelings are the only ones that matter.

While the tone of the letter is somewhat apologetic, it's more narcissistic and self-serving than anything. Especially that bomb she dropped at the end. The old man isn't my father? And what the fuck does she think I'm supposed to do with that revelation at this point in my life. He's been my father for most of my life. The only one I've known. Like it or not, he's been there. She hasn't.

Have I judged him too harshly? Is it possible that the old man has known my entire life that he isn't my real father and raised me anyway? What about that whole confession speech he made about not wanting me but choosing to take care of his responsibilities. Has my mother actually pulled one over on him all of this time? It's hard to believe. One thing Joseph isn't is stupid. If my mother was just a one-night stand for him, or even a casual fling, I can't imagine that he wouldn't have made sure that I was his kid.

Damn, she's a bitch.

I haven't seen or heard from my mother in years and she still is incapable of giving me what I need. The only thing I've ever really wanted from her.

Closure.

Elizabeth

There's nothing sexy about Spanx. I mean let's be honest. They do everything they can to resist being pulled on the human body. It's almost as if they are fighting back the soft and squishy curves of a woman. And let's be real. No man has ever gotten a hard-on looking at a woman's stomach, thighs, and butt encased in a pair of flesh colored, high waisted, spandex shorts. Looking very much like a raw sausage link. Definitely not sexy.

And then there's the fact that most women need to create an entire ritual to get the things on and off. I include myself among that lot. In fact, I've created a simple protocol for putting on these magical pieces of stretchy fabric, which I'm fine-tuning tonight. I'm attempting to get these suckers on by slathering my favorite Jasmine scented body butter all over my thighs to provide a bit more slip, and then wiggling them on while dancing to some sicken-ingly empowering Meghan Trainor song. Another song about how big and beautiful she is. Seems like an ironic song selection, since I'm trying to make myself appear ten pounds lighter.

The goal is that after I slide into the Spanx (and I think my system is working), that I'm going to hopefully glide right into my new, one-size-too-small gold dress; which I purchased for an autism fundraising gala that I'm attending tonight. Juliette is on the planning committee for the event and invited practically the entire city of Philadelphia. Including Roman.

Although we've exchanged several polite chat messages and had three brief phone calls, I haven't actually seen Roman in almost two weeks. I feel like my insides are drying up and not just from the obvious lack of sex, but from way more than that.

I miss his touch. The way his eyes rake across my body whenever he sees me. I miss our late night phone calls. The fun, flirty ones. Not the few we've had lately where all he asks me is if I'm okay, and if I need anything. I know I'm the one who actually requested that we take a little time apart, but I'm seriously starting to regret it.

I'm nervous because both Roman and Jade are going to be at the gala tonight, and I'm way past Jade's forty-eight-hour deadline for telling Roman about the email. He hasn't said anything to me about it yet, so I know that she hasn't spilled the beans yet. But I know she's not going to hold out for long.

While I seriously considered faking the flu to get out of going tonight, Juliette would have been crushed. She worked really hard on this event and is very excited for everyone she loves to experience it with her. I can't let my drama get in the way of my aunt's big night.

I hear a light knock at my front door, and I know already that it's Sloan. Juliette was kind enough to extend the invitation to her as well, so we've decided to meet up and ride together. We'll take an Uber car tonight, so that we both can drink. It's open bar and neither of us wanted to pass up free top shelf liquor.

"You're early, and you're not dressed." I notice as I open the door for Sloan.

"Obviously because I'm getting dressed here, silly. I wasn't going to ride over here in my brand new Givenchy gown. Plus I still need to finish my make up for Christ's sake."

"You bought a Givenchy dress for tonight? Uh, we aren't getting ready for the senior prom or my wedding," I comment snidely as she walks in rolling a small suitcase behind her. I bought my dress for one hundred and twenty-five bucks at TJ Maxx. I've never even heard of the designer.

"Bitchy much? What crawled up your ass?"

"I'm just a little nervous I guess."

"About what?"

"I've never been to a formal event like this."

"What are you talking about? All it is, is a party with better food and drinks."

"And Roman."

"Are you two *still* on a time out? What the hell is he still angry about? Because you didn't want the Viking guy to hear you in the throes of passion? Honestly, I don't see why you bother with the Dark Knight. Oh wait, scratch that, I know why you bother. He must be banging the hell out of you."

"You're so vulgar."

Sloan laughs out loud, "I know."

"We're not arguing. We're just on a time out. At least we won't have to deal with any awkward introductions tonight."

"What awkward introductions? What are you talking about?"

"A lot of Juliette's friends are going to be there tonight. People she serves on boards with. So I was a little concerned about how she would have to introduce us to them. As her niece and stepson? Or as her stepson and his girlfriend? I mean there are a variety of ways she could go about it, and none of them seemed like a good look for me."

"Yeah, especially when they see his hand on your ass all night," she smirks.

"You're not helping."

"It's a moot point anyway. You guys won't be up under each other tonight. I won't allow it. You're my date tonight. So don't get all stressed. When you stress, you start sweating, and then you'll frizz up that perfectly flat ironed hair of yours."

"Actually I probably already broke a sweat trying to get these damn Spanx on."

"I say let all of your jelly jiggle. That's what I do," Sloan chuckles. "I'm going totally commando under my gown. It's not healthy that you're squishing all of your internal organs together like that in that thing. I talk to a lot of doctors in my work, and they all agree that corsets, girdles, or any other sort of medieval waist training device are all completely unhealthy for the female body."

"You work with doctors that write prescriptions for Viagra everyday. None of them even work with women, Sloan."

"That's not the point. They're doctors! They studied the human body for like a million years," she argues.

"This is all easy for you to say. You are some sort of genetic freak. You don't jiggle, and you'll never have to worry about jiggling. Both of your parents look ten years younger than they really are, so chances are that you'll still end up looking like a supermodel when you're a hundred years old."

"Feed me Seymour," she eggs me on with a pretty lame *Little Shop Of Horrors* reference. "Tell me more about my superior genetic code."

"Oh forget it," I laugh. "Let's just finish getting ready."

"I can't wait to see how the Dark Knight acts tonight. Will he act civil and make idle chitchat with you, will he cry about how much he misses you and follow you around like a puppy all night, or will he throw you a cold glare and smack your ass when you walk by."

"Be quiet."

Honestly I'm not sure what to expect from Roman tonight myself, but my plan is that he takes a look at me in this dress and drags me home by my hair, because he can't wait to get his hands all over me. That would be the ideal scenario.

"There's no way that wildebeest will be able to keep his distance from you tonight. I can't even believe I agreed to go with you to this thing. I'm going to be a third wheel once again," she gripes.

"Third wheel." I grin. "Who said you're a third wheel? Juliette told me that both Kings were invited too. I'm sure they'll be there with Roman."

"I can get my own dates thank you very much. I just didn't think it was appropriate for me to ask anyone, because your aunt invited me. Not me and a plus one. From what I've heard, this event has been sold out for at least a month."

"Oh calm down. It's just one of the King brothers. It's not like it's a real date."

"Ugh," she complains. "Don't get me wrong, those Kings are totally hot, and I don't mind flirting with them on occasion, but you know very well they're not my type.

Especially that loud one who thinks he's hot shit. There's not enough time in the world to teach that thug enough social graces to make the evening bearable."

"Well maybe it's a good thing that one of them come. I don't know what tonight's going to be like, and I don't want you sitting alone while Juliette drags me around working the room or something."

"Really?! I'm the bitch who taught *you* how to work a room thank you very much. I will never be sitting alone in a room full of men. Especially men with money. You know I speak their language, and of course it doesn't hurt that they all find me extra interesting, because I'm so *exotic* looking," she grins.

"Whatever, crazy. You're just going to have to make the best of it if one of the Kings shows up. They're Roman's best friends and you're mine. You're going to have to get used to them sooner or later."

"Do I really?"

"Stop being a snob."

She slams her foundation brush down on the counter.

"Oh, guess what I forgot to tell you!"

"What?"

"Another one bites the dust. The guy I met at the bar when we went out for my promotion, just texted me to say that he was in a committed relationship."

"Wow."

"Like he didn't know that shit when he was salivating over my boobs all night. Something really weird is in the air, Bitsy. If I can't make something happen tonight, in this dress, with no panties on? Then I fucking quit."

The gala is way more amazing than I thought it would

be. In fact it's almost magical. No wonder wealthy people are so happy, if they party like this all of the time.

Juliette's planning committee thought of every detail, and I can definitely see my aunt's touches reflected in the beauty of the room. The decorations throughout the event space are elaborate but modern. Long yards of soft, white fabric are draped strategically across the high ceilings. The lighting from the art deco chandeliers bathes the room in a soft and romantic luminescent glow. She once told me that everyone looks five years younger in twilight. So this is definitely her handiwork.

There are also pockets in the room where she has strategically positioned spotlights for press photo opportunities. There's lots of media here, and I notice that my aunt takes a great interest in bringing the right people together in those areas.

So far I've watched from a distance as she's connected two different local news anchors with several city politicians, she has the founder of the sponsoring autism organization posing and shaking hands with the mayor, as well as a professional football player holding up a picture of a child to the cameras. I think I read somewhere that the guy is a popular offensive lineman for the Eagles, and his child is on the autism spectrum.

Watching my aunt in her element has been awe inspiring, and I realize without a doubt that while she's a socialite force to be reckoned with, she would have made an even more amazing lawyer. She definitely commands a room with her presence. Not to mention that Uncle Joseph does as well in his tailored suit. When he's by her side they are by far the most formidable couple in the room. A power couple. Neither of them overshadowing the other, but both truly working the room in tandem.

There are three balcony-like levels to the totally open

event space which allows you to peek down to the first level where the stage is set to showcase two very different local bands. And don't get me started on the food. The food is amazeballs! There are buffet stations on each floor. Each one featuring a different cuisine with servers ready to help fill your plate. One station is serving homemade mini pizzas. Another offers the biggest array of fresh sushi I've ever seen. Then there's a different station offering you your choice of a Philadelphia favorite, hot crab fries or sweet potato fries served in paper cones.

I'm breaking all kinds of carb rules tonight. Well I'm trying to, but these damn Spanx aren't cooperating. The more I eat, the more they continue to roll down over my pouch. I'm literally ten seconds away from shimmying out of these things in the bathroom and stuffing them in my purse.

My aunt has been so busy tonight, that she really hasn't had time to introduce me to anyone. I totally understand it. Hey, I'm just glad to be here. And then there's Roman. I thought he'd try to stick close to me because we haven't seen each other in so long, especially once he saw me in this dress, but I called this one completely wrong. He's still keeping his distance.

"You look beautiful, Elizabeth." Was his simple greeting to me after giving me a soft peck on the cheek.

"Thanks." Was all I could manage to squeak out in response. Stunned by his aloofness. Crushed that he hasn't seemed to have missed me the way I miss him. The way I crave him, cried over him. *Do either of us even remember what we're fighting about?*

Evidently Roman knows quite a few major players in the city, and he has been making polite conversation all night with many of them while avoiding any meaningful conversation with me. Several look like familiar, local politicians that I've seen on television. If I had to guess, a few of the other men he's talking to give me the impression that they're lawyers.

And then there's the other guest he's been chatting with. A striking blonde with long legs, wearing a curve hugging, strapless black dress with a dramatic, long slit up the side. Sort of Angelina Jolie styled. She exudes a brand of confidence, maturity and worldliness that I simply don't have. Not that I'm comparing. All right, maybe I am a little.

She also seems to be hanging onto every word that Roman is saying to a short stocky man whom I've never seen before. Forcing herself to laugh at the funny parts. Looking pensive when he makes a serious comment. Can't he see that this woman is practically panting over him? Oh God, I need to stop watching, because it's starting to annoy the hell out of me. I have the sudden urge to kick her in the shins.

And his too.

"Are you going to stare at him the entire night?" Sloan asks as she walks up on me from behind, startling me for a moment. We lost each other earlier in the evening when she became engrossed in a conversation with some doctor she knows and I went to the restroom.

"I'm not staring."

"You totally are. Stop giving your power away to the asshole."

"He's not an asshole."

Yes he is.

"Did you have the crab fries?" she asks as she absently munches on a few.

"I already had like two mini pizzas and a plate of sushi. I can't eat another bite because of my evil underwear. They're so tight they're making me nauseous."

"That sucks for you. I told you that you should just let it all jiggle, but if you're not going to eat any of the *crack* fries, then why don't you have a drink. They're really good, and you know I'm not big on fruity drinks, but this thing I'm drinking with the fresh strawberry puree is orgasmic. You have to try one. It will change your perspective. You won't even care anymore about what the Dark Knight is up to after two of these."

"Why'd you say *up to*? He's not *up to* anything. He's just talking," I say probably more to convince myself than her. They're definitely doing more than just talking. I think I'm watching Roman do his version of *flirting*.

Sloan snickers. "Talking to a woman that looks like she wants to eat him alive."

"Shut. Up."

"Aww, you definitely need a drink, Bitsy Boo. Come on let's head over to one of the bars and find a cute bartender for you to flirt with. You know you want to."

"Speaking of flirting. Have you bothered speaking to Cutter even once tonight? You didn't mind flirting with him when you first met, and now you're totally ignoring him?"

Turns out that both of the Kings brothers didn't make it, only one did—Cutter a.k.a. The Loud One. No sign of Jade either. I don't know whether I should be relieved or worried that she bailed on coming tonight.

"Calm your panties. I spoke to him briefly."

There's clearly a story behind that, but I'm not inter-ested enough to ask her further about it; I'm too preoccu-pied with blondie. I take another long glance over at Roman who catches my stare with his own. His onyx eyes aren't dancing tonight like they usually do when he sees me, but instead are hard and intense.

We've been polite and cordial for two weeks with each

other, and it's been awkward and painful. I just want him to yell at me, curse me out, or something. Anything that lets me know how much this space we're taking affects him, and how much he misses me, like I so desperately miss him.

The blonde by his side gives me a once over after she notices our eyes locked. Then she touches Roman's shoulder and whispers something in his ear, which breaks our connection. He nods his head at me (whatever that means), slips his hand behind her waist, and they walk away.

I'm two seconds from either balling my eyes out or kneeing Roman in the balls when my ride or die chick steps in.

"Like I said, let's get you a little liquid courage to give you a minute to think this through, and after a drink or two if you want to kick blondie's ass then I'm down. You know I've always got your back."

I don't even respond to that, but instead just start walking. I should have opened my mouth and said more to him. Just end this. Could've, would've should've.

On our way to the bar we run into Juliette.

"Hi, sweetie." My aunt pauses once she notices my watery eyes. "You okay?"

"I'm having a great time," I say with strained enthusiasm. "Everything is beautiful tonight. You really outdid yourself."

"Thanks, sweetie. Listen I ran into someone you know downstairs."

"Someone I know? Who?"

"Mr. Lambert."

My Mr. Lambert from the investment group?

"Really?"

"It's truly a small world, but his wife and I attend the

same spin class over on 14th Street. It didn't take long for us to figure out how we knew each other, and now that they know that you're my niece, Mr. Lambert seems to be interested in taking a second look at School Bucks."

"I don't know, Auntie. They already turned me down flat, and I don't really have any great sales numbers to show him right now."

"I know they turned you down, sweetie, but some time has passed, and I'm sure that he could take a second look at your proposal. People don't always score a win the first time around."

"You didn't ask him to take a second look, did you?"

"Absolutely not, but understand something, Elizabeth. Getting ahead in business is not always about aptitude or fairness, it's mostly about connections. Who you know. I've watched Joseph build his business over the years strictly through meeting the right people. I've planned several big events like these, because I've solidified deep relationships in the community with people who continually support whatever I do. That's what you're going to have to do too with School Bucks.

"All the great press in the world isn't going to do what having one good person with some connections in your corner will do for you. Joseph and I are those people for you until you find your own, or we can be if you let us. I can't guarantee that I can make people fall in love with your app, but I can definitely send people your way to give *you* the opportunity to make them fall in love."

"Well said!" Sloan says while saluting us with her martini glass.

My Spanx feel tighter than they've been all night. I'm suffocating literally and figuratively. I'm not in the right frame of mind to do this, but this is an opportunity I can't pass up. I need to walk the walk, if I'm going to talk the talk about being an independent business owner. This is a second chance to make this happen.

"All right, where is he?" I ask while sucking in my stomach.

"First floor. He's sitting at a table on the right hand side of the room near the stage with his wife. Her name is Mary Lambert."

"Thank you so much."

"Now go and have a good time, and that's an order," she smiles. "Oh by the way, where's Roman? I haven't been able to catch up with him all night."

I hear Sloan mutter behind my back.

"Ah-ha and that is the million dollar question of the night, now isn't it."

19

Elizabeth

I feel as if I'm having an out of body experience. I'm on the third floor of the gala, I've already freed myself from my Spanx (hallelujah!), and I'm watching a bartender named Patrick hand me drink after drink with a grin plastered across his face. I'm also watching myself become drunker and drunker. A loopy drunk. Laughing at every corny joke he makes. Paying very close attention to how he strokes his mustache then wipes the bar top with a white rag in a continuous circular motion. Over and over.

A mirror covers the wall behind the bar from corner to corner. So I can easily see that I look drunk. Glazed over eyes. Flushed cheeks. Frizzy hair. I know that I need to quickly get my ass home and sleep it off, before I make a complete fool of myself, but it's like I can't stop myself. I'm a one woman wrecking ball. A total disaster.

"I think I may have to cut you off young lady," Patrick says in what seems to be very slow motion. Of course I know it's just my liquored up brain translating his slightly midwestern accent into gibberish.

"I know. I know. I should stop shouldn't I?"

"You should have stopped a long time ago, but my guess is that you're trying to numb the pain."

"You're so smart, Patttrickk," I slur. "Did I tell you that you have the same name as my dad?"

You don't have to be smarter than a fifth grader to see that I'm drinking to stop myself from thinking about the flirt, also known as *the cheater,* who I've given my body to night after night since the day we practically met.

My so-called boyfriend.

My cousin.

The asshole extraordinaire.

After I pulled my big panties up and traveled down to the first level to say hello to Mr. Lambert and his wife (a successful endeavor by the way), I spotted Roman again.

New location.

New conversation.

Same blonde.

"You need to say something to him," Sloan chimes in. She's pretty drunk herself and when Sloan gets hammered, she gets confrontational.

"Why!" I protest. "Why should I say anything to Roman El Stupido Masterson?"

She looks over my shoulder.

"Because I'm pretty sure that he's headed right this way."

I whip my head quickly around, but notice that his six foot lying ass hasn't spotted me yet. He's scanning the room and there's the same short guy talking his ear off while he does it. Distracting him.

Good.

I'm *so* out of here.

"I need to dip out of here, Patrick. Is there a side exit to this place?"

"Uh-uh-uh, Elizabeth. We're not dipping out

anywhere," Sloan says. "I'm going to continue sitting here drinking my drink, and you're going to stay seated right here next to me. Plus this isn't some rinky-dink nightclub. Any side door to this place is probably sealed or a fire door. The alarms will go off. Definitely not the way to be discreet. We're in semi-formal wear for God's sake."

"Forget about your Givenchy, I just want to get out of here," I say.

"Stop running. Just confront the bastard. There's no way out and you know it. Space or no fucking space, he's your boyfriend. You should talk to him, especially because the asshole is literally going to spot us in about the next ten seconds. Ten, nine, eight–"

I move my head a little to the left, behind a very wide guy seated on the other side of me with slicked back hair and a glass of beer in his hands. He doesn't notice that I'm using him as a human shield while he continues to laugh about something with two of his equally large friends.

"You're a horrible wingman. I don't know why I continue to go out with you," I whine as I try ducking my head even lower. "You're not my friend. You're not even trying to help me."

"Of course I'm your friend drunkard, and by the way if I was your wingman, I'd be helping you pick up *other* men. Not hiding you from the one you have. Hell, there's no running from the Dark Knight anyway and you know it. He won't sleep until he finds you. He won't let anyone sleep. So suck it up, and deal with him."

I know that what Sloan is saying is one hundred percent correct. I'm not a kid anymore. I just don't know if I'm sober enough for an intelligent conversation with Roman right now. I think I'm just clearheaded enough to curse him out, and then stumble to the street and hail a cab. I'll curse him out good too. I'll use the F word like he's always challenging me to use. Yeah, he'll know I'm done with his cheating butt for sure if I use the F word.

"He sees us," Sloan warns. "Here he comes."

All the bravery I felt a second ago, flies out the window the minute I lay eyes on Roman. I jump up from my stool and try to slink my way in the opposite direction, but moving like a ninja in a place that's packed, when you're three or four drinks deep (I lost count), and in platform heels is not an easy feat. Pros could pull it off, but not an amateur drunk like me.

So I fall.

Flat on my butt.

In my tight gold dress.

A large, sweaty hand helps me up on my feet by pulling me up by my elbow. I'm pretty sure it's the unusually wide guy who I was hiding behind. I can't help but notice how his arms are massively muscular. He probably uses steroids like that Mendez guy I think to myself.

"You okay?" the stranger asks with genuine concern etched across his brow.

I pull down my dress. "Yes, thank you."

I'm pretty sure I just slurred that reply.

"No problem. Are you–"

"Take your hands off the lady please," a gruff voice commands.

I'd know that lying, cheating voice anywhere, even though I've barely heard it the entire night.

"Excuse me?" the stranger says as his back grows rigid and his chest puffs out.

"I said please, motherfucker. Don't make me regret being polite."

Suddenly the guy's two big friends dressed in abnormally tight suits turn around and stand in solidarity with the stranger.

"You need help putting out some trash, bro?" One of them asks in reference to Roman.

"Oh, shit." I hear Sloan mutter behind me.

"That's right!" I exclaim feeling no pain.

Strangely enough I still feel as if I'm out of my dang body. It's like somebody else is doing all the talking while I cheer this mysterious, brazen Elizabeth on.

"Take out the trash." I agree because Roman made me feel like trash tonight. Okay, that may be an exaggeration, but all evening he's been acting like we're casual acquaintances, not as if we are in a loving relationship. I'm so mad at him right now, I could spit.

Then he has the nerve to give me one of his infamous death ray glares for my trash comment, but then turns his attention right back to the three beefy guys who look like they are ready to pound him into dust.

Good! Maybe an old fashioned ass kicking is what he needs right now to recognize everything he is taking for granted. Like how I risked my circulatory health just to look good in this dress for him tonight.

"The lady belongs to me," he says in a voice that I swear is an octave lower than I've ever heard in my life. "So I'm going to say it one more fucking time. Take your hands off of her and step away."

"I don't belong to anybody," I blurt out.

There I go again.

Drunk Elizabeth just keeps talking and talking.

"And he's a liar!" I point to Roman's face.

I know I'm playing with fire now, but I just can't help myself. I'm hurt, and angry, and I know that I'm probably starting some shit. But I just can't seem to bring myself to care right now. I want to piss Roman off, and I think it's working.

"The lady says she doesn't belong to you. So why don't you just go on about your business, Ace."

Then Roman's scar starts twitching.

He cocks back his arm and with the precision of a sharp shooter punches beefy guy number one, my protector, dead in the jaw. And the hit miraculously drops him to the floor like a heavy sack of flour. Next he knees his friend, beefy guy number two, in the lower abdomen, sending him straight to the floor as well with a hard thump. When he steps to make a move towards the final guy, number three quickly throws his hands up in surrender and backs away.

"Sorry, man." He stares down between his two friends on the ground and then proceeds to leave. "I didn't come here for a fucking bar fight."

Something about seeing these two mammoth but well dressed men sprawled across the floor of my aunt's event wakes something up inside of me. My conscience. This is all my fault. If I've ruined my aunt's event, I'll never forgive myself.

Roman cracks his neck to the side once while keeping his eyes dead on the two guys on the floor, while I take a few steps towards him. I've got to calm him down. His jugular vein is engorged, pulsating, and he looks like he's ready to kill someone.

"Don't fucking move."

The words are meant for me, and I stop dead in my tracks.

"Do we understand each other yet?" he says while standing above the two men with a menacing look across his face.

"Fuck, dude. Take her!"

I know I'm still drunk, because I'm actually offended these guys are so willing to pass me off to the dressed up, tatted up, lunatic hovering above them. Well then again, maybe I do understand.

"Pussies." Roman practically spits while throwing a couple of twenty dollar bills on the floor by their heads.

"Uh ... security is coming," Sloan interrupts.

"Can you handle this?" Roman says to the same stocky man I've seen him with all night.

"I got it," he says.

It's interesting that this well dressed, dad-looking guy doesn't even seem fazed by Roman's behavior. He's probably his parole officer I laugh to myself.

Roman nods a good-bye to the man, then stalks over to me, grips my wrist, and pulls me away to a darkened nook of the room on the opposite end of the bar. I think Sloan mouths the words to me "kick him in the nuts" while I stumble clumsily forward. Luckily I manage to walk behind him without falling (which is a miracle), considering I'm in a too tight dress, too high heels, and have had too many strawberry whatever those were.

We're both staring each other silently down. I'm pretty sure he's assessing my intoxication level, and I'm glaring at what almost looks like smeared lipstick on the corner of his mouth.

Did she kiss him?

Did he let her?

I'm going to smack him and run.

After a few moments between us, he's still deadly silent, fuming mad, and I couldn't give one single shit.

He walks me backwards against a wall and slams his palm above my head as if that's supposed to intimidate me. But I'm not scared. I'm loaded with strawberry liquid courage.

"What the fuck, Elizabeth."

I cross my arms in front of me and close my eyes for a

moment to help keep the room from spinning so much.

"What?"

"Don't play fucking games with me."

"What?" I ask again after reopening my eyes.

"Why are you pissy drunk tonight of all nights? Why didn't you respond to my text? Why were you encouraging those assholes back there? And how do you know that bartender?"

How does he know I was talking to Patrick, and what text is he talking about? My phone is on vibrate and in my purse. I must have missed any text he may have sent, but that's totally besides the point, so I lie.

"I didn't feel like returning your text."

Roman slams his hand against the wall above my head again in aggravation. He's got the nerve to be really angry. The nerve!

Then he briskly rubs over the top of his closely shorn head with his palm in utter aggravation. As if he has no clue what part he's played in what's happened tonight. He can't honestly be that *stupid*. Oops, there goes that word again I chuckle under my breath.

"What the fuck is so funny, Elizabeth!"

"You're funny."

"There is nothing funny whatsoever about what happened tonight."

"You're right. This night hasn't been fun at all."

I'm sure he's going to lie. He's going to turn it around on me and try to make me out like I'm some crazy girlfriend. Which is how I kind of feel right about now. Like some trashy, jealous, maniac that you see on reality television.

"I saw you," I say in an accusatory way.

"Saw me what?"

"Who were you talking to all night?"

"Plenty of people. Half of the people here are clients I've done work for at some point or another, so what are you talking about? I don't speak crazy."

"You're hilarious," I say sarcastically. "The blonde, Roman. The blonde."

All of a sudden his facial expression changes and a wide grin spreads across his face as if he's had some sort of delightful epiphany.

"You're jealous?"

He brings one of his hands down off of the wall and begins to lightly caress my face. My reflexes are a little slow, but I do my best to smack it away.

"All of this because of her?" he continues grinning.

"You didn't talk to me all night, but you had plenty of things to say to *her*. I saw her talking about me too. Admit it!"

He doesn't flinch at my words. In fact, all he does is continue to allow his hand to travel down the length of my body until it lands on my butt. He starts rubbing his strong hand in a circular motion and then intermittently kneads each cheek. It's just a light massage, nothing too erotic, but it feels so good that my eyes almost close in rapture.

I missed his touch desperately. I don't ever want to be without it again.

"You're not making any sense, baby. You're drunk. Let me take you home, take care of you properly, and when you sober up I'll tell you all about Kat."

He had me up until he said the name.

Kat.

There's something about him saying her name out loud that sickens me. It's a nickname. Like he knows her well. Like there's a story behind the name.

Women drool and fawn over Roman all the time. At the club. When we go out to eat. When we take Mr. Tibbs for a walk. When we go to the grocery store. That's nothing new to me. I don't like it, but I'm used to it, and I had to get used to it if I was going to be with him.

But this woman is different. She wasn't fawning over Roman or begging for his attention. She didn't need to. He was totally focused on her tonight, and she was quite comfortable being on the receiving end. As if she was quite used to his attentions.

"I don't want you to take me home."

"It wasn't really a request. I'm taking you home."

"Last time I checked, this was a free country, and I have choices."

"You sound like a twelve-year-old right now."

"You like to rub the asses of twelve year olds?" I say sarcastically.

He instantly drops his hands.

"Are you fucking serious right now? All this because I talked to one woman who I've known half my life, when you practically got me jumped tonight by three juice heads?"

"No, this is all because I wouldn't let you *fuck* me in my office with Blake in the other room. Isn't that how we really got here?"

"That prick again."

"This isn't about Blake. This is about how you can't stomach hearing the word no. That and the fact that you don't trust anyone. Not even me."

"That's funny. *You* actually talking about trust issues?"

"I've turned my entire life upside down to be with you, Roman. My parents think I'm some sort of rebellious black sheep. They're waiting for me to come to my senses, meet a nice accountant, move back home and marry him. I've been putting *all* of my trust in you, but now I'm not so sure I made the right decision when you act like this."

Roman grabs my face forcibly with his right hand, tilts it up, and moves his face as close as he can to mine without our faces touching. I can smell and feel his breath. An intoxicating whiff of chocolate and cognac floats over me.

"We had an argument. You said some things I didn't like. I was being a dick about it. I'm sorry. I shouldn't have let it go this long, baby."

I almost crumble when he uses that term of endearment, but I know that it's just the liquor breaking down my defenses.

Remember Kat, Elizabeth.

"You were talking to that woman on every floor of the gala," I shake my head, "I don't know."

Roman holds my face tightly and pulls it in closely to his. "Were you spying on me all night, Duchess? Because I have to tell you, the fact that you were is turning me the fuck on."

He bends down and presses his granite hard pelvis up and against mine. Even though my tight dress won't allow him to position himself completely in between my legs, I can feel him. Every solid inch. He's not lying. He is turned on, and God help me so am I, but I refuse to let my hormones distract me.

That's the liquor messing with you, Elizabeth. Stay focused.

"I saw everything," I say.

"What do you think you saw, baby?"

He starts inching up my dress by the hem. I don't think anyone can see us in this dimly lit corner of the room, but I look around anyway. The last thing I need is to get caught fooling around with my *cousin* at my aunt's fundraising event. I can tell by the look on his face that he's surprised to find me commando.

"No panties a-fucking-gain?" He says in a thick and needy voice.

Ignore that, Elizabeth.

"You were smiling and laughing. You touched her. You had your hand on her back. Damn near her ass. You were looking at her the way you sometimes look at me. It was ... disgusting."

"The way I look at you is disgusting?" he chuckles as one of his hands begins caressing my butt. His fingers teasing the crack of it.

"You think this is funny?"

I'm seriously offended.

"I think it's *very* funny."

"Then you're an even bigger ass than I gave you credit for. Just be a man and tell me who she is."

"Be a man, huh."

"Yes, be a–"

He slides his middle finger inside of me while staring at me with great intensity. I'm drenched, so it's real easy for him to do, but I try my best not to clench down on it like my body normally automatically does. I don't want to give him the satisfaction ... or myself.

"You're always soaking wet for me, but tonight you're like a waterfall," he says in awe.

"Well I haven't had sex in a while, so just talking to the bartender probably made me wet."

He doesn't like what I said and as punishment abruptly inserts a second finger inside of me. I moan shamelessly. Even in anger, his touch feels entirely too good to stay silent.

"That mouth, Elizabeth," he growls as he moves his fingers in and out of me at a languid pace. "It's going to get you in all sorts of trouble."

"So, stop then," I say half-heartedly and still half drunk. "Let's go back to barely speaking. I liked things a lot better that way, and you were so good at it."

He removes his fingers making sure to skim my walls with the curve of them on his way out. Then drops to his knees and asks me a rhetorical question.

"Do you really want me to stop?"

Roman slides my dress back up, but farther this time. Now its hiked up to my waist and his mouth is so close to my exposed pussy, that I don't even care that I'm in a public place.

"I need the words, Duchess."

He spreads me open and licks me from back to front and then he waits.

"This isn't the place for this."

"I disagree. This is exactly the time and the place. In fact, if I had my way I'd toss your pretty ass, naked, across that bar top over there and have every one of these fine people watch me eat you for the next fucking hour."

Roman pulls my thighs wide apart, then pushes his face in between my legs, and devours me. Biting and sucking my clit, then licking me clean as if it's the most delicious thing he's had all day.

There's a live band playing on the first floor, and they're at a part of a familiar song where there's a long drum solo. The drummer is about to reach a part of the solo where he enters a zone. Repeating the same rifts over and over and over. It's intoxicating and primal.

So, between the seductive beat of the drummer, the liquor still traveling through my veins, and the sight of this beautiful man on his knees eating me something fierce ... an orgasm rips right through my core.

"Fuck."

I slam both of my hands against the wall in an effort to restrain myself from yelling the expletive and drawing the attention of anyone who may be within earshot.

I can feel his grin against my sex. He's quite proud of

himself, but his smugness wakes me up like a freezing cold glass of water. I've just had a momentary lapse in judgment.

"This doesn't change anything," I say adamantly.

Roman stands back up and sighs in aggravation.

"I'm over all the dumb shit we were arguing about. Can we just move on from this now?" he asks while pulling my dress back in place.

"My wounds are still fresh. I'm not over mine quite yet."

"What wounds? Kat is an old friend of the family. I haven't seen her in a while. I was just being cordial."

"For two frackin' hours!"

Roman pulls his head back and takes a long look at me.

"Elizabeth, have you been watching me the entire night? Did you even enjoy yourself at all? Did you do any networking?"

As if he gives a hot damn about me networking. It's not like he tried to introduce me to any of the people he was talking to tonight. If he cared so much, he would have made sure that I met some of those movers and shakers he was so busy chatting up tonight.

I don't want to talk about this anymore. He's turning this into some *Elizabeth is a crazy bitch* session, and I'm not doing that. I'm not being irrational. Something about this whole thing doesn't sit right with me.

"As if you care about my business."

"You know I do," he says very seriously.

"I don't know anything anymore." I push against his chest. "I have to pee. Let me out."

"Not until you answer me."

"I have to pee!" I punch him in the gut. He doesn't even flinch.

"Then pee right here in this hallway. I don't give a shit. You're not going anywhere."

Jackass.

"Yes, okay! I watched you. It was easy, because everywhere you were, so was she. I grabbed some sushi and saw you two. I went to the pizza station and saw you two again. I sat at the bar with my new friend Patrick the bartender and watched you yet *again* practically kill yourself fawning all over that whore."

"Not a whore," he callously chuckles. "But a *friend* whom I've known since I was a pimply faced kid."

"I don't care. I don't care if you've known her since you came out of your momma's womb. I don't trust you. Not one bit. Not after seeing what I saw. I'm not going to get played for a fool ever again. I'm not!"

"Playing you!" he exclaims. "Is my name fucking Ethan now? Where is this coming from? Drunk or not, this isn't you talking right now." Roman squints his eyes as if he's looking at a complete stranger.

"Oh my God! Are you implying yet again that Sloan put these doubts inside of my head? Was it Sloan who put a gun to your temple and forced you to talk to Kat instead of your *girlfriend* all night? I'm afraid this is all your doing. Leave Sloan out of it once and for all. She's my friend not a puppet master."

"You know what, Elizabeth, you sure as shit *always* have that chick's back. I wish you had mine like that. Trusted me like that. I wish you would've opened up your fucking mouth just once tonight to ask me about Kat, before you jumped to all these conclusions. Before you got pissy drunk and embarrassed yourself."

"I didn't embarrass myself," I say defensively.

"If you don't think Juliette knows how drunk you are,

you're sadly mistaken. She has eyes and ears all over this place."

"Well if you think she doesn't know that you just beat up some of her guests then YOU are sadly mistaken. I think that is a little worse than me having a few too many cocktails. Don't you?"

"In defense of my drunk cousin? I don't think so. Plus I pay people to shut eyes and close ears for me. The only thing Juliette will hear about is you tonight, sweetheart."

"I hate you sometimes."

"Take it out on me in bed tonight." He licks the corner of his mouth.

"You'll be lucky if I ever sleep with you again."

"Now you and I both know that's a lie. If you were that angry with me, Elizabeth, you should have pulled me aside tonight and used your big girl words."

"I didn't have a chance to ask you diddly squat about that woman. You've been too busy sniffing behind her ass all night for me to say anything!"

"When did I become the bad guy? Have you forgotten that you were the one who asked for some space? I left you alone tonight, because *you* were the one who claimed you needed the distance."

"And you certainly ran with it, didn't you!"

His eyes tighten.

Good, he's getting angry.

Welcome to the club, jerk.

"All right that's enough. Have I ever led you to believe that I want anyone other than you? I thought that I've been making myself pretty fucking crystal clear these last few months. There is only you, Elizabeth. There will *only* ever be you."

He's trying to make me cry. I know it. He's good at this. He knows how to deflect all the attention away from himself by saying all the right things. Isn't that what fixers do?

"I don't want to talk about this anymore. I'm drunk. I can't think straight," I say.

Actually, I think the alcohol is wearing off. Now I'm just sad and confused.

"Well tough titties, because we're not finished talking."

I clamp my lips shut like a pouting child.

"We've been together almost a year, Elizabeth. I know you. You're running. We had one disagreement, which wasn't even that serious, and you immediately go to the extreme and tell me we need time apart.

"Not once over these two weeks did you call me first. Text me first. Think to apologize to me or come to me. You were waiting for me to call you, text you, come after you. Like I always do. Like I'm doing right the fuck now.

"And not only that, but you watched me talk to just one woman tonight, and you're acting like you caught me mid stroke, fucking her. Your reaction isn't normal. It doesn't make sense. The only explanation for it is that you are waiting for me to fuck up. Wanting me to fuck up. Biding your time until the shit hits the fan. Looking for an excuse to run. You're pushing me away, and I want to know why. What are you so scared of? Because all I want to do is make you the happiest woman on the fucking earth."

"You're the one doing the pushing," I say in a knee jerk reaction. Tears pooling in my eyes.

But is he really? I actually consider his words for a moment. Is that what I'm doing? Am I subconsciously pushing him away by making poor decisions? Am I picking a fight with him because I'm almost drowning in guilt? I guess there are two words for that: self and sabotage. Problem is I don't know why I'm doing it, if that's in fact what I'm doing.

"This isn't the place for this conversation," he says, his forehead touching mine, "Let me take you home."

I take my thumb and rub briskly at the corner of his chin. The stain slightly rubs off, and it sure as hell isn't ketchup.

"What's this?" I say in an accusatory tone. Angry that I didn't see it before he put his mouth on me.

"Lipstick," he answers matter of factly as if it's nothing.

"So you admit that you two kissed?"

"I did not put my tongue inside of her mouth if that's what you're asking. She gave me a kiss good-bye. Like I said about a hundred times already, she's an old family friend. We greeted and said good-bye to each other as friends normally do."

"Have you ever slept with her?"

"Elizabeth."

"Well, have you?"

"When I was a kid, yes."

Oh. My. God.

I knew there was something more, but I wasn't really expecting him to say yes. I wasn't expecting him to ever flaunt an old lover right under my nose like he did tonight.

"Were you her first?"

"No and you're still drunk. I'm tired. Let's talk about this later."

And that response tells me everything I need to know. She means something to him, and he doesn't want to talk about it.

I wish that I still had that feeling of being completely out of my body, as I slump back against the wall.

But no.

I recognize exactly whose heart feels like it's breaking and it's mine.

20

Roman

I'm officially out of control. While I don't for one second regret knocking those steroid pumped jerks on their asses for not minding their business at the gala (especially the one with all the mouth), I admit that I could have handled things a lot differently.

I've worked long and hard to learn how to handle things differently. Calmer. Rationally. It's better for business. It's better for me. It's certainly better if I want to maintain a relationship with Elizabeth.

Joseph has been on my ass since I was a kid to master the art of how to punk the shit out of people with words, or money, and not always with violence. But it was a difficult lesson for a boy who spent much of his youth defending himself with his fists. Defending the few friends that I had. Defending my unpredictable and undependable mother. Defending my right to exist and matter in this world. The lesson was especially difficult to learn, because defending myself physically came pretty easily to me. I like easy. Although easy doesn't always mean better.

While I was able to slip out of the fundraiser with Elizabeth in tow, that didn't mean that I didn't leave a mess in my wake. I did. Even though it was a simple bar fight, and I thought my lawyer Ben had it handled, the men I roughed up were special guests of Juliette's. Financial guys or some such bullshit. And they were pissed once their initial embarrassment wore off. They didn't know at first that I was Juliette's stepson, so they went around asking some staff members for my name. Word was that they weren't interested in filing charges against me, but that they wanted blood.

Problem is I welcome blood.

I was hoping Juliette would give them my name, my address *and* my fucking social security number. I was seriously disappointed when she told them who I was and then politely talked them out of pursuing the matter.

That's how I know for sure that I'm spinning out of control, and I'm not entirely sure what can stop me, but I'm going to try like hell to stop. I need to if I want to ever deserve the right to keep Elizabeth by my side.

I met Katherine Lee Dixon (Kat for short) when I was thirteen years old, and she was seventeen. Our fathers were longtime friends and we were visiting her home for some sort of business meeting. Business back in those days usually involved drinks, and drinks meant we were staying a while.

The night we met, Kat asked me if I wanted to go watch music videos in her room for a while, and I thought I'd died and gone to heaven. I was young and horny, and I was hoping like all hell that "watch music videos" was girl code for "touch my boobs."

I was right.

"Have you ever had sex, Roman?" is what she asked me outright, as she pulled her oversized T-shirt over her head, revealing a pretty pink lace bra underneath. I remember my thirteen-year-old penis getting stiff as a board, which probably had a lot to do with my keen interest in women's lingerie. There was no way I was going to pass up the opportunity of a lifetime by telling her the truth that day, so I lied.

"Yep."

"So you know how to make a girl come then?"

"Don't you know how?" I asked like an idiot, basically exposing my lie.

She laughed a little and began stroking the side of my face.

"It's okay if you don't know what to do, Roman. That's what I'm here for. To teach you. If you want."

I didn't actually think whether I wanted to or not was up for decision or debate. Kat was ready to teach me something about sex whether I was ready or not, because at this point she had her pants off and jumped up on her bed in her bra and matching pink panties.

I wasn't sure if I was supposed to be taking off my own clothes or helping her take off her underwear. I'd watched plenty of porn by that age, but this was a real world situation, an actual opportunity, and like a punk kid, I froze under the pressure.

"Well?" she asked. *"Do you want to learn how to make a girl scream your name or not?"*

Well since she put it that way.

"Yep."

"Good let's get to it then. Take off your clothes and get on the bed."

I watched hungrily as Kat unlatched the hooks of her bra, slid down her lace-trimmed panties, and sat up against the headboard with her legs spread eagle. I almost came right in my pants at the sight.

I think that's the moment I truly fell in love with pussy.

A few moments later I learned how to eat it; and then it only took several more moments for me to learn how to push inside of it and seek release. As first times go, I have to admit that I had a great one.

Kat moved to Florida to live with her mother not too long after that, but we occasionally kept in touch over the years. I hadn't seen her in several years when we reconnected at the autism event, but I knew she would be there. We briefly talked before she flew in, and we made a plan to catch up as well as to talk business at the gala. She's a VP at a production company based out of Miami, which is admirable at her age, although I'm sure her daddy's money had a lot to do with it.

She mentioned something about a complicated situation going on with a former employee, and asked about hiring me to take care of it. It was a much welcomed distraction from all the energy it was taking me to avoid Elizabeth all night (a big mistake evidently), so we spoke in great lengths about it.

"So my dad told me that you've broken off with your father and are on your own now. Is that right?"

"That's right. He's retiring. Spending more quality time with Juliette I suppose," I said casually.

"Good for them. You know I love them as a couple. Wish my dad would have found a nice stepmom for me, but you know him. So listen, are you ready to take on a project asap? Or would you need time to wrap up some other commitments if I hired you?"

"I'm available right away. Anything I've got going on here, my partners can handle."

"Wonderful," she smiled. *"You know you look real good, Rome."*

I was well acquainted with the hungry look Kat was giving me. The look of a good woman desperate to erase the bad memories of a love gone wrong. I'd been that man for many women before, but unfortunately I couldn't be that for her. We'd have to keep this strictly business if this was going to work.

"You too, Kat. I'm glad to see that divorce agrees with you."

"It does," she smiled back at me, but it didn't quite reach her eyes. Her divorce must have been tough on her.

"Relationships are a beast, Rome. You've done the smart thing by staying away from anything too serious. I'm barely in my thirties, and I'm already a divorcee."

"Yeah, that sucks," I said with distraction, because my *serious* thing had just entered the building.

I knew the minute that Elizabeth walked into the room. I could feel her, like I always do. I was itching to find her, wrap my hands around her neck, and kiss her long and deep. Making sure that every man in the place knew that she belonged to me, but there was a part of my ego that wouldn't allow it. Part of me was waiting for her to come looking for me that night. I needed her to want me and find me in more ways than one.

It didn't take me long to spot her among the crowd, and once I did, I could not believe what she was wearing. My woman has a mouth-watering shape. Images that I've jerked myself off to many a fucking night when we weren't together. But one of the things that I love about Elizabeth is that she doesn't flaunt it. She likes to keep things covered and casual in jeans or sweats most of the time, but not that night.

That damn dress.

Small, tight, and a subtle gold color that shimmered against her skin. Illuminating her figure. Acting almost as a siren call to every man in the building. The dress was made from a fabric that clung and caressed every hill and valley of her luscious body. It was somewhat modest in the front with zero cleavage, but then it dropped down dangerously low in the back. So low that I was sure every man within a three foot radius around her was trying to see if they could get a good peek at the crack of her ass. If I didn't know better, I would have thought that Elizabeth was purposely wearing that dress to tease me.

Torment me.

Kill me.

I wanted her in the worst way and not just because of how fuckable she looked, but because I missed the hell out of her. I hadn't smiled in days. I hadn't really laughed in weeks. I hadn't touched her in forever. But the words she spoke in her house a few days back hurt me, and sometimes I don't heal quickly or forgive easy. In fact, sometimes I can be a stubborn ass.

So I admit that I didn't say much to her over the course of the evening. I gave myself the excuse that she asked for the space. So even though Kat and I were actually talking business, the type of business that might turn everything around for me and the Kings, I may have paid my old friend a little extra attention when I thought Elizabeth was watching. It was a dick move I know, but I did it anyway.

In fact, I was so preoccupied and inside of my own feelings that I didn't even notice just how much Elizabeth was drinking until it was too late. I had eyes on her most of the night, but when I let her out of my sight for one fucking second, it's like the sharks in the room could smell blood in the water and started circling.

That beefed up fucker was about to go to blows with me over Elizabeth, and he hadn't even had a whiff of her pussy yet. I don't think my Duchess has a clue of the effect that she has on men. She thinks I'm blowing smoke up her ass when I tell her that, but it's true. If I could shrink her ass and tuck her away in my pocket all day, God knows I would.

The deal I'm cutting with Kat is a good one. Not only will I handle the problem she's having with a former line producer at her company, but she's going to retain us to handle various problems with talent at the company. A lot of actors and actresses are nothing but over-indulged children, with a sense of entitlement and money to burn. They get in more trouble than a little bit. It will be my job to get them out of it. It will also get me out of town for a while, which is probably just what I need. Clear my head and get my mind straight, because it seems that all of my insecurities are fucking with me.

My mother's letter brought up a whole lot of shit for me. While her words validated much of what I've always felt growing up, the bottom line is that she still was a shitty mother. Whether she had good reasons or not. Everyone shouldn't be a parent. Sometimes I think bringing me into the world was probably one of the most selfish things she could have done. She was not ready to be a parent and who knows if my real father was. He was never even given the opportunity to find out. Now he's dead. So that's the end of that.

Then there is the other obvious issue glaring me in the face—Joseph. I know that he read the letter. It was opened and taped back. There's no way that he didn't see what my mother wrote. So he must know that he isn't my biological father. Or maybe he's always known.

All of this is making me seriously doubt ever having kids of my own. There's just so many ways to fuck it all up. I wonder if that would be a deal breaker for Elizabeth? No kids. I wonder if just I could be enough for her?

Speaking of Elizabeth, things are still not right between us. I can't put my finger on it, but this isn't just about me giving her the silent treatment for a few days or even about Kat. She's put up a wall. Not a brick wall, but something tantamount to a clear Plexiglas one. A wall where we can clearly see each other, want each other, but we cannot reach out and touch each other. She's pulling back, and I'm pushing hard, but no connection. It's driving me fucking nuts.

I think I better learn how to blow up fucking Plexiglas.
And fast.

Before my blue balls force me to seriously hurt someone.

21

Elizabeth

Ethan: We need to meet.

Me: I told you not to contact me.

Ethan: Then you should have changed your contact information. Maybe there's a reason why you didn't? ☺

Me: Stop texting me.

Ethan: You didn't answer my email so I'm texting.

Me: That was my response to your email. No response.

Ethan: Oh, I thought maybe it just went to your junk folder. ☺

Me: OMG, what do you want Ethan?!

Ethan: Like I said, I need to speak to you. It's about your cousin. Oh, I mean the dude you're fucking.

Me: And f*cking me well.

Ethan: Hopefully he taught you a few things. ☺

Me: He's definitely a better teacher than the one I had.

Ethan: Who is this new and improved spitfire?

Me: Someone you need to leave alone.

Ethan: Only after we meet.

22

Elizabeth

I didn't respond any further to Ethan, because it was clear that he was looking to pick a fight, but I have to admit that the exchange between us has me shaken. I didn't respond to his email, especially now that I know that Jade is watching his inbox, and I changed my cell number after moving in with Joseph and Juliette. So the fact that he was able to find my new cell number worries me. While I know that he likely obtained my new number from a mutual friend from Penn or something, the fact that he went through those sorts of hoops to do so is really troublesome.

While Ethan may have completely fooled me about his drug habit last year when we were dating, there are some things about the guy that I think I know for sure. He's not the type to pine away for me or any girl for that matter. Even though we were dating for over a year, I never felt totally secure about our relationship. Ethan is attractive, arrogant and completely full of himself. Typical frat boy. People are naturally drawn to him, including me, and things always came easy for him. Deep down I never felt worthy. I knew there was a strong possibility that he was looking, if not actually messing around, with other girls the entire time we were together. What we had definitely wasn't real, it wasn't healthy, and it wasn't love. It was the complete opposite of everything that I feel for Roman.

So if Ethan is contacting me out of the blue like this, then my gut is telling me that it must be for a legitimate reason. Not to woo me back, but probably for a reason that only he benefits from. He needs something.

You know what they say about curiosity and the cat. Regardless of what we want, it can't be worth jeopardizing my life to find out, because there's no question that Roman would kill me if he ever found out that I met with Ethan. That's if Sloan didn't beat him to it. Roman may rub her the wrong way sometimes, but after all the shenanigans that Ethan has pulled, she *really* can't stand him. She won't even say his name out loud, just like many of the Harry Potter characters won't say Voldemort's name.

"Every time we bring him up, bad shit happens," she said.

I just can't shake the feeling though, that it isn't just a coincidence that I almost bumped into Shrek one day and then I hear from Ethan the next. The two must be connected in some way, and not in a very good one. I don't want any part of it. I just want to forget about it. So I've decided to ignore both the email and the text.

"You all right?" Blake asks with genuine concern in his voice. He's finishing up some coding while I do a little social media marketing on my laptop.

"I'm fine. Are you almost finished over there?"

He shuts his laptop and turns completely around to face me.

"It's none of my business, but I can see that everything is not all right. I'm a great listener. You've already heard my sad story, so feel free to tell me yours, too."

"This isn't about my boyfriend at all."

"Okay."

I can tell by his tone that Blake doesn't believe me, and I don't even blame him. Roman didn't leave much of a first impression when they first met. The two met at my house. There was a brief handshake, a few hard looks, and then Roman went into the office to make some calls. He told me later that he didn't care for the look of Blake. I was completely embarrassed but Blake was gracious and told me not to worry about it.

Blake probably also doesn't believe me because I'm sure he's overheard me bitching to Sloan about Roman's behavior at the gala as well as the fact that he's now picked up and gone to Miami, the same place that the mysterious family friend Kat lives. So it's certainly more than likely that Blake thinks that Roman is a total asshole, which wouldn't be so off the mark. I'm starting to think he is too. Trouble is I'm in love with the asshole.

"No really," I sigh. "It was just a text I got from an ex."

"You don't have to talk about it, Beth. It's fine. Let's finish this up."

Now I was starting to feel weird. Like Blake thought I was keeping some sort of deep, dark secret.

"He wants to see me," I blurt out. "My ex asked if he could see me."

"Does he want to get back together with you or something?" Blake asks with interest.

"I doubt it, but I didn't really give him the chance to tell me why."

"Well there's probably a good reason why you didn't give him the time of day. I say go with your gut."

"My gut is actually telling me to do the opposite. It's saying that I should find out what he wants. It's my head that's saying hell no. I'm pretty good at holding grudges."

Blake raises an eyebrow at that.

"Is it possible that you still care about this dude?"

"Absolutely not. He's never had my best interest at heart."

"Well why do you think your gut is telling you that the two of you should meet? That seems a little strange if he's a total jerk."

Blake has no idea about the drama I went through last year. I've told so many versions of the story I can't keep track of the lies anymore. I don't want to have to tell another.

"Because I don't think after everything we've been through together, that he would just contact me for no reason."

He's up to something. Plus he mentioned Roman's name.

"Then maybe you should meet with him. It probably can't hurt if you don't have feelings for him."

"It's just not a good idea."

"Is it because of what Roman would think? Is that why you're scared?"

Well sort of, but I think Blake has the wrong idea. He sounds as if he thinks I'm in some sort of abusive relationship. I don't know why it bothers me so much, but I hate that he thinks so ill of him. Sometimes I just wish one person in my life could see Roman the way that I do. The way that he actually is. Imperfect but amazing.

"I'm not afraid of Roman at all, Blake. This is about my ex boyfriend. He and I don't have a good history."

Blake pauses for a moment, takes a sip of his energy drink, then speaks again.

"Well I see things like this. You're totally distracted by this situation. It's affecting your work and probably your personal life. So you should probably just handle it, and get it out of the way. What if I go with you to the meet?"

"Um, that would be above and beyond your call of duty, not to mention a total snoozefest for you."

Blake smiles.

"Would you say that we're friends, Beth?"

"Yes, I'd definitely say that we're friends."

"Then what's so above and beyond the call of duty for a friend to help you out? Especially a friend who works for you? We can make it a working lunch. We meet your ex at a public place. We work. When he comes, I'll continue to work while you two talk. I can even step away to give you two a little privacy, but I won't leave you there alone. I'll just be two steps away. He'd be a fool to try anything shady knowing that I'm there."

Blake is a sweetie. That's all there is to it. Just an all around nice guy. I'm not so sure that I want to pull him into my world of crazy, or if I should go back into it myself. Meeting Ethan would be like a suicide mission. If Roman even got a whiff of it, he'd probably blow up the place to get at Ethan. That's even if I'm still high on his priority list these days.

We've been playing phone tag ever since he decided to go to Miami on his lame work excursion. Something about "getting his head together." I'm not convinced. The only things in Miami are beaches, beautiful girls and Kat. So that's why I may have pressured my aunt to tell me a little more about the woman who practically committed statutory rape when Roman was a kid.

I know that her father is Donald Dixon Jr. and he's a self-made real estate mogul who's been friends with Uncle Joseph since they were around my age. He lived with a woman who is Kat's mother for several years until she left him and moved to Florida. Kat went to live with her mother after graduation, and hasn't left Florida since. She's newly divorced, in the film business, and runs some sort of production company in Miami. Supposedly she's hired Roman to do some work for said company.

Puh-lease.

She's newly single. She's a blast from his past. And she's totally manipulating him. Playing the *friend of the family* card.

"You're doing an awful lot of overthinking on this. Maybe you should tell your guy about it and ask his opinion. If I were your man, I'd definitely want to know what was going on. Especially if there's some risk involved."

"I can't tell him."

"He'd be angry?"

"Yes."

"And would he have a right to be angry?"

"Probably."

"But you're still considering doing it?"

"Yes."

"Do you love both of them or neither of them?"

"I only love Roman."

"Well why don't you text your ex back, and try asking him again for a phone conversation. Maybe he'll agree to it, and you don't have to physically meet him."

Silence falls between us for a moment. I'm thinking about what I've just admitted out loud to Blake, and God only knows what Blake is thinking about me right now. Probably that I am the worst girlfriend that ever lived.

"I want you to understand that my decision about this has nothing to do with Roman. I'm my own woman, and I make my own decisions. It's just that there's a lot that went down with my ex that makes Roman a bit overprotective. And rightly so. But you're right about one thing; I'm totally distracted by all of this. I need to do something."

I'm assuming Ethan won't be open to just a phone call, because he's already asked to meet with me twice, but I figure it can't hurt to ask. I never actually asked. So I pull out my phone and shoot him a quick text.

Me: I can't meet, but I can talk over the phone. Why don't we set up a call.

A few moments later and I receive a response.

Ethan: No texts. No email. No phone. I have my reasons. I can meet you at our diner on Thursday at 3:00. That time good?

I reread his email several times in an effort to process everything he said. Red flags are flying sky high. No texts, no email, no phone? He sounds like he's in trouble. And what does he mean by *our* diner. He's in lala land. It's *my* diner. It was always mine. Not ours.

"What did he say?" Blake asks.

"He said no email or phone and that he'd meet me at a diner we used to go to in college on Thursday. I think I'm going to go. It's a public place and the people know me well there. I should be fine."

"I still think I should go if you're not going to tell anyone."

"Even if I were to tell him, Roman's out of town," I say.

"All the more reason for you to take me up on my offer then."

I'm digging myself an even deeper hole than I was already in. The list of little small truths that I'm keeping from Roman continues to grow.

1. Shrek sighting
2. Ethan email
3. Ethan text
4. Getting Blake involved

Plus Jade is still a wild card out there. I haven't heard anything from her in weeks and it's clearly past her forty-eight hour deadline, so I have no idea when she is going to strike.

On top of everything else, now I've got to deal with this additional problem. Kat. I keep imagining all the things a horny teenaged Roman must have done with the very buxom blond.

I know down in my gut that he'd never be unfaithful to me, even while we're going through a difference of opinion, but I can't help but become emotional over it.

Roman doesn't have a lot of friends. I thought I knew them all. Yet this is the first time I've even heard about him having any sort of long-term friendship with any woman other than Jade. He's *never* mentioned Kat to me, and maybe he hasn't for a reason.

"Sure, let's do it," I say to Blake. I need to get my mind off of this Kat person. "We'll have a working lunch like you said. I'll hear him out for ten minutes, and then we'll eat a really yummy turkey burger and start planning what we want to include in the next update for the app."

"Excellent plan."

"All right, now that that's out of the way, can you pass me a can of Red Bull and show me what this line of code actually does?"

Blake grins triumphantly. "You got it, boss lady."

Elizabeth

I am freezing.

My eyelids feel dense and heavy like two cast iron skillets.

I want to open them, but I'm not sure that I can. I hear random voices but can't really discern any one in particular. None of them sound familiar to me at all. They're all babbling in some sort of strange foreign language. Using words I've never heard before.

That's when I start to panic.

Where am I?

What's the last thing I remember?

The obvious thing to do would be to start with a visual cue. I work really hard to crack one eye open and regret it immediately, once I notice how bright it is in the room. A room with cream walls, and bright fluorescent lighting across the entire ceiling.

I turn my head gingerly to my left, it feels heavy and very sore, and I notice a stainless steel guardrail. The type of rails you would see attached to a hospital bed. Okay, so I guess I'm in the hospital. Shivering under the thinnest blanket known to man. I know germs multiply in warm environments, but at this rate I'll die from frost exposure. Yet there seems to be something about the frigid temperature which seems to be triggering my memory. I remember being ... cold.

It was raining.

No, I think it was storming.

I was in a car. It's not clear if I was driving or riding along, but I know it was moving fast. I hear voices. At first they sound as if they're trying to speak inside of a long tunnel, their voices distorted and distant, but they seem closer now.

Clearer.

Louder.

One of the voices belongs to a man who I think belongs to me, and it grows in intensity after a series of loud booming thuds and clanks.

24

Elizabeth

My head is throbbing.

This must be what a migraine feels like, because I want to throw my shoe at the lights in this room. It's way too bright in here, and I feel nauseous.

I try to turn my head to take a look around. From the little that I can see, I notice that this room looks different then the one I was in before. I notice a mini white board on the wall with my first name written on it and some random numbers under it. One of the numbers written is 142.

Oh my God, is that my weight up there?

I pretend that I don't see that.

I can't see much else, because my head and neck hurt like hell, and I seem to be in some sort of hard plastic contraption that is affixed around my neck.

I can't hear anything, which seems weird.

No machines.

No television.

No people.

I could hear voices the last time I was awake. I thought

I heard familiar ones. So now I'm starting to wonder if I really am awake or am I dreaming?

Why is there no one here to offer me an explanation?

My eyes feel extremely heavy now.

I wish I could stay awake, but it's just too difficult.

25

Elizabeth

I t's still so frackin' cold in here, but I think I'm finally starting to remember more. That's the only good thing about the cold. It's triggering more memories.

I was spinning in a three hundred sixty-degree circle.

Round and round and round.

The rain was falling hard.

Freezing rain.

My foot was on the brake.

I was concentrating really hard not to slam on the brakes, but to pump them like my father taught me to do in case my car ever started slipping and sliding in wet weather.

But the car kept spinning.

The brakes wouldn't cooperate.

Not even the emergency brake was working that ... that Blake pulled.

Blake was with me.

Wait a minute. Maybe Blake was driving. I'm not sure. I'm still confused. Oh my God, is he okay? Holy crap, I hope I didn't hurt Blake.

I try desperately to mouth the word Blake. I want to know his condition. Maybe someone will see me moving my lips. Is there anyone in here?

I notice for the first time that there is a nurse call button in my hand. Someone must have placed it there for me just in case I woke up.

I press it once.

Then again.

And again.

I'm going to press it until someone comes into this room and gives me some answers. I need answers. I've got a ton of questions.

How long have I been here? Where is Roman? Why isn't he here? Where's Sloan? Did she tell my parents? Do they know that I'm in here? Someone needs to tell the doctors about my penicillin allergy before they kill me accidentally.

I continue to fall in an out of a rather loopy state of consciousness.

Now I understand.

They must be drugging the hell out of me.

I'm relieved when a rather obese woman dressed in light blue scrubs enters the room. I can hear her before I see her, because her rubber clogs apparently squeak when she walks across the linoleum floor.

Her head bends over the bed and above mine wearing one of the phoniest smiles I've ever seen. Her disingenuous expression tells me that she's tired. Like she hasn't had any sleep in a week and doesn't want to be here taking care of me. But I don't care. She's the first human being I've seen since ... since I don't know when.

"Well top of the morning to you, Miss Hill."

I try to respond with my own verbal greeting, but I can't talk. I can't even open my mouth.

"Try not to talk Miss Hill. Your head took quite a beating in the accident, but the great thing is that you only have a concussion. Could have been much worse."

That explains the raging migraine, but how do I communicate with her?

"Are you in pain, Miss Hill? Blink once slowly for no and blink rapidly twice for yes."

I blink twice.

"You're on a timed morphine drip, but I can call the doctor in to see if we can give you something different or perhaps more frequently. I'm sure everything hurts right now."

I blink twice.

"Is that why you called me, Miss Hill? For the pain?"

I blink once.

This would be a whole lot easier if I could talk. I'm frightened and alone. Nobody I love is in the room with me. The only explanation I can come up with is that they don't even know anything's happened to me.

"I'm sure you're terribly confused, Miss Hill. I'll call the doctor in to explain everything to you. Dr. Hammond is on rounds, but he's due to swing by here soon. Don't you worry, I'll make sure you see him. We're taking good care of you."

I'm frustrated and frightened. I want to ask this nurse a million questions. I don't want to wait for some Dr. Hammond to finally get to me on his rounds. Just one more person who I won't be able to communicate with, and there's not a damn thing I can do about it.

One lone tear runs down the side of my face and into my hair. I can't even move to wipe it away.

God, I miss Roman.

Where is he?

26

Elizabeth

The next time I wake up, I'm in way less of a fog than I've been in since I've been admitted to the hospital. I'm starting to remember more.

Things are much clearer.

And definitely more painful.

I was in a car accident. An accident that happened after a meeting set with Ethan. Blake was definitely in the car with me, and it happened on a Thursday, although I'm not sure what day it is today.

Blake and I made it to the diner early that day. Ethan wasn't expecting me to arrive so early. He was already seated at a booth directly across from the same man that I saw at Java with the dead, beady eyes. That's when I knew that something was very, very wrong.

"Morning, Miss Hill."

A tall, thin man with a head full of thick, wavy, black hair greets me. He's wearing a set of sea green scrubs with a white doctor's coat on top. The name Jarrett Hammond, MD is written in script lettering on the left hand side, and he doesn't look a day older than thirty even though I'm sure he is by the crinkles at the corners of his eyes.

He must be my doctor.

I remember squeaky shoes nurse telling me that name.

Dr. Hammond.

I make an attempt to smile in response to his greeting, but it hurts too much. My head is still pounding, and it hurts when I swallow.

"My name is Dr. Hammond, and I'm your attending physician. You were in a serious car accident, but you seem to be healing quite nicely. So nicely that you've been moved from intensive care into a regular room. They moved you last night, so that's great news."

Now that he mentioned it, I did notice the room is different. Not as bright as the other. More cozy touches such as curtains and a printed spread on my bed. I also notice flowers. Lots of them.

So people do know I am here.

But where is everyone?

"I'm sure your head is a little sore. No worries, Miss Hill, things are healing nicely. Let me tell you what's going on all right?"

I anxiously blink my eyes yes.

"You were in a car accident ten days ago."

Ten days!

"You suffered multiple injuries including a concussion, a severe vocal cord injury, a broken leg, and a few of your toes were crushed as well on that same leg. You've been in intensive care for eight days, mainly because of the severity of the concussion and the fact that we couldn't keep your temperature down, then you were in a surgical recovery room for one day, and now you've been in this regular bed for one day.

"We had to perform surgery on your leg and toes

which were crushed badly by the impact of the car pinning you inside, and we gave you a bulk injection treatment in the vocal cord area to help facilitate healing there.

"You seem to be moving your fingers and the toes in your other leg well, and you seem to have feeling in all of your other extremities, so we are satisfied that you didn't suffer any permanent damage to your neck or spinal cord. You will need to recover from your surgery for a few days, and then go through some rehabilitation for your leg and vocal cords.

"The best news though is that your baby survived and seems to have suffered no permanent damage by the impact of the crash. It's a miracle really. I'll schedule another sonogram with obstetrics, so you can hear the heartbeat tomorrow, okay?"

BABY?!

27

Roman

I'm completely mind fucked. Spread across the granite island in my kitchen are the parts to three different pieces. My favorite guns. Weapons that have never let me down and have seen me through some serious shit. I'm wiping each piece down with a soft, white cloth, trying to calm myself down, while Jade pours me a highball of Jack.

It's almost like déjà vu.

We've both done this dance before.

The tiny terror is moving around my apartment very stealth like. Quiet. Calculating. She knows me well. I don't feel like talking, so she doesn't say anything to me. I don't want to even think right now. So she gives me a large drink to numb all of the shit swirling around in my head. I probably should just take the bottle and spare her the formalities of pouring the shit in a glass with some ice.

While I appreciate that she isn't asking me questions, Jade's silence speaks volumes. It's like a blaring, painful reminder of how my own girlfriend doesn't know me at fucking all. A reminder of how I had no clue that any of this was coming. A reminder of my failures yet again as a man. Her man.

Doesn't she know I don't like surprises? Doesn't she know that I would put a thousand motherfuckers to ground for her? Why did I let this stupid, not barely speaking "space" shit go on between us for so long. What a waste of time. I don't even remember what the last thing I said to her was.

I angrily chuck a case of ammo across the room and watch as bullets fly in the air and scatter across my living room floor. Jade still says nothing as she slides the drink slowly towards me and then turns around and pours one for herself. I haven't said much these past few weeks to her or anyone else. Not since I got the call from Joseph.

"Are you back in town?"

"Yeah, got in late last night before the storm hit."

"So you haven't heard."

"Heard what?"

"Elizabeth is in Penn Hospital. We're on our way there now."

He waited for me to say something in response, but all I could hear was heavy silence over the phone and a dull ringing in my ear.

"Roman."

I grimaced like a wounded animal but managed to respond.

"Why?"

"She's been in a car accident, son. That's all I know."

I had been having a bad feeling throughout the day. It had been steadily raining and later that night the storm grew even worse as the skies cracked opened wide with thunder and lightning. The roads were a complete mess, and it had been a shitty night for flying or driving. That's why I had flown in the day before from Miami. To avoid the storm. Elizabeth should never have been out in that weather.

I should have listened to my gut and checked on her that morning when I woke up, maybe even the night I touched down, but I figured I was just anxious because I was missing the shit out of her, not because anything ominous was going to happen.

The accident happened on a Thursday, a week away from Thanksgiving, and our date night. Under normal circumstances we would have been together all day. I should have been balls deep inside of her, all fucking night, and making her come until Friday morning. Unfortunately a series of stupid misunderstandings left us barely on speaking terms. I hadn't even checked in to tell her I was back in town yet. I will regret that for the rest of my life.

I've been acting like a fucking imbecile for weeks now. I was trying to basically mark my territory that day when Blake was over the house working with Elizabeth. I might as well have peed around the perimeter of her house. The way I was feeling, if I could have, I would have bent her over her desk, and fucked her hard while keeping the door wide open, so he could watch every stroke. So he would know without a doubt that he had absolutely no chance with her. That she was mine.

But my plan backfired.

I didn't expect her to put up such resistance, and when she did, it pissed me more the fuck off than I thought it would. It made me question us. Doubt myself. And I got angry. It was my anger that muddled everything. I couldn't see things clearly.

I called myself teaching her a lesson by putting her on an extended *cooling out* period. Especially after she was the one who asked for the space. But now I know better. I was taking our time together for granted. Assuming I'd have plenty more days, weeks, and years with her. Which was stupid on my part, because I know better than anyone that tomorrow isn't promised. Half the guys that I grew up with are either dead, in jail, or on drugs, and they're barely even thirty.

In a nutshell, I fucked up on several fronts.

I should have never allowed Ethan or his piece of shit dealer (Shrek) to continue breathing when I first learned about their existence. Then none of this would have ever happened. This shit is on me, and I swear to hell I'm going to fix it.

I don't actually remember getting in my Rover and driving to the hospital that day. I don't remember if I tuned the radio to my favorite satellite station, or if I ever put on my seatbelt. I don't remember handing the valet my keys at the emergency entrance or if I had my wallet on me. What I do remember is this ...

Me sprinting through the emergency entrance.

The old man sitting in the waiting area with his head hung low, staring at his cell phone.

Seeing Juliette with tears rolling down her face.

Me thinking that Duchess was dead.

My heart feeling like it was being ripped completely out of my chest.

"Where is she!" I demanded to know.

More frightened than I've ever been in my life. Wanting to hear the answer, but at the same time not really wanting to know.

"She's in surgery," Juliette said then she ran to me and wrapped her lithe arms around my neck crying softly.

"She'll be in there at least forty-five minutes. That's what the doctor said."

She's alive.

That was all that I cared about, and is what I gratefully asked with a whisper next to Juliette's ear. *"She's alive?"*

She nodded in response.

"Yes, sweetie. She's alive."

Once I knew that Elizabeth was breathing, I kicked into autopilot. I pulled out my phone and sent a group text to Cutter, Camden and Jade.

Me: Elizabeth in accident. Penn Hospital.

Camden: Be there in 15.

Cutter: Hold tight, brother.

Jade: Coming now.

"Who have you called?" I asked Joseph.

"Her parents. The friend."

"Sloan." Juliette corrected him.

"We didn't know who to call for the guy," Joseph said. *"But the doctor said he's going to be fine. Just a broken arm and a few contusions."*

"What. Guy," I asked stone faced.

Juliette looked at me cautiously, then placed her palm on the center of my chest, as she spoke to me like an emotionally unbalanced first grader.

"The young man who works for her, Roman. I think his name is Blake?"

"He was in the car?"

"He was driving."

A sharp pain shot me in the head above my eye.

"Where were they coming from?" My voice rose a little louder.

"Roman," Joseph warned.

"What!" I barked. Not needing his judgmental shit

today of all days. *I need to know everything that happened. She's my responsibility.*

"She's not your responsibility." The old man interjected yet again. *"She's family yes, but she's not your responsibility. She's got parents that will be here in the next few hours to remind you of that very thing."*

"Joseph, now is not the time," Juliette said as she rushed over to his side.

"She's right, old man, now is not the time."

I stomped down those halls in emergency until I found someone who could give me the answers I was looking for. It didn't take long. A middle-aged nurse who told me that I reminded her of her junior prom date told me everything that she could without getting herself fired as a result. Details on Elizabeth's injuries, her condition when they brought her in, what they were trying to fix in surgery, and where I could find that motherfucker Blake. Because I sure as hell wanted to have a conversation with him, and I didn't care if he was in a coma. I'd wake his ass the hell up real quick.

"Are you family, sir?" the doctor asked when I whipped back the curtain to emergency bed number four. He was lifting Blake's eyelids and checking his pupils with a silver pen flashlight.

"Only family members are allowed back here," he said dismissively.

"It's cool," Blake responded when he noticed that it was me. Then he asked me about Elizabeth. It was the wrong way to start a conversation with me.

"How is she?" He had the nerve to ask. *"They won't tell me much."*

"You mean you want to know just how close you came to getting her killed?"

The doctor's hand froze in midair. He stopped what he

was doing and finally turned his head around. He took a long look at me. Scanning his eyes up and down. Stopping at my scar.

Then said to Blake, *"Do you still want this gentleman back here, Mr. Harrison?"*

"I said it's fine."

The tone of Blake's response sounded as if he was offended that the doctor even posed the question. As if he was embarrassed that the doctor assumed he couldn't hold his own against me. Which he can't. That's not even up for debate.

"Can I see her?" Was his response to me.

"Can you see her? I can't believe you asked me that. Hell the fuck no!"

"She's probably worried about me."

"Trust me, she isn't," I seethed.

After my last comment, the prick shifted around on his bed and tried to sit straight up. He grabbed the side of his stomach and winced in pain. Probably just a bruised rib. I've had them plenty of times before. Nothing that warranted the extensive exam he seemed to be getting.

In fact the obvious minor injuries he sustained, made me even angrier, because while he stepped away from the accident pretty much scot-free, Elizabeth was in surgery getting titanium pins put through her entire right leg.

The image of her getting operated on made me think of how scared she must have been after the accident. How much pain she must have been in. It killed me that I wasn't there to help her. I wondered if she called out for me? If she panicked. If she cried.

I should have been there.

"It was an accident. I swerved and we spun out."

"Why were you even together?"

"I was just trying to keep her safe."

"Safe? That's my full time job not yours."

"Well I heard you were on vacation in Miami, Bro. So today it was my job."

This motherfucker.

"Well you didn't do a good fucking job of keeping her safe did you, smart ass. I want a lot less sarcasm from you and more facts. What were you doing with Elizabeth today? I want to know every-thing that happened or I swear to God, I will break your other fucking arm."

"Listen sir," Dr. McPain In My Ass interrupted. *"I'm going to need to call security if you keep threatening my patient. I understand that you're upset about your girlfriend, but this type of language and behavior is not tolerated in the hospital. You need to leave."*

The doctor was looking and talking to me the same way the prick was. As if their non-tatted, pristine skin somehow made them better than me. As if the scar on my face was the mark of a degenerate and not a warrior. I was ten seconds away from taking that pen light of his and shoving it down his throat.

"I suggest you finish wrapping his arm and whatever else it is they overpay you to do and mind your own business," I said to the doctor in the calmest voice I could muster considering the circumstances.

"Listen you—" The doctor started in on me, but I tuned him out, once the prick interrupted.

"You want answers? Here they are. Elizabeth went to meet some ex-boyfriend of hers. The guy asked for the meet. She was nervous about it and didn't want to go alone. She asked ME to go with her. Days ago. I told her she should tell you about it, but she decided against that. Are those the answers you're looking for, asshole?"

"Her ex," I said with a deadly calm. *"What the fuck are you talking about?"*

"You think you're boyfriend of the year don't you? Well think

again. You don't even know what's going on in her life. Did you know that she's afraid of you? She told me those exact words, and now that I've seen you in full action, I understand why. Do you threaten her in the same way that you've been threatening me in here? Do you talk to her like she's a piece of shit? Do you like the way she has to shrink in order to make you look and feel larger than life? No wonder she didn't want to tell you shit."

The words that were flying out of the guy's mouth were laced with nothing but pure disgust. He despises me, and I think it's because he sees me in the same way that I saw that skater kid and his girlfriend in the park. Like I'm detrimental to Elizabeth's health, or that I'm some sort of bad habit that she needs to break. He *actually* thinks he's doing her a favor by getting in between us. I decided right then that I'd take great pleasure in proving him wrong.

"When we arrived to the meet the guy, Beth spotted him sitting with someone, and one look at the dude he was with, and I knew something was very wrong. He looked like trouble, and she was clearly petrified of him. She said we needed to turn around and go before they saw us. So we hightailed it out of there, but they spotted us as we were leaving, and then they jumped in their car and started following us. Then—"

"Shut up." I threw my hand up to stop him from talking. *"Did Elizabeth call the other guy Shrek?"*

"Yeah."

I had to shut my eyes in a moment of deep regret. Over and over in my mind, I asked myself, how could I have let this happen? What universe did I live in that this prick had now become her knight in shining armor? Her rock to lean on?

"And she specifically asked YOU to go with her?"

"That's what I said isn't it."

I knew I fucked up big time, but I didn't believe him.

Not in the way that he was trying to spin it. Elizabeth would never do that.

"I know that's what you said, but I also know that men lie. Especially pricks like you. Acting like they're one thing, when they're clearly another. Pretending to be her buddy and pal, the model employee, when you clearly have a fucking agenda."

"There's no secret to me. No agenda. What you see is what you get. She asked me to go, because she was going back and forth between deciding on whether to meet this guy or not. It was weighing heavily on her mind. I hated to see her struggling like that. So I helped her make the decision she needed to make. I gave her options. She chose door number one."

Then the asshole grinned at me. A smug, self-satisfying grin. I was so ready to get out of there. I knew that if I stayed too much longer, I was definitely going to bash this guy's head in. He was purposely trying to bait me. If I wasn't absolutely sure about his intentions before, I was made crystal clear about them then.

He wanted my girl.

Dr. McPain In The Ass was almost finished with the last of the exam when I decided that I needed to get out of there before I did something I'd regret; but Blake the prick just had to go and say something the fuck else.

"I told her I'd support her regardless of how she wanted to handle things, because that's what a good man does for a woman. Supports her decisions. What he doesn't do is make her question herself so much, that she doesn't feel safe enough to share them."

"Stop bullshitting me. Do you want Elizabeth?"

"I already have her, Bro."

That was it. I couldn't digest any more of this douchebag's shit any longer. The sea of fury that was bubbling inside my chest was growing at a rapidly fast pace, and I couldn't stop it. I was blind with rage, by his words, by his pompous attitude, and by the fact that some of the shit he was saying hit home.

And I hated him for it.

All of a sudden I had the tremendous urge to start breaking some shit up. To exert some energy that caused someone pain. So that's what I did.

Starting with Blake.

28

Elizabeth

There must be a million rooms in Penn's hospital, because now I've woken up in yet another one. A nicer one. They seem to always move me when I'm asleep. You can tell that the hospital hired a professional interior decorator for these particular rooms, and that he or she tried really hard to make it resemble as close to a person's bedroom as possible.

It's a clean, cozy, private single room. The walls are painted the tan color of chocolate chip cookie batter. I'm covered in a bedspread that has a beautiful tan, brown and red Aztec print. Decorative sconces are affixed on the wall above my bed. Mass produced, art work hangs on the walls. It's quite tasteful. All my flowers from the room before are here too as well as a few fresh arrangements. I obviously don't have my contacts in, so I can barely read the fine print on the note cards stuck in them. I think one is from my Aunt Joan. Wow, I haven't talked to her since Joseph's party at the steakhouse.

My room reminds me of one of the hotel rooms my

parents and I stayed at on one of our summer vacations at the shore. The nicer one. I know a little bit about hospitals. Enough to know that there's no way that I can afford this room and neither can my parents. I wonder which Masterson man is responsible for my upgrade.

As my eyes focus on my surroundings I start to recognize a familiar face, balled up in a chair, in the corner of my room. It's Sloan, and she's doing something I've never seen before. Something I didn't think I'd ever see. She's wiping tears from her eyes. Tears of sadness not hysterics.

"Sloan," I croak out.

It hurts like all hell to speak, but I'm excited as hell that I was able to at least get something out. Even if it's just one word. I almost feel like I've been living in a world where I am unable to communicate with the few humans I've seen over the last days, weeks, or however long I've been in here.

Sloan jumps happily up out of the blue pleather armchair she was sitting in, walks over to the bed, and places her hand on my arm.

"Don't talk, Bitsy. I'm so glad you're awake. I thought I was going to lose you for a minute there."

Well damn, did I almost die? Oh my God, is the baby okay? I unconsciously place my hands across my belly. Realization hits me. There's a baby inside of me. I'm pregnant.

Now that I think back, I realize that this is my fault. I ran out of birth control pills about a month ago and procrastinated picking up my new prescription. I missed about three or four pills, but then got back on schedule. It was stupid I know, but I've been taking the pill long enough now that I thought that the hormones were completely in my system. That a few days off wouldn't matter. Guess I was wrong.

I don't know exactly how long I've been in this hospital,

but all the medicine I've been on for the pain can't be good for the baby. Roman's baby. I wanted to ask the technician a million questions when they gave me my sonogram, but my throat is still so sore, so I couldn't ask much. I suppose there's no use in me asking anyway. What's done is done. I've been drinking like a fish, eating crap, and drugged up these last few weeks, but there's not much I can do about it now, but try to do better moving forward.

There are so many things I want to ask Sloan, but there's no way I'll be able to comfortably get the words out. Not all of them anyway. So I just ask the important stuff using one word prompts, starting with Blake. He was in the car too, and I'm worried that his injuries were far more severe than my own. If I remember correctly, I had my seatbelt on and he didn't.

"Blake," I say my second word to her.

Sloan's eyes drop to the floor.

"I'm not going to sugar coat this, babe. You've been through too much for me to do that. Blake ... is still in intensive care, but they expect him to be moved to a regular room really soon."

I close my eyes in painful remorse. What have I done? If I've been in intensive care for days, but he's still in there, what on earth happened to him?

"It wasn't the accident, Bitsy." Sloan assures me after reading my facial expression. "He only broke an arm and I think a rib from the accident. The crash only crushed and pinned your side of the car in. There wasn't as much damage on the driver's side. In fact, Blake's the one who was able to get out and get you some help. He was also here when you went into surgery."

I open my eyes wider and look at Sloan with bewilderment. Hoping she can understand that I am confused as to why he's in intensive care if everything she told me is true.

"It was Roman," she says bitterly.

"Why?" I try saying and cough a bit afterwards.

"Don't talk. Sip on your water." Sloan pours some ice water from a mustard colored pitcher into a Styrofoam cup. She seals it with a plastic top and straw and hands it to me. I take a small sip, almost afraid to swallow.

"It was all too much for him to find out at once. You met with he who will not be named, which you didn't tell me about, but that's an argument for another day. Shrek was also there, then you were in a horrible car accident, Blake was with you when it all happened, and then it was him who ended up saving you. So I think the Dark Knight just lost it. He lost his ever loving mind and beat the shit out of Blake as well as a few security guards for good measure."

That's when the tears start to fall and my body begins to violently shake. Everything I was trying to avoid was happening tenfold right before my eyes, and there wasn't a thing I could do to change it or make it right. Jade's warning suddenly pops into my head about trust and how Roman doesn't give it freely or give it twice.

The urge to vomit is overwhelming. I turn my body as best as I can to the side and throw up all over the floor and apparently Sloan's shoes as she rushes over to hold my hair back for me.

She doesn't at any time ask me about the baby. That pretty much confirms for me that she has no idea. She would have said something already, especially after I puked. I'm actually impressed to see that the doctors really enforce HIPAA laws in this hospital. They probably can't discuss my pregnancy with anyone, because I'm over twenty-one. Not even with my parents. Which reminds me ...

"Parents," I whisper while Sloan cleans up the mess I've made.

"They're here. They've been staying in a hotel close to the hospital. You've been in and out of it. Sleeping a lot. So you missed some of their visits, but they are here all of the time. Listen, Bitsy, I think I should call the nurse in. Tell him you threw up. It's a male nurse, and he's not half bad looking." Sloan smiles, but it doesn't reach her eyes. She's trying to be comforting, but I can tell that she's worried about me.

I try my best to return her smile and ask the question that I've wanted to know since I woke up in this place. The one question that I'm now frightened to ask.

"Where is he?"

She sighs deeply.

"He was arrested for the beating, but he posted bond. So he's home warm in his bed. Your parents convinced Blake to file a restraining order, so that the hospital would be forced to bar him from visiting you. I suppose if it wasn't for the restraining order, he'd be camped out in your room every single moment of the day."

Oh God ... maybe my parents do know about the baby.

"Your parents are at the hotel getting some rest." Sloan tilts my cup of water as a directive to take another sip. "We've all been taking shifts. Me, Juliette, and them. Even if we weren't allowed in your room, you haven't been alone for one second. Someone was in this hospital 24-7. They'll be back tonight, but I can call them now if you want."

I shake my head no as best I can, and I begin to cry harder than I think I ever have in my life. My life is a complete mess, and I have the nerve to be bringing a new life into my mess.

Sloan slides her chair over as close as she can to the side of the bed and starts combing her fingers through my hair. "Shh, Bitsy. It's going to be all right. I promise. It's all going to be fine. I'm just glad you're okay."

I close my eyes as the tears continue to roll down the sides of my face and inside of my ears. Everything is not okay, and all I want to do is go to sleep and wake up ten days ago.

Sloan

"I have to admit that this is very awkward," Is how I start the conversation.

"How so?"

"I don't like you even a little bit."

"The feeling is quite mutual."

"You seem broodier than usual."

"How very astute of you."

"I suggest you adjust your tone if you want my help."

I'm wearing a curve hugging jersey dress, a pair of knee high, leather boots, and my Burberry trench that my parents bought me last season for my birthday. Not only do I look good, but I'm feeling like quite the badass, superior bitch right now. I never thought I'd see the day that I'd have the Dark Knight right where I wanted him. On his fucking knees. Figuratively that is.

With his oversized body, scarred face, and tatted skin, he is the king of his gutter world, but in the soft and safe land of my best friend Elizabeth Hill, he is nothing more than a mere peasant; and I hold the only opportunity for him to gain entrance back into Bitsyland. It's the ultimate example of karma.

Treat people like shit and shit happens to you.

Elizabeth's recovery has been painstakingly slow. The healing process of broken bones, a concussion, and damaged vocal chords is no joke, especially when you're heartsick, and she's definitely heartsick. She misses the jackass like crazy, but she's also carrying around a tremendous amount of guilt over what the lunatic did to her employee Blake.

He beat that beautiful golden-haired Viking of hers so badly, that his jaw is wired shut for eight to ten weeks. I'm not even sure how you pull something like that off in a hospital emergency ward full of doctors, nurses, and security staff, but he managed to get it done. Honestly the guy should be in jail right now, but I suppose he knows a lot of people in very low places who help him maneuver the system and keep him out of jail all the time.

No justice, no peace.

"You listen the fuck up, Glamazon–"

"No, you listen. I have a name. It's on all my official documents. My birth certificate. My license. Hell, my daddy gave me that name." I point directly to his face. "And you're going to call me by that name, or we aren't going to continue this conversation. *You feel me?*" I say satirically mimicking one of his usual go to phrases.

He thumps his fist on the table we're sitting at in The Lotus in anger. Maybe to get my attention, or maybe to get a reaction out of me, but his temper tantrums mean nothing at this point. He needs me, and I don't need him. Pure and simple. He's the one that better play nice.

"All right, *Sloan.*" He says my name like there's garbage in his mouth.

"Good!" I clap my hands together. "Now we're getting

somewhere. What do you want to know?"

Roman is on the outside of the circle of trust. Even though he isn't in jail, he's been barred from the hospital. I think forever. Bitsy's parents won't take or return any of his calls. Juliette and Joseph were so angry with him for embarrassing the hell out of them in the hospital that they've cut off his Elizabeth information pipeline. At least temporarily. Juliette has been known to slip when it comes to her stepson. She has a soft spot for him.

Elizabeth's phone was trashed in the accident, and she doesn't want another one until she's out of the hospital. I figure she doesn't want to field calls all day from fair weathered friends and curious extended family members. So I am the only direct connection the Dark Knight has to his beloved cousin, and it's a fantastic feeling. I am now the overlord.

Cue my evil laughter!

"What's up with the parents?"

"They're leaving in two days, but they're coming back for her."

"What do you mean *for* her?"

"Obviously they want her to finish her recovery at home with them. It's normal for a girl's parents to want her close after something traumatic happens like this."

I love seeing him sweat.

"I've been trying to be respectful, *Sloan*, but I'm running out of patience," he blusters. "They're trying to take her from me. Everyone is trying to take her from me."

He sounds like he's going a bit batshit if you ask me.

"And that is never going to happen. She's mine, and she belongs with me."

"And how exactly have you been *respectful*? You've only stayed away from the hospital, because legally you aren't permitted within twenty feet of the building. Don't act like you're staying away out of respect for Bitsy or her parent's wishes. The reality is that you don't have a choice."

"I would think that *you* of all people would know better than that. I could throw some money at that place, and in ten minutes they'd throw a red carpet down for me that leads straight to Elizabeth's room. Trust me, I'm giving her parents what they want ... for now."

"You mean what Elizabeth wants."

"She doesn't want this."

"You sure about that?"

"Let me get you up to speed. Elizabeth is having my baby."

I almost choke on my own salvia. What the hell did he just say?

"Your baby?"

"That's right." He grins triumphantly. Like he's won some sort of prize.

"She never told me anything about being pregnant. We were just out drinking–"

"She didn't know she was pregnant then. She just found out. So like I said, I'm pretty sure that distance isn't what she wants. We just need to talk. I have to clear some things up."

"Oh you mean clear up the fact that you went to Miami to see about a kitty *Kat*?"

For a moment there, it looked like I caught him by surprise. I wonder if Bitsy is seriously considering having this guy's baby.

"There's nothing going on there."

"Really? So you go to Miami and barely say good-bye to Elizabeth, because there's nothing going on? That's real confusing."

"I didn't ask you here to talk about Miami."

"Listen, I don't know what I can do for you or if I even

want to do anything for you. You don't seem remorseful one iota about Blake, you have some mystery bitch in your life, and you always complain about Bitsy spending any time with me. Her cutting you off actually works out for everyone's benefit if you ask me. There's no real motivation for me to help you."

If looks could kill, I'd be at the bottom of the Delaware River right now. The Dark Knight wants to throttle me. Good. He needs to feel a little pain right now. Baby on the way or not, he fucked up. We were all frightened about what happened to Bitsy, and maybe Blake did say something out of pocket to him back in that exam room. I don't know. None of us will really ever know all the words that passed between the two of them, but what I do know is that taking it out on his face like that was not the answer. It only made things a hundred times worse. Maybe in his world that's what you do, but not in ours, and I come from a crazy family of professional athletes. They fight all the damn time, but they definitely don't put people in intensive care.

Roman doesn't just punish, he obliterates.

Bitsy is smart, driven, and non-confrontational. She's supposed to be with men like Blake, or Jagger, or some other good looking square who just wants to marry her, put nerdy babies in her tummy, and move her back to the 'burbs.

"When's the last time you've been out on a date?"

What a strange question. Probably trying to mess with my head.

"What does that have to do with anything that we're talking about right now?"

Weirdo.

"Answer the question."

"I don't know," I lie. "It's been a minute."

"Don't you think that's odd?"

"I just haven't met the right guy. Again, what does this have to do with you?"

"I know exactly why you haven't been on a *real* date in almost two months."

This is getting borderline creepy. How does he know how long it's been? Maybe Bitsy's been telling him my business. I'm going to kill her once she gets better!

"Who's counting." I say nonchalantly.

"I bet your hard up ass is." He smirks.

"I've never been hard up a day in my life."

"I'm sure you can get dick quite easily, *Sloan*. Plenty of men like skin and bones and a disrespectful mouth. But this need of yours to go out every weekend, and get wasted, get laid, and take my woman with you while you do it? That's what women who are fucked up in the head do. Women searching for something. Desperately seeking daddy. I'm not falling one second for this *I've got my shit together* act you put on for the world, and so I'll ask you again. Do you want to know why you no one bothers to call you after you meet?"

I squint my eyes and glare at the asshole for a few moments. It reminds me of the times when I was in third grade, and I would stare really hard at Cynthia Martin's head during recess. Hoping I had telekinetic powers that would blow her two long ponytails, clear off of her head and over to the nearby baseball field.

"What have you done now, you psychopath?"

This isn't the Dark Knight trying to give me a few words of wisdom. It's almost as if he's done something or knows something very specific. I can feel it.

"I haven't done anything," he smiles. "You really have me pegged as some sort of criminal mastermind don't you? I'm glad you think so highly of me."

"Mastermind, no. Criminal? Most definitely."

"Your boy Blake had that shit coming."

"If that smart, hot guy had something coming to him, then you *definitely* have some shit coming to you, too."

"You know what, *Sloan.* I've never hit a woman, but you make a strong case for why a man would want to."

"I'm sure cowards across America salute you."

"Bitch."

"What did you say?"

Them's fighting words!

"I am going to see Elizabeth today come hell or high water."

"Hope you can swim then."

The Dark Knight growls in frustration, pops a couple of candies in his mouth, and takes a deep breath.

"Look, I mishandled this today. I don't want to fight with you."

"Then what do you want, because you have a funny way of showing it."

"I want us to stop this bickering thing between us before it gets out of hand. Our mutual dislike for each other is growing into more, and we need to squash it now, because it will crush Elizabeth if she has to cut you out of her life and our baby's life."

"Cut *me* off?! You self-centered prick. You can't be serious. She would never choose you over me. That's what's really bothering you isn't it? The fact that she'd choose her best friend over you. The fact that she *already* chooses me over you all the time. Your delicate ego can't take it can you?"

"I can't even believe you two are even friends, because you don't know Elizabeth at all. First of all she hates that childhood nickname you still call her, but she's too polite to tell you to shut the fuck up. Secondly she has never chosen you over me, *because* I have never asked her to. Not yet anyway. I think you need to ask yourself why you're so angry with me. I've never done anything to you. In fact, I barely know you.

"Maybe you're pissed that Elizabeth isn't as dependent on you or in need of your attention as she once was, because she's with me. Or is it that she isn't as available to you as she's normally been. Your go to, on call, built-in therapist. Your wingman. Your subordinate. Your lesser than."

He pinches his pointer finger and thumb together. "Someone to make you feel just a wee bit better about yourself. Or maybe the real issue here is that you want to *fuck* me yourself, which is unfortunate for you if that's the case. There was a time I didn't mind a little ménage between friends, but I'm a one woman man nowadays."

He's disgusting.

"I'd sooner jump off a bridge than ever spread my legs for you, and as for all the other shit you just said, go fuck yourself."

The Dark Knight finishes off a shot of dark liquor he had sitting on the table, slams the shot glass back on the table, and starts laughing hysterically. It's the first genuine bit of glee I've seen from him since Bitsy's accident. I don't know how many days it's been since I've given myself permission to laugh either, and so his deep rolling laughter acts almost as a healing balm for the both of us. I let go of my disdain for him for just a moment and crack a genuine smile.

"I've never asked you for shit, Glamazon, and I don't plan on ever doing it again, but I need your help. I love her, and I feel like I may be losing her. I can't let that happen. It will kill me. I need you to let go of the fact that you don't like me and take into account that Elizabeth loves me. I need for the two of us to try and be friends."

He stares at me straight on waiting for an answer.

I cross and uncross my legs. Take a sip of my cocktail and then another. Shit, I'm still sober.

I'm not sure what just happened. I had the upper hand at the beginning of this conversation, and now he's telling me about my best friend's pregnancy, which I knew absolutely zilch about, and making friendship requests.

"Under one condition."

"What?"

"I have two questions that I need answered. Truthfully."

"What are they?" he asks impatiently.

"First, I want to know if you've dealt with Ethan and the dealer."

"I have."

"For the record, I told Bitsy to tell you about the whole Shrek thing right away."

"Noted."

"Are they–?"

"They won't be bothering Elizabeth anymore if that's what you're asking."

"Did you do something illegal?"

"Is this your second question, because that's all I'm giving you. Two questions."

"Okay, forget the whole illegal thing. What I really want to know is why none of the guys I'm meeting are asking me out?"

"Well shit that's easy, I can give you that reason in two words," he says with amusement.

I'm waiting for one of the Dark Knight's usual smart-ass responses, but am totally shocked by his actual answer.

"Cutter King."

30

Roman

I'm standing on the opposite side of a closed door to Elizabeth's hospital room. My hands flat on the cool metal door and my eyes closed. She's just within reach, but I've convinced myself that she needs more time to heal, before I dredge up all the shit that's happened in the last few weeks.

So I don't go in.

Punk.

The only nurse who has been helpful to me since the whole Blake incident stares at me sympathetically, like I'm a pitiful soul. She's right. I am a sorry excuse. She also taps her watch to let me know that I don't have much time. I make sure to respect the boundaries she's given me though, because she's given me a gift today.

Information and access.

I'm not permitted to see Elizabeth, in fact legally I'm not even supposed to be inside hospital walls, but I just wanted a moment. A moment to be near my girl and to talk to her. Even if it's just for a moment. Even if it's just through this door. Nurse Price told me that Elizabeth's been awake and alert for most of the day now, and so I figure that if I just say a few words through the door that there's a chance that she'll hear me.

I knock lightly on the door.

"Yes?" Her voice sounds weak and strained, like it hurts for her to speak.

"Don't talk, Duchess. It's me."

Heavy silence.

"I'm just going to talk for a moment, and I want you to listen."

I lean my head closer to the door, so she can hear me clearer.

"Once you heal up, I'm going to spank that pretty little ass of yours for going rogue on me. Obviously I know you were meeting with the ex, and he brought some company along. I even think I understand why you didn't tell me, but that doesn't matter anymore. What matters is that I've taken care of that problem. You'll never hear from either of them again."

I think I hear her moving around in bed.

"Keep still."

The movement stops.

"It was all a set up, Duchess. From the very beginning. Back then in your apartment, Ethan knew that asshole was going to break in. They planned it. He may not have known the amount you had stashed, but Ethan knew about the money in the house. He and Shrek were actually more like partners than dealer and seller. Fucked up, whacked out partners. And then this time, they were going to try to extort money from me by using you once again."

Turns out Shrek and asshole hatched a very poorly thought out and ridiculous plan to get cash out of me by using Elizabeth as bait. Evidently Ethan convinced his dumb ass partner that I was sitting on a lot of money, but neither of them must have done their homework on *how* I make my money. If they had, they would have learned that I shoot dickweeds and lowlifes for fun, and I'm the wrong one to fuck with.

I think they are very clear about that shit now.

"But everything is fine now." I assure her.

I hear her moving around again. So disobedient. It takes everything in me not to fling open the door and keep her still with my own hands. I don't want her to injure herself any further, but I also promised Nurse Price that I wouldn't do anything to get her fired. So, I have to stay outside of the room, and I've got to make this quick.

"I haven't talked to you in so long. I miss that you know. Us just talking. I've been so inside of my own head, I haven't had the chance to tell you that I read the letter from my mother. I didn't exactly ask Joseph for it, but regardless of how it came to be in my possession, I read it.

"It was basically a lame ass twelve-step inspired apology letter. She said sorry for being such a fucked up mother. At least I think it was an apology. Either that or an explanation for her bad mothering thinly veiled as an apology.

"She also told me something very important and very fucked up. Interestingly enough Joseph isn't my biological father. Can you believe that shit? That probably explains why we don't get along. He isn't even my blood. Now we really have zero in common."

I pop a couple of M&M's in my mouth and keep talking.

"Listen, Duchess, I also wanted to say that I'm sorry about your coder. I mean I'm not sorry that I whipped his ass, but I'm sorry that I did it here in the hospital, in front of witnesses, and that your parents saw me lose control like that. That's why I arranged to have his medical bills paid, and I plan on sending him a check for whatever income he's missing out on while you're both in the hospital. I also went to explain things to your parents at their hotel room. To apologize."

I hear a labored one-legged hop and wheels rolling. Probably the ones from her IV stand. She's out of bed, and I'm not sure how she did it with that shattered leg of hers.

"Get back in the bed, Elizabeth," I order and then continue telling her my story, because I'm running low on time. "So needless to say, they weren't happy to see me, especially your father, but I still stood my ground and made my case. You may be mad as hell with me for it, but I told them everything. I told them about Ethan and what a little drug addict he was. I told them about the attack in your apartment, and the whole story of why you moved in with Joseph and Juliette. I told them how I was so angry that Blake took you to meet those vile bastards without checking in with me, that I couldn't see straight and regrettably lost control."

I don't tell her everything that Blake said, because this isn't the time or the place. I'm not even sure that she would believe me if I did tell her.

I lean my forehead on the door just so I can get a bit closer.

God, I want to touch her.

"I told them how we met. How we didn't know we were related to each other at first, and by the time we found out it was much too late. I admitted to them that I have a history of making bad decisions sometimes and worrying about the consequences later; I also told them that I'd never hurt you, and that I'd never let anyone else hurt you, and how that's a guarantee that not many men can make and truly deliver on. And lastly I told them how much I fucking love you, how that's never going to change, and how I'll never let it change."

There must be a set of crutches beside her bed, because I can definitely now hear her clopping towards the door, the IV stand rolling, and her breathing heavy. I can tell that she's working hard to get to the door. To get to me. I wonder if she's anxious to see me or smack me. I most definitely deserve the latter.

I look over at Nurse Price, because I can feel her eyes drilling a hole in the side of my head. She taps her watch a bit angrily to hurry me. I have to get moving. Fuck. I just want to hold Elizabeth. Just once.

I lightly thump my forehead several times against the door in frustration.

"I have to go now, Duchess, but you do what the doctors tell you all right? You need to heal and get better. You need to be strong for School Bucks and for the baby."

I nod in deep gratitude to Nurse Price, who told me about the baby today and who bought me quite a bit of time with Elizabeth in this hallway, and then I turn to make my way down the hall. I'm about midway to the elevator when I hear the door to Elizabeth's room creak open. If I turn my head to look at her, I'll fucking lose it. So I pretend that I can't hear her. I pretend that I can't tell that she's peeping her head out of the door. I pretend that I don't hear her bang her fist against the doorframe several times to get my attention, because she can't yell down the hall after me.

There was a reason why she didn't want to tell me she was pregnant before the accident, or maybe she didn't even know she was, and this is not the time to push for the reason why. I'm still processing the fact that I'm going to be someone's father. That's a mind fuck for your ass.

It's a good thing that I never got around to sharing with

Elizabeth some of my new found reservations about having that squad of kids I mentioned before, because neither one of us can afford to second-guess how to move forward now. A baby is coming, and it's like I've won the damn lottery. A part of me is growing inside of Elizabeth. A connection that links me to the woman I love forever.

But I'm not going to lie.

I'm also scared shitless.

31

Roman

I'm sitting again in Longwood Park on what is becoming *my* bench. Well mine and Cecil's. I wonder what kind of man this Cecil person was that he deserved a bench dedicated to him and in such a place like this. I wonder if it was something as simple as him making a financial donation, or if he was some sort of pillar of the community, or maybe just a really great father.

Typically I do a little investigation on things I wonder about. I've been known to have an insatiable appetite for knowledge about very specific things. I mean it doesn't take much to Google a name and get a little history on someone, but this time there's something about me not knowing who Cecil is that I like. I know enough. He was respected and he's remembered. And sometimes that's all a man wants out of life.

A legacy.

Longwood is humming with energy today. It's the week after Christmas and before New Years and evidently in this neck of the woods that's a big deal. Everywhere I look there are shitloads of young couples, in matching North

Face jackets, pushing strollers and sipping on expensive lattes. Looking like they do this all the time.

According to a posted schedule, they have some sort of small celebration in the park every night until New Years Day, and tonight it's a troop of young girls dancing a scene from the Nutcracker. I remember the ballet, because it was one of the few holiday traditions my mother stuck to. Watching The Nutcracker every time it aired on television. We only had one TV in our house, and I hated when she watched that damn special. I'd rather have been watching wrestling or something, not to mention that it made her cry every single time.

Jade spots me and walks hesitantly over. We haven't spoken much since Elizabeth's accident. Mostly because all I've had on my brain is Elizabeth's surgery, her recovery, and the baby that is growing inside of her. I haven't been in the mood to argue with yet another person close to me, but we were overdue for an argument. There was no putting it off any longer.

"Hey."

"Jade." I nod hello. "Have a seat."

She sits down next to me, but doesn't really look at me. Then she starts to nervously tap her leg.

"Why are you nervous?" I ask.

"I think we both know why."

"Why don't you tell me."

"I was keeping an eye on the ex, saw that he contacted Elizabeth, but I didn't tell you about it."

"Why?"

She finally looks up at me. I think she's surprised by my calm response.

"I was waiting for Elizabeth to tell you about it."

"Why?"

"Because I knew she wouldn't."

"So you put her in danger to prove some sort of point?"

"Obviously, I didn't know it was a set up. I didn't think the ass would try to hurt her."

"All he's ever done is hurt her." My voice rises slightly. "So forgive me if I don't understand your line of reasoning. You are quite familiar with drug users are you not?"

I not so subtly remind her of her drug addicted ex.

"I didn't even know he was in contact with that other asshole. I don't have access to his text messages, Roman. Just his email. She didn't even email him back. I honestly didn't think she would agree to meet him."

"Camden could have helped you get access to the text messages or put a tail on him once you saw that email."

"I thought I had it handled."

"But the point is that you didn't. You didn't have it handled at all."

She looks away while cracking a piece of gum that's in her mouth.

"You're right."

"I've always appreciated how you look out for me, Jade. You are way more than an assistant. You're one of my best friends. One of my only friends. But you're dead wrong about Elizabeth. She's the one. She's IT for me, and the sooner you get on board with that, the better off we're both going to be. Because if I have to make a choice, Jade, it will be her. It will always be her."

Jade clears her throat for a moment.

"I did try and talk to her about Ethan."

"When?"

"When I found out about the email. We talked. I told her then to tell you about the email. To tell you about Ethan. I knew you'd handle it from there. I gave her two days, long before the accident, but she didn't do it."

"What happened after the two days passed?"

"I didn't address it," she pauses, "I became distracted with something else."

"Doesn't matter either way. You had no right to order her or to strong arm her into doing anything, Jade. That's the part you're not getting. You work for me, and you're my friend, but that doesn't mean you have the authority to unilaterally manage my life and the people in it."

"Understood."

"She's having my baby. Did you know that?"

"No," she says with genuine surprise in her voice.

"She was pregnant with my child when she went to meet those douches. Elizabeth and my baby could have both been hurt badly or worse."

I hate to even think about an outcome like that. I would have set the whole city on fire if I had lost Elizabeth that day. Those assholes were dumb enough to make a mistake that could have cost her life. The truth of that hits me like a thunderbolt. What were they even planning to do with Elizabeth once they stopped the car? It's too bad I'll never know.

"I'm sorry, Roman. I didn't know. If I had, maybe I would have handled things differently."

"Just handle them the way I pay you to handle them. If I ask for surveillance, then I expect you to report back exactly what you've seen and heard. I don't pay you to make judgment calls about what you find out."

"I got it."

"All right, so are we good now?"

"I don't know, are we?"

"Well you're not fired, if that's what you're asking."

"Ok."

She looks as if she's almost in tears.

"What did you think I was going to say, Jade?" I ask a bit puzzled by her uncharacteristically emotional reaction.

"I don't know. I mean ... I was afraid that you'd cut me off."

"Listen, we have a very complicated relationship. You're my friend and you also work for me. Those are two very different positions in my life. You jeopardized the business relationship, but it would take a lot more for me to dump the friend. Just don't fuck up again." I give her a small smile.

"I won't," she says relieved and more relaxed now. I imagine that if either of us were huggers, we'd be hugging right now. But we're not.

"Now that we've got that out of the way, little Minion, we need to talk about why I brought you back out to Longwood today."

"All right, why? What's the deal with you and this place?"

"I've got something that I need you to do for me."

32

Elizabeth

I can't wait to see the inside of my apartment. My simple furniture. My exposed picture windows. My dusty wood floors. My empty stainless steel refrigerator. My three fig plants, that are all probably dead. I can't imagine who would have put forth the effort to water them over these past few weeks. Only two people have a key, Sloan and Roman, and I seriously doubt that either of them even bothered.

I was hoping to sleep in my own bed for the first time in almost eight weeks, but I have no idea how I'm going to make it up the ladder to my loft. Not just because I basically now have a bionic leg filled with pins and screws, which is still healing, but also because I'm pregnant. If I fall climbing up the ladder, I have more than myself to consider. I'm responsible for another life. So I guess I'll just have to make do with some pillows and a comforter on my sofa. That's fine though. I'm just grateful to be back home.

I was ten seconds away from being practically kidnapped and taken back to Penn-Washington by my parents, but thankfully I was able to convince them that I'd much rather recuperate back in my own space. I convinc-ingly spit out a couple of totally exaggerated statistics about the speed of healing in a familiar, relaxed environ-ment. Blah, blah, blah. That and the fact that I told them I wanted to keep a close eye on Blake. Which is totally true. He's going through his own hell of a recuperation. Stuck on a liquid diet and pretty much homebound. I feel responsible for his condition.

He wouldn't have been involved in any part of this drama if I hadn't dragged him into it. If it hadn't been Roman who hurt him, it would have been Ethan. Somehow Blake would have gotten hurt, and I have no one to blame but myself. How can someone as smart as me make so many dumb decisions at the same time?

My parents didn't actually put up as much resistance to me staying as I thought they would. I'm a little frightened that it's because they've developed a soft spot for Blake. According to Sloan, they visited him several times in the hospital and practically begged his parents for their forgiveness. Especially once my mother found out that his family was from Washington Falls. While she was truly sorry that Blake was hurt because of me, she was probably more mortified that our parents shared mutual friends. Tongues would be wagging back home about my torrid love affair with my cousin and the fact that he assaulted one of Washington Falls own. My mother was desperate to put that fire out before it started.

"I guess I should have fished for your keys while we were still driving, Bitsy." My mother fusses with a smile. "Your bag is as deep as the bottom of the black lagoon."

"I know. I know. They're in there somewhere, Mom. I just need to get a smaller keychain, so I can drop them in the pocket of my bag. That pouch thing they're on makes them too big to stuff in the pocket."

I'm waiting for my mom by the door, leaning on my crutches, while my father walks around to the trunk of their Subaru to get the bags of groceries we purchased after I was discharged.

"Found them," she cheers. "Don't forget to bring in the flowers too," she says to my dad.

I smile to myself, because I realize just how much people can surprise me. Neither one of my parents have given me a lecture about not telling them about Ethan or why I never reported the assault by Shrek. All my dad said was, "We live with our own choices." And left it at that. They didn't even address the fact that I was now pregnant out of wedlock or about the fact it's Roman's.

While I doubt they'll be shouting the announcement of my pregnancy from the rooftops, they seem to have come to terms with it in a way that works for them. In fact, I was really amused by how my mother was being really particular about the groceries she picked up on our way home. Everything organic, wild-caught or grass fed. She's so cute. I think she's only been inside of a Whole Foods literally twice in her life.

"Welcome home, darling," she chirps.

When my mom finally gets the door open, I'm stunned by the condition of my home. It's cleaner than I think it was when I first moved in. The windows are crystal clear, the wood floors have a freshly lacquered sheen to them, the counters are spotless, my mail is sorted and put in manageable piles for me to sift through. The leaves of my plants are clean, shiny and perky, and the soil in the pots looks slightly moist. Someone has been taking wonderful care of my house!

There's even a tastefully decorated, fresh Christmas tree in the corner where my biggest fig plant was. Someone moved it to place the tree there. The lights on the tree emit a warm white glow and the bulbs are mostly gold with a few red ones sprinkled around. There are five wrapped presents underneath the tree and they all are labeled with my name.

"A tree!" I say almost like a kid.

"The lights are on a timer, so don't worry about unplugging them later."

"You did all of this, Mom?"

"Not really."

"Aunt Juliette too?"

My father grumbles something incoherent under his breath while I continue hobbling around my apartment. Now I'm curious to see what else my family has done while I've been recuperating. I peek inside of my office. It's clean and spotless. Nothing out of place. Except that there's a copy of the blog interview I did before the accident, printed out, and framed. Why is my mother not taking credit? This is totally her handiwork. Only a mother would be proud enough of a blog interview to frame it, I laugh to myself.

"Sloan helped too," my mother says. "She'll be over after work and blow out your hair for you. Make you look pretty."

"All right," I say rolling my eyes.

I hobble on my crutches to the other office. I haven't quite got the feel for these things. They hurt my armpits, and sometimes I just want to chuck them to the side and hop on one leg.

Everything looks pristine in here too. I notice an envelope in the middle of the desk with some scribbling on it. Roman's handwriting.

Look inside is written across it.

Inside is the gold bracelet he gave me. I thought it had been mangled and lost in the car wreck. I even asked one of the nurses about it, and she assured me that there was no gold bracelet on her inventory list when I was admitted. I thought it was some sort of awful karmic sign that I had lost it, but here it is.

I dump the delicate chain onto the surface of the desk and spread it out with my fingers. It's evident that the clasp has been replaced with a more secure lobster claw and a new charm has been added. A different one.

A sunflower.

Almost in tears, I awkwardly unclasp it and latch it around my left wrist, which is infinitely harder to do when you're leaning on a pair of crutches. Then I jingle my wrist back and forth watching my new charm slide around my arm.

I was devastated that day in the hospital when Roman wouldn't turn around and acknowledge me. I didn't think it had anything to do with the restraining order, because if it did, he wouldn't have come to the hospital at all. It felt to me like he was rejecting me. Punishing me. I couldn't get Jade's words out of my head. I'd lost his trust, and I didn't know what I could do to earn it back.

I know to him it looks like the minute he set his foot on that plane to Miami, that I made plans with Ethan out of spite. It looks bad, but it wasn't like that at all. I knew Ethan was up to something and once he brought Roman's name into it, I couldn't let it go. I just forgot the fact that drug addicts are big fat liars, and I shouldn't have believed anything that came out of his mouth. I should have told Roman the minute he contacted me, then none of this would have happened.

"You all right?" My father startles me.

"Yeah, I'm fine," I lie.

"You have a visitor."

My heart jumps inside of my chest. Is it Roman?

"Here I come," I say hopeful.

When I enter the living room, I see my mother smiling from ear to ear. She's taking Blake's jacket for him while he moves to sit on a stool at my kitchen island. I'm surprised at how good he looks. His hair is a bit longer, and he's definitely thinner, but other than that he looks totally normal until he spreads his mouth open.

It's full of titanium.

"Hey, boss lady." He tries articulating his words through a clamped mouth of metal.

Once he notices my unsteadiness on my feet, he stands back up and quickly walks over to me.

"I've got crutches, Blake." I reassure him smiling.

He doesn't respond, probably because it hurts too much to talk, and instead replaces himself as one of my crutches. I wrap my arm around his waist and lean into him as he helps me hobble over to my dining table.

"Blake brought you a present, Bitsy," my mother says as if she's pleased that someone else has a little Christmas spirit around here but her.

I can't possibly accept a Christmas present from this man after everything I've put him through.

"No, Blake."

He ignores me after I'm comfortably seated, and goes to grab two boxes out of a large shopping bag. My mother hands him a pad of paper and a pen. He starts writing furiously.

It's for the sake of School Bucks.

Let's open them at the same time.

I already know what it is. I've opened this same gift before from a very different man, which makes this feel even more wrong. A new laptop. Both of our computers were ruined in the car accident. They had both been sitting on the floor of the car in a laptop bag by my feet. When my leg became pinned, they were crushed.

Thankfully I saved all the files to the cloud the night before.

We can continue with the app just like it was eight weeks ago.

I could kiss him. So my update is not as behind as I originally thought. At this rate we'd be able to relaunch the app for the new year. Instead of a kiss, which would be wildly inappropriate, I thought at least a hug was in order.

I clumsily lean over in my chair and give him a hug, which puts a huge smile on his face. A smile that I think is painful for him because he flinches. I place my hand on the side of his face.

"Ooh, that must hurt," I say chuckling. "Stop smiling, you goofball."

It's at that very moment, with my hand on Blake's cheek, that I can hear a key being turned inside the lock of my front door and it swiftly being pushed open.

Before I can react, a large ball of fur charges in first and lifts his huge paws onto my knees, then starts licking my face. An even larger man is standing in the doorway giving me a very unforgiving glare.

The one where he either wants to fight me or fuck me.

33

Elizabeth

"**D**uchess."

I've never been more thrilled to hear that simple, panty-dropping greeting. Low, gritty, and heavy with tension. As soon as I spot him in the doorway my stomach spins, and although I know it's impossible this early in the pregnancy, I feel like the baby is flipping and fluttering around in my stomach. Excited to hear his father's voice.

I say *his* because, I've decided that my baby is a boy based on the fact that I admittedly have a glow, and according to old wives' tales, girls steal a mother's looks. Boys don't. So even with a smashed leg, a jiggled head, nausea, sore boobs and jacked up vocal cords, I've never looked more vibrant if I do say so myself.

"Hi." Is all I manage to say. Wishing I had come up with a more eloquent greeting for my baby's daddy.

"You want to take your hand off of your employee's face, Elizabeth?"

It just really hits me that Roman is wearing a severe facial expression. Very serious. He doesn't look exactly happy to see me or happy at all. Not that he ever does, but at least this time I think I understand why. I quickly drop my hand away from Blake's face. The sunflower charm on my bracelet delicately dangling mid air.

You can literally hear a pin drop in the room. Blake is obviously quiet because he can't talk that much, but he is watching Roman's every moment with an eagle eye. My mother stops making my salmon salad, and walks over to stand beside my father at the dining table. The two of them standing behind Blake and myself at the table as if we're forming some sort of alliance against Roman.

Crap, this looks really bad.

"You used your key," I say through a forced smile in an attempt to diffuse the tension in the room.

"I did."

Mr. Tibbs is still basically lounging with his paws on my lap. I scratch under his chin and ears, which he seems to enjoy tremendously. So much that I think I see his eyes almost roll towards the back of his head in total bliss. This is the friendliest he's ever been with me. I'm always joking with Roman how he is more aloof like a cat instead of outgoing like a dog. He's usually so subdued, but today he seems really happy to see me, and I've got to admit that I feel the same exact way.

"Tibbs missed you." Roman acknowledges proudly. "Hello Mr. Hill, Mrs. Hill," he greets my parents politely as they continue to stare at him, like he's some sort of unusual attraction at a county fair or better yet a motorcycle convention.

Tall, tatted, massive, muscular, scarred and covered in denim and leather. Roman looks like the type who spends his days on the back of a Harley and his nights inside of whatever woman would be willing to spread her legs as long as she does what she's told. But that's not who he is at all. In fact I think for the first time in a long time, I'm starting to understand all that he really is, and what I mean to him.

He's a complicated man that loves me.

My layered onion.

And me? Well, I'm the dumb chick who didn't trust it.

"Hello, Roman," my mother says pleasantly enough.

My father doesn't respond at all. I'm thinking Roman's talk with them didn't go as well as he let on that day he visited me in the hospital.

"Blake."

Roman gives Blake a simple but polite greeting, although I know it's strictly for my benefit only. I'm not sure how I feel about that. In fact my feelings are all over the place. On one hand I want to jump up and wrap my one good leg around Roman's waist and lick his face, and on the other hand I want to slap him for being such a brute.

"It probably would have been a good idea to have called first before you came over," my father says.

"Dad-"

"Elizabeth doesn't have a new cell phone yet. So I thought I'd just stop by and make sure she settled in. I knew she was being released today."

"Blake's restraining order is still in place," my father stiffly responds.

Roman looks pained. I'm pretty sure he's dying to tell my father to shove the restraining order up his ass, but he's trying very hard to be respectful. Which makes me feel all fuzzy inside. The fact that he's trying when my father is being down right rude is appreciated.

"Elizabeth, you really should get a landline," my mother interjects. "I know your generation does everything on your cell phones, but what if there was an emergency?"

"I planned on replacing my cell this week. No one has a cell and a landline anymore, Mom. That's just a waste of money."

Roman's nostrils flare for a moment as his inky eyes roam my face. I realize that I'm still sitting quite close to Blake, and that my father just made that comment about the restraining order. He can't control this situation, and I think that's driving him crazier than anything.

"Elizabeth, you know I would never hurt you, and if I promise not to touch *him* again, could I talk to you for a moment? Alone," Roman asks carefully.

"That's interesting. When you came by unannounced and unwelcomed to our hotel room, you had a lot to say to us. Now you just want to speak to Elizabeth privately? I think that whatever you have to say should be said in front of all of us. Including her friend who you assaulted."

"Dad! This is my house and–"

"It's fine, Elizabeth," Roman quiets my protest. "I can say this in front of your family, your *employee*, whoever. Just as long as I say it."

"Ok," I say a bit stunned by his words, especially because I know this isn't what he wants to do or how he wants to do it. Roman is a very private person, and we have a lot of things left unsaid between us. I figure the number one issue on the discussion table is our baby.

Roman pulls one of the chairs from under the dining table out and takes a seat facing me. There is a cumbersome leg cast around the entire length of my leg, so I do my best to turn myself around without hurting Mr. Tibbs who is interestingly enough still resting half of his body on my lap.

Roman snaps his fingers once and Mr. Tibbs ears perk up, then he jumps off of me and goes to his usual corner of my living room where he lies down. Then Roman pulls my chair forward, away from Blake, and facing him.

"You should have this leg elevated," he says as he lifts my leg onto one of his massively muscular thighs. I wince a bit from the movement.

"Too high?" he asks. His jaw hard with worry.

"No, it's fine."

My stomach lets out an angry growl that fills the entire room. Everyone looks at me, and then my mother who scurries back to the kitchen to grab my lunch.

"Let me get your salad finished, sweetie," she says. "You must be starving."

"I went to Miami to meet with Kat," Roman starts. Not exactly what I wanted to hear from him, but I'll bite.

"I know," I say.

"To meet with her about business. Her production company put me and the Kings on retainer for the near foreseeable future."

"*Retainer* for what?" my father snickers. "Lawyers get retainers. Not thugs."

Roman keeps his eyes on me but responds to my father's accusation.

"I help keep her actors out of trouble, out of the court system, and hopefully away from bad press. That's what I get paid a lot of money to do, *Sir*."

"By whatever means necessary?" my father snidely asks.

Roman doesn't flinch. "That's right."

"That's how you plan on taking care of this baby?"

Blake furiously begins scribbling on his note paper. For a moment I forgot he was even sitting here, and now I've just remembered that he had no idea about my pregnancy. I haven't seen him since the accident and my parents definitely wouldn't have told him. Knowing them they were probably worried he wouldn't want me, after he found out I was carrying another man's child. They're so delusional.

Blake finishes writing and slides the paper next to me at the table.

"One second," I say to Roman so that I can read the note, but he stops me from reading by slapping his hand on top of the note and sliding it back across the table towards Blake.

"I'm not finished talking," he says sternly. Keeping his steely eyes on Blake's for an elongated moment, then on my father's, and then back on mine.

"There is no one but you, Elizabeth. There will only be you. There could only ever be you. We don't need any more space or distance from each other. Not now and not ever again.

"It kills me that I wasn't here when you needed me. It infuriates me that I gave the illusion to your *employee* here that there was even a sliver of a chance for him to move in and claim you. There is none. It incenses me that somewhere along the way you started feeling as if you couldn't trust me, because you can. You can tell me anything, Elizabeth, and I swear to fucking God that I will always listen, and that I will move heaven and earth to make whatever is wrong right for you.

"I love you. I didn't know exactly what that was at first. Loving another person like this. Loving someone without all the conflict or the hate that I've usually felt for people in my life who claimed to love me. So when I actually recognized what this was between us, that it was real, I didn't know if I deserved it at first. Especially from someone as smart, and beautiful, and innocent as you. But once I accepted it, and embraced it, then I became scared as hell to lose it. So I made some mistakes. Ones that I hope you will forgive me for, because it's going to make it awfully difficult for us to raise this baby together if you don't."

I hang my head low to hide the tears that are rolling down my cheeks. I don't know if he's saying all of this because of the baby or because my accident scared the hell out of him, but the weight of his words tear through my chest violently.

I know Roman, and this couldn't have been easy for him. Baring his soul to me in front of two people who have never been kind to him and one who I now suspect may have been hoping for our demise for quite a while now.

In the middle of all of this, my mom places a mixed green salad with a piece of blackened salmon on top in front of me. Something about the poor timing of the gesture spurs me to say what I should have said the moment he entered the house.

"I need everyone to leave," I say firmly.

"Elizabeth, you just got out of the hospital!" my mother exclaims.

"That's right I did, and it's my prerogative if I want to rest and recover by myself. And that's what I want to do. So could you guys come back tomorrow maybe? And Blake—" I turn around and look at my poor coder. My flirty friend. His mouth wired three quarters shut. I need to remember what Roman has done to him. Regardless of the reason, he didn't deserve this. Even if he does have more than friendly feelings towards me. Nobody deserves *this*.

"Blake, thank you so much for the generous gift and for checking on me today, but I just need a moment to myself now. I will definitely start putting the computer to use sometime this week, and I'll try texting you tomorrow, okay?"

Blake nods his head in agreement, but he doesn't look happy about it.

"Elizabeth—" my father starts to lecture.

"No, Dad. I want you all to leave. Roman and I need to talk ... alone."

I couldn't make it any clearer than that without becoming rude.

After five minutes of gathering their jackets and a few awkward good-byes, the three of them left, and I was now finally alone with one very intense looking Roman Masterson.

34

Roman

"Why are you still in so much pain?"

Elizabeth is oblivious to just how well I know her. She doesn't need to say a word. Her pained facial expressions tell me everything I need to know.

"It's not *so much* pain like you're thinking, it's just a little. I'm not on any painkillers."

"Because of the baby?"

"Yes."

I grin.

"Let's talk about the baby, but first take a bite of your salad."

I slide the plate of salad and salmon Elizabeth's mother made for her in front of me, pick up her fork, and attempt to feed her.

"Open wide."

"I don't need to be fed."

"Actually you do. That stay in the hospital caused you to lose too much of your hips and ass. So what the hell am I going to hold onto while you're riding me, if we don't get your weight back up?"

"Ha. Ha."

I'm not kidding.

"Was the food gross or something?"

"I was asleep most of the time, so I didn't spend much time eating. Are you saying I look bad?"

I look at her like she's crazy, because she is. Elizabeth Hill has never had a bad looking day in her life.

"You need to eat for the baby. Speaking of my baby. How exactly did we get into this predicament?"

I rub my palm across her abdomen.

"I'm pretty sure you know how we managed to get in the family way. You were there. Repeatedly."

"I'm also pretty sure you told me you were on the pill."

She snaps her eyes up to mine. "Are you angry?"

A flash of worry crosses her face.

"Of course not. I'm just curious as to how we created this human being when I've seen you pop your pill practically every morning."

"I may have skipped a few pills a while back when my prescription ran out. I thought I'd be fine as long as I got back on track a few days later. Honestly I thought my system was so flooded with birth control hormones that missing a few days wouldn't make a difference."

"Did you ever think about not having it?"

"Never." She looks like she wants to slit my throat right now. "Is that what you want?"

"Calm down, mama bear. I'm just trying to see where your head is at about all of this. You've got a lot going on, and you've never talked about wanting kids. You can't blame me for being a little surprised by it all."

"I haven't talked about kids before?"

"Not in a positive way."

"Well I suppose I'm a little afraid of the sticky little troublemakers, especially when I'm barely an adult myself, but getting rid of our baby was never a consideration. Listen, I know I've just complicated what is already a pretty complicated relationship between us but–"

She sounds like she's apologizing.

Shit.

I didn't mean to put her on the defensive, so I cut her off.

"It's not complicated. I mean it is, but it doesn't have to be. I admit that I don't know shit about raising a kid. I'll also admit that I never seriously considered bringing kids into this world because of who I am, what I come from, and what I do for a living, but all that's changed now. I *want* this baby. I want our baby."

That puts a beautiful smile on her face, and I can't help but reach out and finger a few strands of her hair. I've missed her so fucking much. Talking to her. Touching her. But I better let go of her hair, because I can't help but think about how I'd rather be pulling back on it, while I'm deeply rooted inside of her.

She's got one good leg, asshole. Get control of yourself.

"Have you talked to Joseph?" she asks, which breaks through my lust filled daze.

"No."

"Why not?"

"He knows I took the letter. He's probably waiting for me to call him and curse him out about it."

"And you haven't?"

"I've been a little preoccupied."

"Worrying about me?" She grins.

"Every single moment of every single day. Here, take another bite for me."

I feed Elizabeth another forkful of her salad. It's important that I shove as many veggies and healthy proteins I can down her throat so that my baby will overcome being jostled around and scared to death by the car accident. I don't care what those doctors say. I'm sure my little bambina or bambino was scared as shit inside of there.

I also feed her to stop myself from doing what I really want to do, and that's to move in between her legs and never leave. I can't get her pussy off of my brain. My horny ass is already sitting here planning how I'm going to need to strategically position her, so that she can receive all of my cock without getting hurt. It's going to be tricky to get around this neon yellow leg cast she's wearing, but if anyone can figure out how to get it done, it's me. I'm highly fucking motivated.

"We have a lot to talk about, Roman."

"So talk."

I want us to put everything on the table, so that we can get past it and get on to the making up part.

"I don't see how I can work with Blake, now that you've beaten him to a pulp."

"I agree." I smirk. "There's no way you can work with him now."

"I'm not kidding."

I sigh. She doesn't get the humor I guess.

"He seems to be taking it rather well if you ask me. Over here for a holiday lunch with your family. Buying you expensive Christmas gifts with *my* fucking money."

"Seriously!?"

"I paid his bills, AND I gave the prick extra. So yeah, seriously. He bought you a fucking laptop with my money."

"You've got some nerve. He wouldn't need your money if you hadn't broke his frackin' jaw."

"All right, all right. Maybe the money comment was a cheap shot, but I'm serious when I tell you that he doesn't give two shits about making School Bucks a household name. All he wants is to get in your pants."

"I'm flattered that you think I have this universal sex appeal, but I thought that we were in agreement that you're a bit over the top with it."

"What agreement? We're talking for the first time in weeks, and I told you in the hospital that I *wasn't* sorry that I beat Blake's ass. I meant that shit. He deserved it. He said some very foul shit to me while you were fighting for your life—"

"I wasn't dying, Roman. Stop being dramatic."

"He wants you, and he can't have you. He seemed to need some clarity on the topic, so I gave it to him. I'm just sorry that your parents had to see it. So really you should admit that not everything I tell you comes from a place of insane jealousy, and that I actually know a lot more about the deviant nature of people, especially men. I knew early on, maybe even before he knew himself, that Blake was interested in you."

I lower her injured leg on the floor and pull her chair in even closer towards me.

"I don't blame him for wanting your pretty ass, but he picked the wrong woman to crush on."

"So you want me to fire him?" she asks distracted by my intimate proximity.

"Is he still working for you?" I feed her a little more salad. "Chew."

"I think so," she says with a mouthful of salad. I push a spinach leaf that's sticking out of the corner of her mouth back inside with my finger.

"Would you fire him?" I ask with my face now in the crook of her neck.

She swallows. "Would you fire Jade?"

"What's she got to do with this?" I ask a little defensively.

"She basically blackmailed me."

Oh yeah, that.

"I talked to her. I made it very clear that she over-stepped her boundaries, and it won't happen again."

"A conversation and it's taken care of, huh?"

"Yep."

"Okay, well Blake is now very much aware that I am pregnant with our love child, so even if what you say about him is true, I don't think we have to worry about any issues with him in the future. So can we both agree that both of those topics are settled and off the table?"

"All this bargaining and negotiating is turning me on, Duchess."

"You can't be serious right now."

"Very." I assure her while pulling her in the last few inches that I can without spreading her bum leg too far. I really wish that she could sit on me and straddle my waist, but I'm being greedy at this point.

"My leg—"

"Is easy to work around."

"Wait, I'm not done talking," she says as I wrap my hand around the base of her neck and pull her in for a long, overdue kiss. Taking great care not to jostle her leg.

"I'm listening," I whisper by her ear after my momentary exploration of her mouth.

"I don't want to ask but—"

"Then don't ask," I say while licking and lightly sucking along her neck.

"I have to."

I already know what she wants to know, and I don't want to talk about that shit. Ever. I don't even want her thinking about it.

"What, Duchess?"

I brush my fingertips lightly across the tops of her

breasts. I figure my best offense is to distract her as much as possible.

"What happened with Ethan?"

I ignore the question and rub my knuckles lightly across her right nipple. Her saying his name out loud actually makes me want to bite her damn nipple.

"If I never hear that name for the rest of my life it would be too soon."

"What. Happened." She insists.

I exhale heavily in annoyance more than anything. Even as she arches her breasts into my touch, she's not going to drop the shit. So I might as well get it over with, so I can get back to what I'd rather be doing.

"Your safety is my number one priority, Elizabeth."

"I realize that."

"So you think I could let go the fact that those two were planning on using you to get to me? Maybe blackmail you or kidnap you? Maybe even rape you. I don't know what the fuck they had planned, but I couldn't let that shit stand, Elizabeth. Just the possibility of what could have happened is too much for me to bear. You feel me?" I ask through flared nostrils.

"Yes, but–"

"I promise you that I can live with what had to be done, and if you're going to be with me for the long haul, you're going to have to learn to accept that there is shit you're never going to get all the details on. That's just how I do things. I deal with all the dirty, and then I sink myself inside of you and make myself clean again."

I know this is going to be difficult for her to let go. Maybe I need to tell her something. Anything, so I can end this conversation for good.

"Now can we stop talking about this?"

"Are they ... still breathing?"

"And what if they weren't? How would you feel about that?"

"Well ... I'd be worried about you. The last thing I need is the father of my child locked up."

"Then it's a good thing you don't have to worry about that."

"Really?"

"Really. Are we good now?"

She takes a minute to consider everything I've said. I've tried to assure her without really having to commit to an answer either way. I think I've succeeded based on the expression on her face.

"Yeah, we're good."

"Good. Now finish this last bite, so I can put you to bed. Both my girls need their rest."

"Both of your girls? Uh-uh, we're having a boy, and he's going to grow up to be just like his stubborn father."

I laugh out loud.

"Let's make a bet." I challenge.

"What kind of bet?"

"If we find out that we're having a boy, I'll grant one wish for you. Anything you want, and I won't give you any shit about it."

"Okay and if it's a girl?"

"You'll grant one for me. Anything I want."

"No ménage," she warns.

"No ménage," I say with heavy laughter as I recall my hysterical exchange with the Glamazon.

"What's so funny?" she asks suspiciously as I lift her up in my arms, and grab her jacket, handbag, and crutches to help her walk towards the front door. "Wait, where are you taking me?"

"Exactly where you belong, baby. Home with me and Mr. Tibbs."

35

Elizabeth

I t's New Year's Eve and I've been holed up in Roman's penthouse for several days eating some of my favorite foods, binge watching *Walking Dead* episodes, and getting ready to release School Bucks' latest update in the app store. It sucks to be stuck in the house during the holidays, but I couldn't have wished for a better place to become an invalid. Roman makes sure that I have everything that I need, even before I realize that I want it for myself. Food, drinks, pillows, my Kindle, my laptop. He's the perfect host.

Unfortunately that's about all he is. A perfect host. He hasn't touched me except for a few chaste kisses that have done nothing but made me angry ... and horny. A few days ago he couldn't keep his hands off of me, but now nothing. I think my visiting nurse must have gotten into his head, and convinced him that I was some sort of fragile porcelain doll. I'm going to fire her and fix his ass soon enough.

I get a text message on my new cell phone (one of my many Christmas gifts from Roman) alerting me that a package has been delivered. My new cell is a private number added as a second line to his main account, so I haven't had many calls. My parents, Sloan, and Juliette.

Almost twenty-four hours after I texted Blake that I'd be working from Roman's house for a while, he sent me a long email explaining how he has suddenly decided to recuperate back in Washington Falls and will do freelance work from there. He finished my latest update, uploaded it to the cloud, and basically told me to have a fantastic life. I haven't told Roman yet. I'm not in the mood for how elated the news is going to make him, especially because I'm not totally happy about it. I'm out one amazing coder and possibly a friend.

"Roman," I call out to the man who refuses to leave my side, much less leave the house.

"Yeah, babe."

"I've got a package downstairs. Can you get it?"

"I'll have Darren bring it up."

Darren is the building's doorman.

"All right." I roll my eyes to myself. He won't even leave to get a package. He thinks I may roll out of bed and bump my head or something. Talk about overprotective. *Good grief.*

"Your box is here."

Roman tosses the box next to me on the bed.

"What is it?" he asks curiously.

"I'm sick of these bird baths the nurse has been giving me. I want a real shower."

I open the box and pull out a seal tight cast protector that I bought on Amazon.

"It says that it will cover and keep my cast completely dry. I'll be able to get in the shower. Or better yet, I can even take a bath." I bat my eyelashes in an exaggerated fashion.

"Not in my tub. The sides are too high. You might hurt yourself getting in or out."

Seriously?

"You can help me get in and out."

"Still too dangerous."

"I'd have to stand in the shower though. Isn't that a hazard as well?"

"No. I have a waterproof stool you can use in the shower."

I roll my eyes.

"Fine."

"Does Raina know how to put this thing on?" he asks while examining the plastic package.

Raina is that damn visiting nurse Roman has hired to come three times a week to check on me, and that's only because I talked him out of having her come everyday.

"Raina? I'm not waiting until tomorrow to take a shower. You can help me."

I laugh a little to myself, because Roman makes an expression like he'd rather swallow nails than help me in the shower. He's been trying to avoid looking at or touching my naked body for days.

"Elizabeth," he warns.

"What?" I act clueless.

"Why can't you wait for Raina? You just had a bird bath this morning. You're totally clean."

"There's nothing totally clean about a bird bath, and I'm not bringing in the new year dirty."

"You're hardly dirty," he says dismissively.

"You want me to call Juliette over then?"

There's no way Roman would want Juliette and Joseph to think that he wasn't taking the best care of me. I knew I had him with that. I think that something Joseph said to him during their little lunch messed with his head. That might not have been the best idea Juliette and I came up with. He refuses to ask for their help with anything.

"Fuck," he says in a defeated voice. "All right. You get undressed, and I'll start the shower. Don't try and walk. When you're ready, I'll come and get you. Understand?"

"Yes, sir."

It doesn't get past me that Roman has to adjust the rather large bulge swelling inside of his sweats after hearing me respond with the word *sir*.

After stripping off my sweats, it only takes me a few minutes to figure out how to pull the plastic protector over my cast. It's actually quite ingenious. There's a rubber gasket at the top of the protector that creates a watertight seal around my thigh.

I think I hear a few indiscernible curse words when Roman comes back to grab me for the shower. He bends over the bed, and lifts me up as if I weigh two pounds, then walks me inside of the bathroom. I'm pretty sure he tries to stealthily take a whiff of my neck.

Roman's master bath is gorgeous. It's covered completely in creme Italian tile with caramel colored veining. The shower is huge and spans the entire length of one side of the bathroom. There's a large showerhead that hangs from the ceiling and the water falls like gentle rainfall. Then there's another showerhead strategically placed on the opposite wall which is tilted to spray directly on your body and pulses like a therapeutic massage.

The size of the room, the multiple shower heads, and the attention to detail makes his bathroom feel very much like one you'd see in a five star hotel or a spa, and it's one of my favorite rooms in his apartment. So relaxing, especially once it fills with steam.

"I'm going to sit you on this stool. See it has a wide seat and short, stubby legs. I'm leaning your crutches right here. Your bodywash is on the table. Use the handheld sprayer to wash yourself. Don't try and stand up for anything. Call me if you need to reach something, and call me when you're finished."

"And where in the ham sandwich do you think you're going?" I demand to know.

"I'll be right next door in the bedroom if you need me. I have a few calls to make, but I'll keep the door open. You enjoy your shower, baby."

Oh for Pete's sake! He is being so infuriating.

"Roman."

"What."

"Are you just going to let me take a shower by myself with a broken leg and a baby in my belly? What the hell."

More expletives under his breath and a sigh later, he starts getting undressed; and just the sight of him getting undressed to come into the shower with me is making me salivate.

What's so beautiful about Roman is that he doesn't even have to try hard. There's just the way that he moves in this world, with hard edges and confident swagger that makes me wet every single solitary time that I'm near him. I'm actually waiting for this effect he has on me to finally wear off, because there's nothing more annoying than sitting around in soaked underwear all the damn time. Luckily today I'm already undressed and under a stream of water.

"Have you been working out more lately?" I ask him practically panting. Knowing full well he has been working out like a maniac. Anything to keep his hands off of his *delicate* baby's momma. *Eye roll.*

"No, Elizabeth," he says tensely. "Why are you acting

like you haven't seen my body before. I sleep with you every night."

Covered in sweats and on his back barely touching me. He forgot to mention that part.

"Oh, it's just that you look even more cut lately," I say in mock appreciation. Although it's totally true. Watching Roman's thick, hard muscles stretch and flex in motion, especially the parts covered in ink, is better than watching porn.

"It's the protein shakes."

"So how do I look?" I ask while adjusting myself on the stool.

"Beautiful as always."

"Have I gained some of my weight back?" I ask worried a bit about the weight I'll gain during this pregnancy.

"A little." He says in a grumpy tone. "You could stand to gain a couple more pounds though."

I smile at that comment. Only a man like Roman would want me to actually gain weight instead of lose it.

"I think you just want to fatten me up so no other men look at me." I joke.

"Not possible," he grumbles. "Men will always look at you. Assholes."

Roman enters the shower in all of his commanding magnificence and swiftly helps me up off of the stool. He carries me over to a corner of the shower and places me gently down on my feet. He leans us both against the wall, so that the tilted showerhead is hitting us directly.

I'm a little unsure about standing in this position because of my leg until he tells me firmly to, "Lean back on me."

His strong arms encircle my waist as I lean back with

my head against his chest. A soft stream of water to my front. Hardness at my back. It feels heavenly.

"Can you hand me the body wash?" I ask.

"I'll do it." He practically growls in response. As if he's angry I even suggested that I'd wash my own self.

I grin triumphantly to myself as he grabs one of the Dead Sea sponges on the shelf and pours a generous amount of my favorite jasmine body wash on it.

He starts washing me at my neck first and meticulously begins washing me with the sponge in a slow, sensual, circular motion. I close my eyes and settle farther back into his body. Melting from his touch.

"Is this what you wanted?" he asks through gritted teeth by my ear.

"Mmmm, yes," I say raising my arms above my head and behind his neck.

"Me rubbing this sponge all over your body? Across your breasts? Down your back? Between your legs?" he asks while completing the motions.

"Yessss."

"Or were you hoping my hands would replace this sponge? Maybe hoping I'd slide my hands underneath these heavy tits and squeeze until your pussy starts gushing for me."

I yelp a little from his rough pinch of my nipple, but my one good knee becomes limp like a noodle as the blood rushes back into my breast once he releases it. I'm dying to come. I think these pregnancy hormones are doing a number on my libido. I'm aroused all the time.

"So responsive," he growls in my ear.

One of Romans hands cradles me in a possessive way around my neck while the other holds me at my waist. The hand at my neck reminding me that I belong to him. The other hand claiming his baby. I finally relax a hundred percent into his embrace. My full weight against him. I trust that he has me. I've never felt safer in my whole life.

"That's it, Duchess. Give yourself completely over to me."

His words spur me to softly moan in compliance.

"I wasn't planning on touching you tonight," he says. His voice thick with need. "But maybe just a little taste."

My pussy is throbbing, and I nod my head eagerly in agreement and bumble over my words like an idiot. "Yesss. A taste."

"Ask me," he demands.

"What happens next, Masterson?"

"That's a good girl," he says by my ear while holding both of his hands underneath my breasts and rubbing his thumbs along my pebbling nipples.

"What happens next is that I'm going to turn you around to face the corner, like that bad girl that you are. You're going to lean into that corner and spread your legs. Keeping all your weight on the only good leg you have. It's going to be difficult, but you're going to do it, because you've been begging for me to plow inside of you for days. And I always give my girl what she wants, even if it really isn't what she needs don't I?

"See I planned on waiting until your leg and throat were fully healed, and your belly was good and swollen with my seed, and then I was going to pound that pussy until you had to literally beg me to stop. And even then, I don't think I could stop myself. You know why, Duchess?"

"No," I say with a very dry mouth. My throat constricting.

"No, what?"

"No, I don't know why, Masterson."

"That's real good, baby," he says as he slides the fingers of his right hand between my folds. "Because this sopping wet cunt was custom built for my dick. That's why you've never been nor will ever be fucked by anyone the likes of me. This is mine."

He slides one finger inside of me.

"Today," he says.

Two fingers.

"Tomorrow."

Then he compresses my left nipple, my extra sensitive one, with his thumb and pointer finger. First softly. Then hard.

"And forever," he growls.

My orgasm is coiling inside of me like a fast moving, angry snake. It's going to be quick, powerful, and bite me in the ass. If I fall in this shower, I'm going to kick Roman's butt.

Then he stops completely. One hand back around my waist, the other totally out of my pussy. Yep, it's official. My orgasm bully is back in full force. He's not even taking any sort of pity on the cripple that I am.

He switches positions with me. Turning me around face first and leaning me into the corner, holding me at the waist the entire time. He uses his hand to guide my legs farther apart, making sure I'm leaning most of my weight on my good leg and my arms.

Then he drops on his knees behind me.

Still only holding me at the waist, but I can feel his breath on my ass. His lips are just an inch away from my pussy, but he doesn't do anything. He just waits for me to calm down a bit.

Controlling jerk.

"That's not going to work," I say snidely to the wall.

I probably shouldn't have said that.

Whack!

Roman slaps me firmly on the ass. I should have

known it was coming, but it took me by surprise. A mixture of shock and carnal pleasure escapes between my lips.

"What the fuck did you say?"

I don't say anything in response. I can't talk, or I swear I'll come before I get two words out.

Whack!

"Are you deaf now, too?"

Oh. My. God.

"No." Is all I manage to eek out.

"What's not going to work?" he asks insistently.

"I'm not going to settle down. In fact if you slap my ass one more time I'm going to come so hard, and scream so loud, that I may traumatize Mr. Tibbs."

I notice that one of his hands drops low and he uses it to begin slowly stroking himself.

"You've got a greedy pussy, Elizabeth," he says as if he's almost in pain. Still stroking himself. Harder and harder.

Everything he says, everything he does, and every noise he makes seems so erotic to me right now, that I swear I'm about to lick one of these shower tiles. I wish he'd shut up, and take care of business.

This is so mean.

"What are you doing right now, Masterson?" I demand to know.

I hear him mumble a few unintelligible words to himself.

"What did you say?" I ask getting bolder by the minute.

"I *said* that I'm stroking my cock to relieve some pressure, because I'd rather be ramming it up inside of you, Duchess."

"So why don't you?" I reply with a bit of sass.

"You know why dammit."

"Don't act like you care about my safety now. You've

got a one-legged woman barely holding onto a wall inside of a wet shower."

"Shit," he grumbles as if he's just realized his error.

He stops jerking off and drags the shower stool over.

"Sit," he orders. "Now."

He helps me comfortably adjust myself on the stool.

"Spread your legs as best you can," he commands. "Lean your head against the wall."

It's hard to take commands right now. I'm still a little wound up.

"Wider," he orders. "Now relax, Duchess."

Roman kneels back down in between my legs looking like a powerful, stony warrior. His beautiful hard body, adorned with swirls of ink, wet with shower water, and the shiny scar under his eye seems to glisten in this light.

He looks up at me with lust filled, obsidian eyes. His dick hard as steel and stiffly bobbing up and down. He's trying to decide how he's going to move forward with me. I can almost see him working various scenarios through his head.

"Just one taste."

"Okay," I say knowing good and well it will lead to a lot more. At least I hope it does. To encourage him, I try to spread my legs a little farther.

He's hesitant at first. He begins by softly brushing the insides of my thighs with his knuckles. They move inch by inch closer to my sex but not quite the center. I shamelessly try to roll my hips forward, so that he gets the hint, but he chooses to continue teasing and torturing me. I think it's his favorite thing to do.

When spread apart, Roman's hands are huge. The span of them like the wings of a large eagle. To stop me from fidgeting, he holds me still at the crease of my hips with both hands. His beautiful mouth only millimeters away from my pussy.

My eyes are closed and all I hear is water falling and heavy breathing. Then as if we're in sync, I lean my body against the wall of the shower and he moves forward.

His mouth on my clit.

Suctioning softly.

Then a stronger pull.

A release.

Then a lick from as far back as he can reach with his tongue towards my ass and then moving forward, all the way to the tip of my clit and the top of my mound.

Roman likes rituals. They soothe him. And so he continues with this pattern of suction, release, and licking over and over and over.

I'm writhing.

I hate this damn cast.

I want to find the sharpest knife in Roman's kitchen and saw this thing the frack off. I want to wrap my legs completely around his head and ride his mouth.

But I can't.

And even if I could, he won't let me. He gets off on this crap. Bringing me to the edge, to the precipice, but controlling exactly when I fall over. But not this time. I've got a plan.

I'm going to draw on all the inner strength that I know I have and control my own orgasm for once. Hell, I'm a woman. I'm Wonder Woman. I'm oh mighty Isis. I'm about to give another human being life in a couple of months. I can do this.

I'm going to pretend to settle myself down, so that he thinks I'm not close to coming, when really I'm about to ignite. And then I'm going to scream bloody murder when there's not a damn thing he can do about it. Of course this is all good in theory, because he is way deep into his ritualistic rotation of eating me out.

And the shit is damn good.

I clench my eyes shut and ball my hands into fists. Rubbing his head or grabbing onto his shoulders would be a dead giveaway. It's my tell. But my orgasm is coming in like a runaway train. I try to take several normal breaths to try and bottom out the erratic shallow ones I'm taking, but it doesn't work.

He knows.

And he stops.

And then he has the nerve to start asking questions.

"Do you trust me, Duchess?"

"Yes." I practically snap.

"Do you love me?"

"Yes."

"Is this my pussy?"

"Yes!"

"And you promise you won't do any more stupid shit with my pussy."

"I promise."

"What did you say?"

"I promise, Masterson."

"That's my baby."

Then he gives my pussy a hard slap and descends upon it with his mouth.

Devouring me.

It doesn't take long before I start screaming. My heart beating rapidly like a wild rabbit. I think I now understand why some older men die inside of a woman. Coming is some serious shit. I feel like I'm going to pass out.

"I'm dizzy," I breathe.

Roman stands up grinning proudly. His mouth glistening from being covered with me. He lifts me up, kicks the stool away, and returns us to our original standing position in the corner of the shower.

Him standing behind me.

Holding me.

The water streaming across our bodies.

I can feel his steel length almost angrily poking me in the back, and just when I think this shower is about to go in another Rated X direction, he does a full one-eighty and begins to pull back emotionally.

Instead of giving me what I really want, him inside of me, he decides instead to return to his ritualistic washing of me again. This time giving a lot of attention to scrubbing and rinsing my scalp. Then repeating it all again. It's a half an hour of more torturous foreplay in my opinion, but I'm not complaining, because my eyes have been closed for the last fifteen minutes in total bliss. No one gives a hair wash like he does.

I only know that the shower is over once I hear him shut the water off. Sheesh, his building must have one hell of a hot water heater. We were in there a long time, and the water stayed the perfect temperature the entire time.

Roman scoops me up out of the shower and places me gingerly on the countertop. Even though he has a wide double sink bathroom counter, there's also a pretty large section of free countertop space where he keeps toiletries and freshly folded towels, and that's where he places me.

He grabs one of the plush white towels on the counter and wraps it around his waist. He lets the rest of his body air dry while he grabs another towel and starts silently drying me off. He's starting to piss me off all over again. I'm reaching the end of my patience with him. My pregnancy hormones won't allow this to go on for much longer.

"Roman."

"Yes."

"Why won't you touch me?"

"What are you talking about. I just gave you the best orgasm of your life."

He wraps a towel around my shoulders, which drapes over my breasts, almost as if he wants to hide them from his line of sight, while he figures out how to take the cast protector off of my leg.

"I'm not the Virgin Mary. So why are you handling me with kid gloves? I have had sex before you know. Plenty of it!" I try to yell at him but it's difficult, because my vocal chords are still somewhat sore and that bloody loud orgasm I just had didn't help matters.

"I'm trying to be good, Elizabeth. I told you just a taste. Don't push me."

"Good for what?"

"You're hurt."

"I'm fine. I have a broken leg."

"It's selfish."

"What is?"

"Sex is a very physical act. It's selfish of me to push you when you're hurt like this. We shouldn't have even done that shit we just did in the shower."

"You are aware that this cast has to stay on for *eight* weeks right?"

I see a flicker of something pass through his eyes.

"I'm aware."

"So we aren't going to have sex, real sex, for eight weeks? Is that what you're saying?"

"That's what I'm saying."

And now I want to strangle him. I don't think I can last two months without having sex with Roman. Not if we're living in the same city. On the same planet. Breathing the same air. I might spontaneously combust. Then he'll have to explain to my parents why there are bits of me all over his penthouse walls. Ugh!

"I'm dry now," I say seething. "Hand me my crutches please."

"Here," he says seemingly amused by my sour mood. "Oh by the way, we're going out later."

"Most couples stay in and have sex on New Years Eve." I deadpan.

He laughs out loud. Usually one of my favorite sounds ever, but right now not so much.

"No, Duchess. Most people bring in the new year by going out and partying. So go get pretty."

I wasn't in the mood to do all that it required to *get pretty*, but I also didn't want to spend New Years Eve in the house either. I already missed Thanksgiving and Christmas in the hospital and rehabilitation center. I didn't want to bring in the new year reading a book on my Kindle while he was in bed dreaming about dancing M&Ms.

"Can I invite Sloan?"

"I just want it to be the two of us."

Why am I not surprised that he doesn't want my best friend to tag along.

"Fine," I agree angrily.

I swear by this time next week, I'm going to be back in my own house and my own bed. I've got a long standing date with my battery operated boyfriend, and he doesn't care if I have a broken leg or try to draw out my orgasms. In fact, my battery operated boyfriend likes to get me there as fast as he can. Especially if he has a fresh set of double A batteries!

36

Roman

"I can't believe we're going to this place tonight."

"Maybe your New Year's resolution should be to broaden your horizons," I say to Cam on my speaker phone.

I just picked up Mr. Tibbs from the groomers, and I think he's pissed at me. He hates getting his nails trimmed, and he's just sitting in the passenger seat with what I swear is a scowl.

"If this is what comes with broadening my horizons, then I'm all good. Thanks anyway."

Cam is the only one I've told where I want to bring in the new year tonight and why. Well he and Jade, and that's only because I needed her help to orchestrate the whole thing. God knows it wasn't easy. I've planned blackmail schemes that were easier to pull off than this.

"You know you're going to eventually have to go to Miami," I say to him.

"I can handle all my shit for Kat from behind a computer in Philadelphia. What the hell do I need to go to Miami for?"

"She needs to meet you at least. She's not going to pay someone she's never met. You should have come to the gala, then you could have knocked it out then."

"She knows you."

"You went to Baltimore right?"

"This again."

"I'm just saying."

"So this Kat chick will funnel us the type of work we like right?"

"Absolutely. Miami is a cesspool. They're all on drugs and fucked up. We'll have plenty of messes to clean up for her. She already has two situations for us to work."

"Cool. This sounds like just what we need."

"It is. She's good people."

"Maybe I'll figure out a weekend me and Cutt can shoot down there with you."

"Good. You know with all that's happened, I didn't get a chance to say–"

"You better not be opening up your mouth to say thanks or some stupid shit like that."

"Cam–"

"We did what we always do, Rome. Shit is never fifty-fifty between us. This time me and Cutt handled things. Next time it will probably be you. We've never said thank you to each other before, and we don't need to start now."

"I had more on the line than usual though, brother."

"I know that and we did what had to be done. It's over. Forget about those two motherfuckers, and concentrate on what's in front of you. The good shit you have going on with Elizabeth. That's rare, man. Enjoy it."

"Can I ask you a question?"

"Sounds like you're going to ask something stupid with or without my permission."

"I just want to know what happened in Baltimore and what Jade has to do with it."

"That's two questions."

"Whatever is going down, and however strong she may appear to be now, I need you to remember the land of fucked up she came from. So don't mess with her head."

"Not your business, Rome."

"I know it's not, but I'm asking you anyway. She's important to me. To all of us."

"I was there too you know. I remember exactly what Jade went through, and I'm a little offended that you think I don't have better shit to do than to fuck with her head."

"I'm not saying that you'd do it on purpose, but shit happens. Right, brother?"

I'm referring to a trail of heartbroken women Camden has left in his wake. Where I was the type that slept with a different woman every night, Camden is a serial dater, which in my opinion is worse. At least my women knew what they were getting with me. One night only. With Camden, they saw marriage, babies, and forever after in their futures, and it wasn't always their fault.

"I'll see you tonight, Rome."

"Remember what I said."

Then the asshole hung up on me.

I was just about to call him back and tear him a new asshole when another call comes in.

"It's me."

The old man.

"Hey."

"How's our girl?"

"She's doing good, but I'm sure you know that already. Juliette calls like every other minute for an update."

"Well it's like you have Elizabeth on some sort of lock down over there. She's just being a good aunt and making sure her niece is begin well taken care of."

"As if I'd do anything less. Hey you guys kept her away from me while she was in the hospital, so it's only fair I get her to myself now."

"I guess."

"You coming tonight?"

"I'm coming."

"I know you don't approve."

"I'm coming anyway."

There's a pregnant pause over the line. One of us has to say something.

"Should we talk about the letter?" I ask.

"I don't have anything to say about it."

"You didn't want me to see it."

"No I didn't, but as usual you've made it a point to get your way."

"Why didn't you want me to read it?"

"She's a shitty mother, that's why."

"I already knew that."

"And I didn't want you to think that the fact that I'm not your biological father changes things. It doesn't."

"And you're sure that you aren't?"

I'd be lying if I said that I wasn't hoping that my mother was wrong or lying. Joseph is the only father I've known.

"Yeah, I had us tested a long time ago. Way before you came to live with me. Stole some of your hair when I dropped off some money. I've known most of your life."

What. The. Fuck.

"Why didn't you tell me, or better yet, why did you do it? Why raise me?"

"That neighborhood would have swallowed you up

whole like all the boys before you. I'm not dead inside, Roman. I couldn't leave the block and not try to save someone besides myself. So it made total sense that it would be you. Give or take a week, you actually could have been mine. It's just that some other man beat me to it."

"Does she know that you know?"

"No. I thought if she knew that I was aware you weren't mine that she would hold it over me. That she'd try to come back in our lives at some point and threaten to take you back or extort me for money. I wouldn't put it past her. Especially when she was acting nuts. Which I didn't know back then, but must have been the times when she was manic. But anyway, I let her believe she was pulling something over on me. It made things easier."

"Did Juliette know?"

"No. It's part of the reason why I'm taking her around the world. She's mad as hell at me."

"I didn't think you ever lied to Juliette."

"I don't usually. Just about this one thing. I had my reasons."

"So that whole story you told me before. Not wanting me and then finally stepping up? I still don't get it."

"That part was true. For a time, I thought I was your father and I didn't want to be anyone's father. I was too busy trying to make a name for myself. To build a life that would be so far removed from the old neighborhood that people there would barely remember my name. Your mother was beautiful and fun, but we were never supposed to form a lifetime connection. I didn't want connections to that place. You were a connection.

"When I decided to have you tested, it was because I heard from a few people that she'd been seeing another man the same time I had been. Someone regularly. A guy she hadn't told me about for obvious reasons. He'd long disappeared from the neighborhood, so the minute I discovered you weren't mine, I thought I could help you by at least giving your mother money to raise you right. Send you to a better school. Enroll you in extracurriculars. But I learned pretty soon that your mother was incapable of holding up her end, and like I said, while it took me a minute, I finally stepped up and got you out of there. You not being mine biologically didn't factor into the decision."

"Really, because you've been tough as shit on me, Joseph. Don't you think it might be because we're not related? Maybe you resented me a little?"

"Hell, no. I've been tough on you, because it was all I knew how to be. It was the only way I knew how to save you. How to raise you. How to keep you safe. I'm your father in every way that counts, and I did a damn good job of it. I won't apologize for any of it. I'll be the best grandfather that I can be too."

And that was it. All I ever wanted from the old coot. Validation. Acceptance.

"Are you planning on looking for her?" he asks me about my mother.

"Don't you know exactly where she is?"

He pauses.

"I do."

"I don't plan on it. I think this conversation we just had is all the closure I need. No need to open up that can of worms."

"I don't think anything good could come of it, but she is your mother, and you do have the right."

I decide not to acknowledge his last statement, and just say my good-byes.

"See you tonight, old man."

"All right, son, see you then."

37

Elizabeth

To: Elizabeth Hill
From: Henry Lambert
Re: School Bucks

Dear Miss Hill,

I just wanted to follow up personally on our conversation from the night of the Autism Alliance Gala. I'd love for us to meet about a possible source of funding that might work for your app expansion. Let's pencil in a time during the second week of January. Call Daniella and she'll set it all up. Happy New Year.

Sincerely,
Henry Lambert

38

Elizabeth

"**E**lizabeth, are you ready?"

Roman calls out for me from the kitchen, but I can't stop staring at my phone long enough to respond. I keep reading and rereading the email, resulting in a permanent grin across my face, because Roman says something about it as soon as he comes looking for me.

"Why do you have that goofy grin on your face?"

I turn my phone and show him the email.

"Nice."

"That's it? Nice."

"I'm proud of you?"

"Is that a question or a statement?"

"Hey, I 'm a little surprised that you managed to have a coherent conversation with the man considering you were blasted out of your mind that night."

"Stop being dramatic and a Debbie Downer. I wasn't even drunk at that point."

"Or stalking me yet."

"Whatever," I say, not even wanting to think about anything in regards to that night especially Kat.

Even though I know she's just an old friend and a client, she's still a drop dead gorgeous woman from his past. And I'm pregnant with raging hormones. So I'm giving myself a pass to feel a little jealous right now.

"I know that Aunt Juliette probably had a lot to do with making this happen for me, but I've decided that a little help is okay nowadays."

"Is that right?"

"That's right."

"Well I could have helped you with the money for your business a very long time ago. I can still help since you're starting to see the light and all."

"I don't need your money now. I've got Mr. Lambert's." I start doing a little victory dance using my crutches.

"Stop it, nerd, before you fall and break your other leg."

"Shush it. So do I look pretty enough for whatever lame plans you have for us tonight?" I give him an exaggerated twirl and curtsy in my little black dress, which is harder than you would imagine when you're on crutches.

"You're really mad that we're going out aren't you?" He chuckles.

Yes, I'd rather be underneath you.

"I'll make the best of it." I try to say nonchalantly.

Roman and I drive for what seems like forever in the direction away from the city. Traffic is especially bad because of the simple fact that it's New Year's Eve, and it's close to midnight. We just finished having a late dinner at what will probably be my new favorite restaurant. My lobster and rib eye were perfect. So were the grilled asparagus and lobster macaroni and cheese. The only thing that was missing was a nice glass of merlot, but it's all worth it for this little blessing growing inside of me.

I recognize the exit ramp we're on. It leads to one of the biggest malls in the area, although I can't imagine why we'd be going there at eleven at night on New Year's Eve. It's not even open.

Roman pulls over on the side of the road for a moment. It's terribly dark on this stretch of road.

"What's wrong?" I ask nervously. Worried that something may be wrong with the car. He opens the glove compartment and pulls out a piece of yellow satin fabric.

"I want you to put this blindfold on."

"What?! Why do you have a blindfold in your car?"

"I don't want you to see where we're going just yet."

"Okayyy," I say hesitantly. "But I hope this isn't the part in the movie where the girl is about to be murdered."

"There's no murder movie with a blindfolded, pregnant girl, wearing a yellow leg cast inside of a Range Rover." He makes fun of me.

"Fine." I turn my head and he ties the fabric around my head.

"Comfy?" he asks.

I nod my head.

"All right, I'm going to get back on the road now. Try to sit back and relax."

A few minutes later I hear the car drive across what sounds like gravel. If I didn't trust and love this man so much, I'd swear that he was about to murder me and dump my body at a construction site.

Stop going to sleep watching shows like Criminal Minds, Elizabeth.

Roman turns the ignition off and tells me to, "wait." I

hear him exit the car and walk around to the passenger side. First he grabs my crutches then helps me out of the Rover, which has noticeably high seats when you have a broken leg.

When I'm totally on my feet and have the crutches under my arms, he growls in my ear. "Pull your teeny tiny dress down. I can see your panties. I should spank you later for that."

I grin. "You told me to look pretty."

"That I did. Keep the blindfold on and keep walking," he orders with a smile in his voice.

If you think walking on crutches is difficult, just imagine walking blindfolded, on a variety of surfaces, on crutches. First gravel, then concrete, then earth. It isn't easy.

"Okay, stop."

Roman unties the blindfold, and as I survey my surroundings I'm utterly speechless. We're in a park. Longwood Park to be exact. I know it well, because I've been here twice before after meeting friends at the mall. I just didn't know Roman knew anything about it.

The park is beautiful. No, it's magical. It's bathed in holiday splendor. There are hundreds and hundreds of white lights decorating every single tree around us. There are even some covering the trunk of a large weeping willow tree, which we are standing under.

"It's so beautiful, Roman. How did you–"

"Have a seat, Duchess."

There's a wrought iron bench with wooden slats under the tree. On one of the slats is an engraved metal plaque. The plaque looks brand new because of the metal's sheen and the bench might be new too based on the fresh mulch surrounding the base of it. All details which make me curious. So I sit down, turn my body around, and read the plaque.

There is only you.
There will only ever be you.
Will you marry me, Elizabeth?
On bended knee ...
Roman

Oh. My. God.

I whip my head around and see that Roman has bent down on one knee holding a black velvet box in his hand. I can't really say anything. I'm speechless. This is unreal. Like a fairytale. And here come the tears. I'm hormonal anyway, so I expect nothing less from myself than the waterworks.

"Elizabeth, when I first noticed you dancing in the middle of the club like no one was watching, I knew that I had to have you. I didn't realize at the time that my desire for you wouldn't be for just that one night, or one month, or one year, but for all my nights. I love you. I need you. I want you. So under the moon and the stars, I'm asking you, will you marry me? Let's officially let all these asshats in the world know that you're mine, and as they say, let me put a ring on it."

He opens the box and inside is a flawless princess cut diamond on a simple platinum band. It's a pretty big stone. Almost Elizabeth Taylor big, yet it's tasteful at the same time. A classic cut stone in a simple setting. It's totally me.

In this moment, there is not a moment of doubt, of fear, or concern about who he is, who I am, how we met, or the timing of it all. All there is, is a tremendous amount of surety that I'm with the person that I'm supposed to be with for the rest of my life.

So I immediately give him my answer.

"Yes!"

He slides the ring on my finger, sits on the bench next to me, and kisses me like he never has before. His tongue plunging inside of my mouth, claiming it, devouring it. I love that I can taste a blend of the salt of my tears mixed with a little of his chocolate and whiskey.

"I see you had a stiff drink already," I observe happily. "Were you nervous I'd say no?"

"I have a drink every night, smart ass."

Roman pulls out his cell and sends a quick text.

"Take a picture of the bench with your phone," I say wanting to make sure he gets a picture of the plaque.

"It's our bench, Duchess. We're going to sit here for the rest of our lives and watch our children and grandchildren play in this pretty ass park. We don't need to take a picture. We can see it anytime we want."

I start crying again. "Take one anyway."

"Are you going to cry this entire pregnancy?"

"Yep, and who were you texting just now anyway?"

"I'll show you," he says. "Come on."

"I don't want to leave our bench!" I exclaim while hugging the bench.

"It's not going anywhere, baby," he chuckles. "We can come back. I promise, but right now there are a few people waiting on us."

Roman effortlessly scoops me up in his arms and walks me over to another section of the park where there is a large gazebo also decorated in tons of white lights, vases of sunflowers, and filled with all of the people we love and who love us.

"Congratulations!" I hear voices cheer.

There's my mom, my dad, Juliette, Joseph, Sloan, Cutter, Camden, Tiny, Jade and even Jagger. I can't believe that Roman did all of this. I'm dumbfounded at all the effort he went through to propose to me. It's the most romantic, beautiful proposal ever.

After a lot of congratulatory hugs and kisses, music starts playing from a speaker that's mounted high up in the gazebo.

"It's one of Juliette's mixes, so you know we'll be bringing in the new year to a lot of 90's music." Roman laughs.

"It's the music we first danced to." I laugh too.

He pulls me in closely and hands my crutches to a nearby Jade.

"It's the music we fell in love to," he says.

I wrap my arms around his neck and stare into his eyes. A long gaze that I can't break away from. I'm falling deeper into him just when I didn't think there was anywhere further to tumble.

All the way to Oz.

Juliette interrupts us to hand us champagne flutes. One has actual champagne for Roman, and the other has sparkling cider for me.

"Only ten more minutes until the new year!" she says excitedly.

"Thanks, Auntie," I say.

"When do we get to start planning the wedding?" she asks grinning from ear to ear.

"You mean when do *you* get to start?" I ask.

"You, me, us. It takes a village. Especially if we're short on time," she says rubbing my stomach.

"I think we'll wait until after the baby is born. I'd like a flat stomach in my wedding pictures," I joke (but not really).

"I don't see why we have to wait," Roman pouts.

"Because it's the bride's day," I respond. "And I want to look stunning."

He threads his fingers in my hair. "You already do, Duchess."

"Okay love birds, I see you may need to iron out the details, before I get involved."

We watch my aunt flit away as if she's walking on sunshine over to both of my parents. They exchange a few words that I can't hear but then start laughing together. Actually laughing. And then she places her hand on my father's upper arm as they continue smiling, and for once I'm hopeful that our union may bring the family finally together. They all seem so genuinely happy for us. Happy to be together.

I didn't notice earlier, but at some point Roman must have pulled one of the smaller sunflowers from one of the vases. It's in his hand. He snaps half of the stem off and places the remaining flower behind my ear.

"You've grown as tall as a sunflower, Duchess."

I know what he means. I'm excited about who I'm becoming too.

I'm growing, evolving, and blossoming.

A business owner. A mother. A wife.

"That's because you watered me and I grew," I say.

"Happy New Year, baby."

Then my fiancé pulls me in tightly and kisses me senseless as our friends and family begin cheering and roaring the new year in.

"HAPPY NEW YEAR!!"

"And don't worry," he says after breaking off our kiss and savoring it a little further by licking his bottom lip. "I was just messing with you earlier today. I'm going to fuck you senseless as soon as we get home."

"Promises. Promises."

Epilogue

Zoe Clarkson

I'm an artist, and I'm sensitive about my shit. I specialize in creating meaningful, permanent works of art on the human canvas. Some people call them tattoos, ink, or body art.

I require every client to have a thirty minute, consultation with me before I design any permanent art for them. After the consultation, I immediately start drawing the design in my head while the inspiration is fresh. While clients are waiting I prep them for their experience.

They relax in my sitting area where they can eat, listen to music, watch television or just nap. Due to the nature of my work I prefer to take only three clients a day. Elizabeth and Roman are my last appointment.

I tend to work a lot with couples. Couples seem to be more drawn to the type of work that I do, because my art has to mean something. It has to be important to the person first and foremost, to the couple secondly, and then to me third. Everyone has to be in agreement with the design or it doesn't work.

After listening to Roman and Elizabeth's story during our consult, I am very clear about what I will create for these complicated lovers. Especially after reading Elizabeth's email that she sent me prior to this session.

She's quite pregnant, which I knew beforehand, so I've made especially sure to make the accommodations soothing and comfortable. This needs to be a totally pleasant experience. Especially with that huge fiancé of hers out there stewing. He isn't happy, but he will be when he sees the final result.

I've decided that he has to stay outside of my workspace tonight because for one, the permanent art is a surprise for him, and two because his energy consumes the oxygen in the room. It's very important for me that I have a clear space to concentrate on my design, and Elizabeth needs to just *be*. Not fret after him.

I prep the room and have her lie in my elevated, oversized chaise lounger. After approving the design, she's ready. Sometimes I create intricate, painstaking works of art that take many sessions to complete, and other times I just etch a few meaningful words that take an hour tops. She has chosen the latter.

"Turn on your side, Elizabeth. This won't take long."

I stick my earbuds in my ears and get to work.

Then after about an hour of careful writing and shading it's done. Etched above Elizabeth's right buttock and a little to the right, close to her hip, are the words she selected in a midnight blue script with a variety of swirls and shadows of lighter shades of blue highlighting it.

"Masterson Made"

Evidently her guy mentioned to her a dream he had

about tatting the words Masterson Made on both of her butt cheeks. Something about him being totally responsible for her new and improved hips and butt. Unbeknownst to either of them at the time though, the real reason why Elizabeth was spreading is because she is pregnant with their first child.

A boy.

And now she's won some sort of bet between the two of them.

"How do you feel?" I ask her. Spreading a little salve on the design and covering it temporarily with gauze before the big reveal.

"It stung, but it wasn't as bad as I thought it was going to be."

"Exactly what I wanted to hear. Here, let me help you up so you can take a look. Here's a mirror."

She smiles brightly, and I know that I've done well.

"I love it," she says to me.

"I'm so glad. Should you bring your fiancé in now?"

"Yep, let's do it."

I go out to the waiting area to get her guy. He's big in stature and in presence. Right now he's sitting in one of my chairs with his legs spread wide, and his body bent over with his elbows and forearms on his knees, staring absent-mindedly at his phone.

"She's finished, Mr. Masterson."

His head pops up as if he's been on the edge the entire time we've been in here. God help them (or really her) when it's time for that baby to come. He's going to be a nervous wreck.

"Did you hurt her?" he asks gruffly.

Like I would say yes if I did. Puh-lease.

"No, sir. She barely felt a thing."

"I don't know why I couldn't be in there," he grumbles.

"It's a surprise," I say excitedly. "Of course you couldn't be in there."

"Whatever."

Elizabeth's eyes almost shimmer when her man enters the room, as if their hour apart was excruciating for the both of them to bear.

"Are you still grumpy?" she asks him.

He stares at the gauze and shakes his head.

"What the fuck have you done, Elizabeth?"

I turn my back to the couple and start cleaning up my workspace to keep busy while the two of them spar.

"Lift the bandage, and take a look."

"Why are you so stubborn. If you had to get this damn tat while you're still pregnant, then why didn't you use my guy? No offense," he says to me.

"None taken," I reply.

"If you would stop grumbling for one second and take a look."

I love how this woman doesn't take his shit. They are a great match. I'm glad she trusted me to do this for them.

When he lifts the bandage and reads the words, he grins, and looks up at her as if she's the most amazing woman on the planet.

"Do you see the colors I used?" she asks him.

"Blue."

She waits a second for it to register.

"Blue? We're having a boy?"

"Yes!" she says excitedly.

He grabs her face with his palms and plants a huge kiss on her lips. I don't want to watch, but then again I can't look away. Their obvious connection makes my ovaries want to applaud.

"And you know what that means," she continues. "It means that I won the bet."

His face drops.

"Oh shit."

"Oh shit is right, Mr. Masterson." She smirks.

"What do you want?" he asks with a wariness to his voice.

"You have to give it to me. A bet is a bet."

"What. Do. You. Want. Nerd."

"I-want-us-to-get-married-in-Vegas-so-your-mother-can-come," she blurts out.

"You've got to be fucking kidding me."

"Uh-uh."

"Um, Zoe, we're going to need the room."

Is he kicking me out of my own space?

"Well, I'm going to be closing–" I say before he cuts me off.

"Here's a hundred as a tip for the nice work, but we'll be needing the fucking room, or you can stay and watch. Your choice."

Uh ...

"On your feet, Duchess."

"A bet is a bet," she says again teasingly.

I can't believe she's still egging this maniac on with a victorious look on her face. I was scared to leave her alone with him for a moment, but now I'm starting to think that she's totally got this. Maybe she does realize her own power over this man.

"And I'm going to honor your bullshit bet, because I love the ground that your pretty little ass walks on; but right now you're going to lean on the chaise, lift up your dress, and spread your fucking legs."

"Masterson," she exhales harshly.

"Good thing your panties are already off, or I'd rip those fuckers to shreds right now. Now let me have a taste," he growls.

And that's my cue to leave.
My work here is done.
Well done.

Roman and Elizabeth are officially a couple with a brand new baby, but sometimes happily-ever-afters are easier said than done. Sometimes you have to fight like HELL for them!
MASTERSON MADE
TAP TO ORDER THE BOOK INSTANTLY.

Bonus Scene

Cutter & Sloan At The Gala

Author's Note: This is a scene from the Autism Gala that didn't make the book, but one which I thought was fun between Sloan and Cutter. I thought you'd enjoy it:)

"Here to catch an investment banker tonight, Ms. Pearson?"

"Very witty," I say with sarcasm to the dressed up caveman seated next to me.

He grins like he thinks that I'm actually amused by his degrading question, even though it's closer to the truth than I would like to admit.

"Me see that you found suit," I retort in the manner that Jane would speak to Tarzan.

Then he lets out a deep belly laugh that garners us a few glances from the other guests at our table.

"Let's dance, Princess."

Ick! I hate that overused, unimaginative term of endearment.

"If you're going to address me, please use my name. It

seems like you and your friend have a problem with calling people by their God given names. Is that how they do things in your *'hood*. Everyone gets a ridiculous nickname."

"You were much nicer when we first met. Why can't you be *that* girl again?"

"I'm not even going to dignify that with a response. Now go away before people think we're here together. As if."

I motion for him to shoo with the back of my hand.

"Scoot. Shoo!"

The asshole laughs even harder.

I swear I don't know what on earth I'm doing to encourage this guy. I sat on his lap for ten seconds when we first met at The Lotus, and he's been giving me googly eyes ever since. Why am I not inspiring this type of adoration from the gazillion other men whom I've met over the last few weeks?

"Fine," I say in frustration. "I'll move then."

As I motion to stand up, Cutter King grabs me around my waist with clear purpose. His eyes dancing. His grip strong. And he pulls me in toward his very large pecs. Then he stands up slowly. Making sure to slide his chest against my breasts as he rises to his full height.

He's tall. Really tall.

Muscular. Massive.

Brick hard and built like a caveman.

Strong enough to bash the head in of any intruder. Fast enough to catch any prey. And I'm not going to lie, big enough in all the right places to give me the fuck of a lifetime.

"Save that dance for me, Princess."

Now I understand. This is why Bitsy wears panties, and me going commando was a bad idea.

What the hell is going to soak up all the wetness that the bass in his voice just produced between my legs?

"I need to excuse myself please."

And all I hear is Cutter King's arrogant, rumbling laughter echoing behind me, as I hightail it from the table to find the nearest ladies room.

Note From Lisa

Thank you *soooo* much for reading Masterson In Love. When I first came up with the idea of Roman, his story was only supposed to be a duet (a two book series). It was my first novel, and I wasn't sure that I could handle writing a longer series.

Well, things have just organically evolved, and now it has grown into a longer series. Readers wanted to know more about Roman and Elizabeth as well as what would happen with The King brothers. So now it's seven books! Yippee! Thank you for all the encouragement and support along the way:)

Also, your feedback is critical to my writing process. So please write me at Lisa@LisaLangBlakeney.com or join my fan group and tell me your thoughts. I love to hear from readers, and I respond to all letters.

Finally, I need a favor. If you have enjoyed any book in the series, I humbly ask that you please leave a review for any or all of them on your favorite retailer and recommend the series to your friends. This really helps me as an author, as those ratings are so very important to us independent authors and allows other readers to find our books.

xoxo,
Lisa

P.S. Make sure to *Join My VIP Readers List* or my <u>Private Facebook</u> Group to be notified immediately of my next release.

The Masterson Series
Devour this addictive series about the possessive bad boy,
Roman Masterson, who falls hard and fast for the girl he's
promised his family to protect.
Masterson
Masterson Unleashed
Masterson In Love
Masterson Made
Joseph Loves Juliette
Masterson Box Set

Masterson Next Generation Series
The crazy hot fruit doesn't fall far from the tree. Dive into
this second generation of Masterson men!
Knox - Knox & Gigi
Bronx - Bronx & Karma
Seven - Coming soon!

The King Brothers Series
Dive into this series of interconnected standalones

featuring 3 alpha hot brothers and the women they lay
claim to without apology.
Claimed - Camden & Jade
Indebted - Cutter & Sloan
Broken - Stone & Tiny
Promised - All King Brothers
King Brothers Box Set

The Nighthawk Series
Sexy & sweet sports romances set in the professional world
of football. All standalones.
Saint - Saint & Sabrina
Wolf - Cooper & Ursula
Diesel - Mason & Olivia
Jett - Jett & Adrienne
Rush - Rush & Mia
Freak - Freak & Willow
Brick - coming soon!

Acknowledgments

When I met my husband **Deric** at 18 years old, I told him I wanted to be an author. Then life got in the way, but now I am. I want to thank him for all his pushing, prodding and support during this quite extended period of growth! He's the best alpha a girl could have! Thank you to my wonderful daughters, my extended family members (Yes, my mother-in-law reads my books!), and my personal group of cheerleaders and champions: **Tracy, Vicki, Erica, Robin, Kelly, Donna, Stacey, Kelly J. & Trina**.

Thank you to my ever patient editor & fellow NYU alumnus: **Marla Esposito**. Thanks for working with my inability to stick to my own deadlines:) Thank you to my author mentors: **Liv Morris & Jordan Silver**.

A BIG thank you to all my **Ninja Alpha Romance Warriors** and my bomb ass **Street Ninjas**. You ladies are amazeballs! You've injected enthusiasm in many a diffi-cult writing day for me and support me all day, everyday. I'm humbled. I'm honored. I appreciate it so very much. Special shout out to my super ninjas who lead the charge: **Johnnie-Marie Howard, Kathryn Dunaway, Lainey De Silva, Leann Frantz & Devine Warnes**.

Shout out to all of the fantastic bloggers who support indie authors everyday. None of you have ever said no to anything I've asked, and it makes me feel all warm and fuzzy inside that women are out here supporting each other in such a major way. Special thanks to: **Deb Carroll of "The Club" & Crystal Grizzard Burnette of "BBB Romance Book Pimps".** You ladies rock and have supported me in a big way that I sincerely and deeply appreciate.

Finally, I want to thank every single reader who has taken a chance on the Fixer Series so far. I appreciate that you could have spent your money elsewhere. On a more established author. Or something at Target:) But you invested in me and that means so very much.

Gratitude,
  Lisa

About the Author

Lisa Lang Blakeney is a USA Today Bestselling author of contemporary romance sold in more than 28 countries. Worried that her fellow PTO moms might disapprove, she wrote and published her steamy debut novel Masterson under a different title and pen name in August of 2015.

Thanks to strong reader support of her alpha male character, Roman Masterson, she was encouraged to continue with the series and published the entire Masterson Trilogy the following year. She hasn't looked back since and continues to write novels featuring strong alpha men and the smart women they seek to claim.

A romance junkie for sure, you can find Lisa watching a romantic comedy, reading a romance novel, or writing one of her own most days of the week. If she's not doing that, she's outside in the garden tending to her roses.

Lisa is the wife of one alpha (whom she met in college), mother to four girls, and two labradoodles. Get news on releases, sales and giveaways when you become one of Lisa's VIP readers at : http://LisaLangBlakeney.com/VIP

facebook.com/authorlisalangblakeney

twitter.com/LisaLangWrites

instagram.com/LisaLangBlakeney

amazon.com/author/lisalangblakeney

bookbub.com/authors/lisa-lang-blakeney

goodreads.com/Lisa_Lang_Blakeney

pinterest.com/lisalangwrites

tiktok.com/@lisalangblakeney

patreon.com/lisalangblakeney